THE SAFE BOX

a perfect crime

ALLAN BARRIE

THE SAFE BOX
A PERFECT CRIME

iUniverse books may be ordered through booksellers or by contacting:

iUniverse
1663 Liberty Drive
Bloomington, IN 47403
www.iuniverse.com
1-800-Authors (1-800-288-4677)

ISBN: 978-1-5320-0511-4 (sc)
ISBN: 978-1-5320-0510-7 (e)

Library of Congress Control Number: 2016915407

Print information available on the last page.

iUniverse rev. date: 09/14/2016

For Cynthia
The World's best reader, contributor and
supporter and an even better friend.
Thank you for everything you have done for me

For Norman
Your inspiration and undying belief in me
has been the foundation of writing.
May you always rest in peace

Prologue

January 1, 2016

MY NAME IS SAMUEL WEST AND THIS IS A STORY ABOUT A part of my life that happened many years ago. As a-matter-of fact I was a young man, only twenty-four years old and fresh out of NYU. I was a good looking guy, about six feet tall and carried my one hundred and eighty pounds nicely. I had beautiful dark hair with great big brown eyes and a very warm smile. I was quite a ladies man at the NYU but decided to put all that behind me and start looking for a job. I was filled with hopes especially with a bachelor's degree in my back pocket. In those days, a college degree was a coveted thing and was supposed to help one get a job. Not just any job, but one that paid better, and offered far greater avenues for advancement than somebody with only a high school diploma could expect. Much to my surprise that turned out not to be the case, and I was forced to accept a position that was well beneath the level my esteemed degree indicated. Nevertheless, I took a job that proved to be the one that defined my future, and this is the story of how that happened.

This journal is the only link I have with my past, and, if you stop and think about it, my only legacy. I hope that when you read these notes of mine you will not judge me too harshly and instead, perhaps applaud me, (just a little) for the ability to pull off the one perfect crime of the century. Perhaps I'm being a little flippant when I brag about a perfect crime. There is no doubt that when one commits the perfect crime, no one else knows about it. How else how could it be perfect? That logic makes me believe that I was not the first to commit the perfect crime and probably won't be the last.

By the time you read this and the attached notes about my perfect crime I will have left this planet for my final resting place. Being as old as I am, each day is a bonus and before I take that final trip, I'd like to add a few comments. I am beyond the law now, as I'm sure the passage of time has more than exceeded the limits of the hands of justice. Of course, I am being rewarded by a greater power which has decided that soon my time on this planet will have expired.

I wrote this as it happened and just wanted you to know all about the events that took place, and I'm very happy to share them with you. I do hope you enjoy this short but exciting adventure. It certainly made my life much more interesting than it would have been otherwise, and it may entitle me to my fifteen minutes of fame. Come along with me and enjoy the ride.

Introduction:

OFTEN, IN THE COURSE OF MY JOB, I MEET A LOT OF PEOPLE. Some I like, some I don't, and others are just people passing me by. The year is 1955, my name is Samuel West, my friends call me Sam and that suits me fine as Samuel is too formal. I worked at the Sy Johnson Clothing Company, one of the largest men's clothing operations in New York. I was lucky enough, as my Father always said, 'To land a job immediately after completing college was God's doing.' I was a customer representative, a fancy name for a salesperson.

It was my job to greet a prospective client and make sure I showed them the best of our suits and other men's wear when entering our main store located on Fifth Avenue and Twentieth Street. The shop had been here since the beginning of the twentieth century and has since grown into a chain of three stores, all in Manhattan. It was a nothing job as far as I was concerned. The best I could hope for would be a promotion to manager in about twenty years, after our present manager and his underlings retire. Nevertheless, I discovered that when one graduates with a Bachelor of Arts degree, he is qualified to look for a job and very little else.

I made each day as interesting as I possibly could. I felt this was a temporary position and soon I'll find my calling. The best part of this dead-end job was that I felt I would meet people. This was a perfect place for me to network and meet the go-getters, the winners, those who wanted more, the others, who like me, want riches and a taste of the good life and knew how to get it.

In the meantime I learned how to handle a client and make him feel comfortable in our store. I learned all the right things to say to each type of person. I was a great people person and knew how to make a man feel good about himself through the proper selection of clothes, as well as a right word here and there.

I kept my mind open and listened very intently to all my customers. I found that the less I said the more I learned and learn was what I wanted to do. I also discovered a certain intimacy existed between myself and my customer when measuring them for a new suit. The nuances I used made them feel good. I was their friend and personal clothing designer as well as their best listener.

Under this environment I was getting an education that I hoped would stand me in good stead in later years. Their tutelage was invaluable in my post graduate course on understanding life and reaching my goal, and that is success at whatever I choose to do.

The Foundation:

THE FUNNY THING ABOUT LIFE IS HOW WE CHOOSE OUR paths. As we all know life has many forks in the road and choosing the right one is the most difficult task we are faced with. I found that out as I toiled at my job, making men look professional, or should I say very respectable. Lawyers don't flinch for a second when fleecing a client as long as they are wearing a beautiful suit of clothes, their uniform of respectability. Doctors and dentists and other professional men feel superior wearing their suits, it makes them feel that they are far better than anyone else. Yes, it's true, suits do it all the time. Just look at an accountant, the suit makes him look like one and the same is true with others like a salesman or a banker. No matter how we put it, a well-dressed man gives off the aura of respectability and success. It even makes killers look good and feel better about their jobs, after all, a well-dressed killer is a man of distinction and would never be considered any differently.

I have learned in my time as a haberdashery expert that there is an endless supply of valuable information if I listen, and at times, ask the right questions. During this time I built some very nice relationships and began to learn a lot of things that I should not have been privy to. One of those talkers was Benny Guarino, a soldier in the Bonnano Family. He was a nice man that loved new suits and insisted I call him whenever a sale was about to take place. He was a big man, standing at least six foot-five and weighing in at three hundred pounds. His goal was to work his way up in the Mob Family's hierarchy and with some luck, he could become a capo or hold some other important title. When one was in the Mob the title was very important as it made others look-up to him. I only throw these titles around because he loved to confide in me and told me, many times, what he was aspiring to be. I, of course, was very impressed, or so I let him think. In any case he stops in often because, as he told me, he drops off money at a bank that is located only a few doors down from the store. Once he was so stoked with his integrity that he actually opened his briefcase to show me a bundle of cash that he was taking to the bank for safe keeping. He is here at least twice a week and starts off by asking what's new in men's clothing. It is his excuse for stopping in and spending some time in the shop and with me. I also believe that he likes me and wants me to know what an important guy he is. To prove his point he reminds me that he is trusted with a lot of cash and always delivers it exactly as ordered. I asked him the other day, "Doesn't the Bank wonder where all this cash comes from?" He laughed and looked at me like I was pretty dumb and he was very smart and said, "Sam, I don't put it in the Bank. I put it in the boxes and when one of them is full I get another one and fill it as well. Can you believe it, Sam, I'm trusted with so much bread it's mind boggling, and they don't know exactly how much is there. They trust me to handle their cash, there is never a question of my loyalty. Soon they will recognize how valuable I am and I'll be moving up, there is no doubt."

Of course, I let the subject go over my head as I didn't want to arouse any suspicion that I was interested in any way. My mind was working overtime as I wondered just how much money must be in those boxes. My imagination was running away with me, all I could think about was the cash. I really didn't know what I could do with this information but it was the kind of stuff that made me feel alive. If I could ever figure out how to get into those boxes what could anyone do about it? The fact that there was nothing anyone could say excited me even more. I never knew I could be so motivated, but Benny's regular trips to the bank was an intoxicating elixir. I'll bet that most of the cash kept in safety deposit boxes doesn't get reported. If these boxes were knocked off, no one would say a word on how much cash they actually had in there. This could be the perfect crime, all I had to do was figure out how to pull it off!

The Beginning:

I COULDN'T GET IT OUT OF MY HEAD. SO MUCH ILL-GOTTEN money sitting there for the taking. Easy to say, and even easier to fantasize about, but in reality how can it be done? I certainly didn't have the know-how but I was sure I could learn, all I needed was determination, and that I certainly had. I just couldn't contain myself as the days passed, all I could do was to dream about the riches I would find if I could only find a way into those safety boxes. I think I understood how a gold miner felt when he was looking for that illusive treasure. I was bitten by the bug and I couldn't get it out of my head. If it took me four years to graduate from college with a brain full of knowledge, then how long will it take me to learn how to pull off the perfect crime? As far as I was concerned it shouldn't take me too long. All I had to do was to be very committed to detail. I must be very careful about every step that had to be taken. Best of all I had plenty of time to get involved in this project and get my degree in perfection. If I do things with determination and meticulous planning there isn't any reason why I can't do this one job and do it perfectly. And best of all, to never worry about money again.

The BNZ Bank was located just down the street from my workplace and that was my target, thanks to Benny. How does one learn about a bank? How does one learn about the inner sanctum of safety deposit boxes? Easy, open an account at the Bank and rent a safety deposit box and find out exactly what the inside of the vault looks like. There is nothing like first-hand knowledge, on-the-job training so to speak.

Friday was payday and what better reason than to take my pay package and open an account. When Friday arrived along with my pay envelope, I walked over to the Bank and introduced myself and told the Banker that I wanted to open an account. I was directed to a very nice woman in her early thirties. Her name was Terry Donovan, she was this and very pretty with beautiful blond hair and blue eyes and seemed to have a great disposition. "Hi," I said, "I'm Samuel West, I work just down the road at the Sy Johnson Clothing Company. I'd like to open a Bank account and a safety deposit box."

"That is great Mr. West, it is a pleasure to have you as a valued customer. I need to ask you a few questions and, I also need some I.D." she said. I spent another fifteen minutes answering her questions as she filled in the information. She handed me a signature card which I signed and then asked me what type of account I wanted. She recommended a savings account and asked me how much I wish to deposit to open the account. She was really very nice and most informative. I removed my pay envelope from my pocket and opened it up and gave her one hundred dollars. I asked her if that was enough to open the account and she smiled and said, "That will be fine Mr. West, the more you put into your bank account the more you will earn. Remember Mr. West, money grows when you leave it in your savings account," she said.

"That is great, I'm going to like having a bank account," I said.

"That will be fine Mr. West. We welcome you to our Bank and would like to let you know a few things that will help you when using your Bank account. Our check policy is that if the check is larger than the balance in your account, we will not be able to advance you any cash until the check clears. Usually that takes about three to five days. If the check is drawn on our Bank then the waiting period is not required. I want you to know our policy in order to avoid any misunderstandings in the future," she said. She took my savings account book and entered my deposit amount in the book and returned it to me.

"I understand and thank you for letting me know. I'm sure my relationship with your Bank will be a good one. By the way, I want the smallest safety deposit box possible. All I need is a place to keep a few important papers safe and this is the best way to do it, don't you think so? How much does a box cost?" I said.

"As an account holder the fee will be six dollars a year for the smallest box. Let me show you the various sizes of boxes that are available," she said.

I spent another fifteen minutes with Terry as she completed the forms for the box rental. She then took me downstairs where the boxes were kept and took me inside the actual vault and showed me where my box was. "Would you like to use your box now?" she said.

"Yes, even though I didn't bring my papers along but I might as well see how it works. I'll leave a dollar bill in the box It is good luck to leave something that is good when you open a new place. This box is a new place for me so I won't break tradition," I said.

She explained to me that all interactions with the box itself was private and that one could retire to a private, secure room to add, place, or remove their belongings from the box. There are no devices that watch or record what you do with your box. A representative of the Bank must go into the vault area with you because, as an added precaution, two keys are required to open your box. Of course, she pointed out that access to my box must be during Banking hours. During this first time I carefully studied the entire layout of the vault and decided that to do it right I needed to take pictures of the vault area. It will make it easier for me to work out the logistics on how to tackle this area and get away with it. I did notice that there were many different sizes of boxes and for just a moment, I imagined Benny was there stuffing his cash into the biggest ones. Just the very sight of all these safe boxes made me feel warm all over. I knew, right there and then, that this treasure was going to be mine, all I had to do was to remove it from here and, standing there in that vault I knew I could do it. I was stoked and ready for the most important project of my life.

I made it back to work just as my lunch period ended. I was very excited about this project, more excited than I have ever been. This made my day a little harder, work was the farthest thing on my mind. I realized how important emotions could be when involving oneself in a venture such as this. My first lesson was to control these emotions so no one will detect that anything out of the ordinary is taking place, either in my mind or physically. It had to be business as usual no matter how excited or nervous I was. If push came to shove the report on Samuel West must always be the same. I had to maintain my persona as a very conservative and conscientious sales person who always came to work on time and did his job well. I was quite satisfied with my actions so far. The account was open and I had a box of my own thus allowing me the right to enter the vault as often as I felt was necessary. Of course, I was determined not to raise any suspicions by hanging around too much. I was going to be very careful, this project was far too important.

Assembly:

ANOTHER WEEK PASSED AND I MADE ANOTHER DEPOSIT IN my new bank account. I was getting to know the Bank and the people who worked there. I was chatty with the people who mattered at the Bank, but never too much, just enough to be known as a lowly employee at a clothing store. The plan was progressing very nicely, and although I did not set an exact date for the project to take place, I wanted it to be soon, but not too soon, certainly not until I had made certain beyond a shadow of a doubt that every aspect of the project would be covered flawlessly. There could be no traces of my involvement in this caper. I must remain invisible at all times and with careful planning I will be able to achieve this. My task now was to create a script and go over it a few times to make sure it was flawless. I cannot be lazy as that could result in clues being left behind and that may lead the cops to me or to anyone else involved. I will write the script, revise it until I make sure it is perfect before moving forward.

My work schedule has been the same ever since I came to work here. I got Monday and Tuesday off on a regular basis but I needed to change that. I needed to make that change now so it would not appear to be out of the ordinary if and when an investigation brought the cops to this doorstep. I went to see my Boss and requested that my days off be changed to Sunday and Monday. I used the excuse that I bought a small piece of land in the Adirondacks and I would love to spend Sundays there while I fix up my small cabin. My boss thought that would not be a problem and told me that my new days off will begin the following week when he makes the new schedule. I was pleased how simple it was to make the change and felt very confident that this change would not be construed as a red flag. I felt quite comfortable with the results of this step in my plan.

My next task was to find a costume shop where I could buy some material for my new play. This was not an unusual thing to do, especially in Manhattan where Broadway wanna-bees are always trying to get that big break. On Monday I went out to one of the four costume shops that I found in the yellow pages. The first shop was the most dangerous because I entered the shop as myself, Sam West. I must be as forgettable as possible and keep my conversations to a minimum. I just wanted to be another guy looking for that big break on Broadway. I realized if the cops learn that disguises were used, they would be canvassing costume stores. Because the project will be many months from now I probably should not worry, but making certain that this project will be perfect means not to leave any detail to chance. I met a very nice but very curious sales girl and decided I would make certain my part was convincing, complete with the excitement of someone who was getting a big try out for a part as a suave, bank executive. I took out a note pad that I previously set-up to look like a script and began scanning it and said to the salesgirl, "*I will need a mustache, a pair of glasses and a wig to match the mustache.*"

"*I'm sure we'll be able to find the right accessories to suit,*" the short, pudgy salesgirl said, "*is this a major show or just some small acting group*" she asked.

I realized she was only making conversation as she was finding the items I had requested. It is the same way I treat customers when they come in for a suit. Make them feel comfortable and welcome in our store and, most of all, getting them to like dealing with you. "*Yes, it's just a small group, an actor's workshop where I hope, if I get the part, to be noticed. I need the experience as I just moved here from Plattsburg and am hoping to get some experience. In the meantime*

I wait tables at the Deli. One has to pay the rent, you know!" I said in a jovial tone of voice.

She gave me a smile and said, *"I know exactly how it is. I was hoping to become an actress but so far I haven't been able to crack the ice. This job is only temporary, I hope I'll soon land a part in a show and I'll be on my way."*

"I know what you mean, I've wanted to be an actor for years. I now know how hard it is to break into show business. It's not how good you are, it's who you know." I said.

"I sure do and hope that I might be discovered one day. There are so many people trying to get a break that it seems almost impossible. Let's hope this costume will help me get the part," I said as she showed me a wig that didn't look bad at all. I got all I needed and went back home where I donned my new look and went back out again to another costume shop on the West Side. It took me all day to find the right costume and go home, change and move on to the next shop. By nightfall I had all the costumes I would need for now and spent a whopping four hundred and ninety dollars. I realized that I'd better watch my expenses as my budget was not unlimited.

On Tuesday I took advantage of my day off and found a shop on Canal Street that sold cameras of all sorts and sizes. I played with the camera for a few minutes and then signaled the clerk that I will take one. I told the clerk, "It will go over real well at my friend's party next week, I'm sure everyone will get a kick out of it." I also picked up a few additional rolls of film and was ready to begin the project.

I needed a very small camera and remember seeing an ad for a camera, it was called Minolta. It was the smallest camera I have ever heard of. It was small enough to be hidden in the palm of one's hand and easily slipped into one's pocket without anyone noticing, it was perfect for my purpose. I was sure I saw one of those cameras while watching an episode of Foreign Intrigue, a spy movie on television. I remembered one of the spies used a very small camera to take pictures of a set of maps. This was the kind of camera I needed and there it was in this store. I was very happy with the purchase and also with the fact that my disguise will protect me if this should ever become part of the investigation.

I waited until Friday when my pay check arrived then took my lunch hour and went over to the Bank to deposit it. I also made a visit to the vault, but this time I had a briefcase with some papers in it as well as my camera. As soon as the girl opened the door to my box I took my time in sliding the drawer out. *"This is the first time I have ever used a box like this, I hope you don't mind, it won't take me more than a minute or two,"* I said. *"I only have some important papers to place in my box and I'm done."*

"No problem, please take all the time you need. Do you know you can use one of the private rooms any time you like? I'll wait outside at my desk, please let me know when you are done," she said as she went out of the vault leaving me all alone. Perhaps I lucked out because she left me alone and probably wasn't supposed to although there wasn't anything anyone could steal out of the vault as all boxes were locked. I didn't waste any time as I took my camera out of the briefcase and snapped pictures as quickly as possible. I made certain I got every inch of the vault area and took a couple extra photos of the large boxes so I could count them when I'm home alone. I put the camera back into my briefcase and then peeked my head out of vault and called out, *"I'm all done here."* She came over and I slid my drawer back into its slot, she closed the door and inserting her key and waited while I inserted mine. I thanked her for her time and kind service and left the Bank. I had spent no more than four minutes in the vault area and accomplished all I wanted.

I could hardly contain my excitement that my plan was moving along very nicely. I realized that the next few steps were going to be very crucial to the success of this project. The most important part of it all was to remain anonymous at all times. No one can ever know about my involvement in this deal, ever! The thing that usually helps the cops catch people who live outside the law is their tendency to talk too much, this term is referred to as 'loose lips'. The cops use this common flaw that is why they make deals with bartenders and other snitches to reward them for tips. Most criminals wonder how the cops found out, never realizing that they we're responsible because they couldn't button-up their loose-lips. It shall not happen in this case, I simply won't let it. And if it should happen that one of my associates should suffer from that terrible affliction, the only story they will be able to tell would be baseless, because the person they dealt with didn't really exist.

Let's break this down step by step. My first task was to obtain the photos of the vault, it was now completed. The next step was to develop these photos and that is where my *trust no one policy* comes into play. Although I do not know how to develop films, I am going to learn and will develop these on my own. I have picked up a couple of books on the art of developing film. I am converting my closet into a dark room and even though it is cramped, it will suffice. Once I have developed the film I will get rid of the equipment and the books. This step is essential in my efforts to remain totally invisible. I want to be known as a simple clothing salesman and nothing else, no one must ever know the other side of me! Of course, I really don't have much to worry about because there is no reason for the cops to ever suspect me, but just in case, there will be no trace of anything out of the ordinary. I will not ever leave any clues behind, I'm certain of that.

Each day after work I went home as usual and studied how to develop film. I took some unimportant photos to use as experiments while learning how to develop black and white photos. I purchased the necessary materials like developing fluid, etc. When doing so, I was in disguise even though it was not necessary as there wasn't a remote possibility I would be under suspicion, but I was not taking any unnecessary risks. I enjoyed the challenge and it consumed my time for the next two weeks, but one thing was for sure, I now knew how to develop film. I now had photos of the entire vault and began an in depth study of the layout. I counted how many large boxes would have to be opened. This was important as it gave me an idea how many there are, how many small, medium, and large boxes that I must open. The vault area became very familiar to me, I could close my eyes and see the entire area. It also gave me an idea of where I was to drill when I find a way into the vault area. The layout was very essential to a successful plan, at least it would help me in my attempt to eliminate errors.

I was very satisfied with my progress and now I had to embark on step two. How to get into the vault area when the Bank is closed? That was my first priority, after all, if I can't gain access to the vault area I really don't have to worry about getting the money out of there. My mindset is that I will find a way and will succeed in my objective, therefore I must plan ahead. The project can only be successful if it is thought out very carefully and each phase is thoroughly laid out. How to get out carrying a great deal of money is another big problem but I'm certain I will be able to solve that very soon. The amount of cash I believe is in those boxes must be staggering. I say that because of what Benny has told me and that there are other people who also have safety boxes beside Benny and I'll bet they hide their cash there too. The next step would be where to hide the money. Just imagine how much space a few million dollars will take up. Not having any experience with this sort of task I imagine that a great deal of the cash would be in smaller denominations, thus making the load a lot heavier and more bulky. So how to get the money away from the job site was a major concern. Of course, the next phase would also be a very big problem as it was simply unwise for anyone who pulled off a job like this to suddenly appear to be wealthy. The very first thing the cops will be looking for is anyone who starts to spend money in a manner that would raise suspicion. It's easy to arouse suspicions when one starts to throw money around or talk about their new found wealth. For this very reason alone the cops usually pay bartenders, and other people, who have a lot of contact with people a finder's fee for clues that lead to the apprehension of crooks. Usually people who spend time in bars like to talk and with the help of a drink or two often say things to impress others. They think no one hears when, in fact, the bartender is already heading towards the phone. Human nature dictates people's desire to brag about their accomplishments and thus the road to prison is paved with best of intentions. Keeping one's mouth shut is harder than committing the deed itself and has undone many a perfect crime. There was a lot of work still to be done, but I didn't mind it at all. Something as important, and as exciting as this, must be well planned and expertly executed to be successful. I will make sure that every base is covered and that this will be the perfect and most successful crime of all time.

Reconnaissance:

WITHOUT A CLEAR CUT LINE OF ATTACK THE PLAN WOULD fail before it is even off the ground. There are so many things I must clear-up and make sure that every question is answered before I can move forward. For example---how to get a copy of the layout of the Bank? Where will I find some type of plan? How and where each adjoining structure meets the Bank wall? Without doubt, the Bank must have built a very thick wall of concrete when putting in the safe boxes. No doubt the Bank must have thought of every angle when it constructed the safe box room and now I must find how to deconstruct it quickly and gain access to the area, an area no one is supposed to penetrate.

I discovered nothing by walking the area as there wasn't any clues as what was the closest access point to the proximity of the safe box area. The Bank was built over the old subway system and has been in this location for years. Did they take steps to secure the floors or did they trust the original construction? My supposition was that they built things a lot stronger and better many years ago so it was logical that the designers of the Bank left the floor area as is. If that was the case, and I felt it was, at least at this juncture, they could not really improve on the safety of the floor.

I was getting very discouraged as my daily walks past the Bank produced nothing. The pizza shop next to the Bank didn't have any distinguishing things about it but was on the wrong side of the building so their basement was not of any value. The fact that they stayed open late, especially on weekends, made the place worthless. On the left side of the Bank was Mario's Bar and Grill. It had a basement and possibly could be an entry point to the vault. The problem here, once again, was that they stayed open until four in the morning and kept all their beer kegs in there. If one of the beers on draft would malfunction or they ran out of beer, they would be forced to go into the basement to correct the problem. No, the Bar was out of the question and that left only one other access area. The front of the Bank faced Fifth Avenue with a side entrance on Twenty-Third and right underneath was the subway entrance. Needless to say we cannot use that way to burrow under the Bank as it is in use twenty-four hours a day and, besides, how the hell would we ever get our equipment in and our loot out? It didn't look good at this point and although knocking over the safety deposit boxes of a bank was a great idea, implementation was not so simple! As a matter-of-fact it seemed impossible and that made me more determined. There had to be a way, and as far as I was concerned, I was positive that the Bank did not take any additional safety steps to protect the safety box floor area because of the other businesses surrounding them. The fact that three of the surrounding occupants operated on a seven day schedule and remained open close to twenty-four hours a day and a subway station that remained in use twenty-four hours-a-day, there would not be any need to fool with the floor. The only other access to the Bank would be the roof and I'm sure they have reinforced that. Anyone who would be foolish enough to try to get through the roof would find it an impossible task and would probably be arrested the moment they started to hack their way in. I did some research and found that banks as far back as 1870 had safety deposit boxes for their customers so this was not new in any way. Way back then, when this Bank took over this property about thirty years earlier, no one would think there were any weak spots in the Bank's structure especially in the safe box area. It was my job to find that weak spot and exploit it and that is what I was about to do!

Needless to say I was bummed out. All these weeks of planning, dreaming, and now what? I can't explain how I felt, thinking about the tremendous amount of cash sitting there, and now it seemed way out of reach. I refused to believe that I was stymied so soon into the project-all because we can't get in and can't get out. No wonder they are called safety deposit boxes, stuff is pretty safe while in these boxes.

I was sitting at home one evening and wondering if I should just take my loss and scrap the entire project when a thought ran through my head. Where is the weakest spot in this puzzle? I was not thinking clearly until this very moment, of course, it's the subway.

It was late in the day on a hot and muggy Tuesday in July when I finally closed up shop and walked the three blocks to the subway station. I guess because of the weather and the time of year, and being after rush hour, the platform was nearly empty. Trains were slow this time of day as usage was not heavy at all. Also a lot of people were on vacation so traffic was light. As I stood there, feeling pretty low, I may add, I noticed a door in the wall. The door looked as if it was never ever used as the paint seemed to be covering it entirely. If I wasn't mistaken the door was on the Bank side and possibly could lead right underneath it. Of course, I couldn't tell much until I opened the door and checked things out. I walked over to the door, I tried to be very casual like when someone is waiting for a train they wander aimlessly, well I tried to do just that and when no one was paying any attention, I tried the handle expecting it to be locked. Much to my surprise the handle turned and with some effort I was able to push the door open with my shoulder. I looked behind to make sure no one was curious and slipped into the room very quickly. I was in a large area of nothing but a few maintenance tools. I didn't need a light as there was plenty of overhead lights, some were burnt out but a few were still working. They weren't very bright but bright enough to see where I was going. Obviously the lights were on a circuit that must be attached to a timer. I really did not understand why they were on or what this room was used for. No one was in the room and it appeared to me that no one ever comes to it. There was dust on the floor but no footprints that meant that no one has been in here for a long time. The tools that were scattered around had a layer of dust on them as well and had to be many years old. One broom that was leaning against the wall had a cobweb on it. My spirits started to rise as I began exploring this area more thoroughly. My mood changed from low to high, "*Maybe*," I said to myself, "*maybe this could be the answer.*" I began to open doors that led to more rooms but they didn't have lights that worked. I felt like I had discovered a hidden land, a place that no one has been to in years. The darkness was darker than I have ever experienced, I thought it would be best if I got out of here and returned with the proper equipment so I could explore these areas, the sooner the better. I could see dropping and paw prints on the floor, I was now certain that the tenants down here were of the four legged variety, the ones I didn't like. I made a mental note to make sure I also bring a tape measure, a pad of paper and a powerful light. I will have to measure this area and ascertain where the floor of the Bank is and then find the vault area. I also needed to locate an area where I can store and hide the loot from the job. There was no way I could just cart out bags and bags of money with people waiting for trains. I decided not to worry about that for now, at least not at this juncture of the project. Who knows, the areas I have just discovered could prove to be useless, so the concern over the disposition of the loot was really meaningless. I left the area and went back to the platform to wait for my train. My mind was spinning, the project was back on track and so was I.

It took another week before I could get into that room again. Mostly because I had to work a lot that week due to a sale that was planned without consideration that I had a project in my mind. This was our annual sale to try and drum up business during a slow summer season. Finally my shift had ended, I now had two days off and could get to see just what I am up against in my new found areas. First thing Sunday morning I left my apartment carrying a small bag that contained the equipment I needed to explore the area. I dressed in a disguise and looked like a janitor on his way to work. I was carrying a small bag that looked like a lunch bag, nothing unusual for a working man. I followed the same routine and found the door locked and realized that when I left the room I didn't leave the lock on the off position and it locked automatically when closing. I had a tool in my bag that I brought with in case I found some doors locked inside and needed to open them. It took me only thirty seconds or less to get the door open, the lock was old and easy to manipulate. I stepped inside and found nothing different than I'd found the first time I was there. I immediately went into the other areas with my flashlight and was able to see that this entire area was an abandon tunnel that perhaps was once a main artery for the subway but hasn't been used in many years. This was the original subway line from way back at the beginning, sometime in the 1900's. I took out my pad and drew a map of the area complete with measurements. It seemed to me that this was the place and I was actually standing directly under the safe box vault. My heart was beating so fast I had to stop and take a few deep breaths to compose myself. This was the place, I could feel it in my bones this area would play a big part in my plan. I decided to take a walk through the tunnel to see how far it goes and where it may lead. I had to see if there were other access areas attached to this tunnel? Are there additional exits that might be more convenient to insure success of the plan? There was so many things I needed to know and I was going to find out everything I possibly could about this tunnel. I'm certain that the moment the cops get on the scene they will block off the tunnels as well as any other avenues of escape. There was no sense in doing all this work and then losing the rewards. Leaving the money anywhere in these tunnels would be the wrong thing to do. I might as well not do the job if I elect to that. The cops will shut this place down and make sure there is no way one could enter or leave this area ever again, so the plan will have to include removing the cash before anyone becomes aware that there has been a robbery committed. I will have to be very thorough no matter how long it takes.

I spent the next four hours in the tunnels checking every nook and cranny. I could not leave anything to chance, I had to make sure I knew exactly what existed down there. I made a floor plan and made sure I had every room located and completely explored. I was very thorough and made sure I wouldn't have any surprises! I found many rooms that probably served as service areas but have not been touched in many years and led nowhere. I am sure these tunnels haven't been used since the early thirties, perhaps even longer. I will research all that over the next few weeks. I discovered that I could not exit the tunnel from the other end. It seemed that when they constructed the new tunnel they closed off one end of the tunnel with concrete blocks and debris they didn't want to haul out. I guess that once the new line was complete, they had no more use for the old and just left everything there, time will take care of the rest. It also reinforced my theory that no one really comes down here, there is no reason to as it is a thing of the past and probably never comes into mind, after all, there is no reason to. If I took the old tunnel further north, I would be boxed in and could not possibly escape, it ended somewhere in the middle of the run between Forty-Second Street and Thirty-Fourth Street and in between two different stops. Even if there was a way out in this direction we would have to walk along the active tracks and that would be dangerous and slow, especially when carrying sacks of money, not only that, how would it look if two or three people emerged from the tracks carrying a heavy pack? It would not be wise to do that, I was sure of that. I completed my reconnaissance and made sure I didn't leave any clues that I had been there. I could not help but leave some footprints on the floor simply because the dust was so thick. If I didn't pass this way again, time will cover these footprints with a new layer of dust. I really didn't worry because I didn't feel anyone would come down here to look around. It didn't appear to me that anyone has been here for many years except the rats.

I had brought a different door lock so I could lock the room and open it whenever I wanted and keep any curious souls out of my new found space. I changed the lock in a matter of a few minutes. I bought the replacement lock at a new and used shop on Canal Street, I wanted a used and old looking one that didn't look out of place. I was pleased with the look of the replacement door handle and lock. I would sleep better knowing that I protected this area especially after I start leaving equipment there. The subway platform was, as most of the stations are, a flat surface that faces the tracks where the riders wait for their train to arrive. Next to one of the pillars is a short hallway that leads to nothing and is fairly dark except one small bulb. That is where my special door was located and it leads to the room directly under the safety box vault, there was no doubt about it.

I spent a few hours on the platform trying to see if there is a pattern I could rely upon. The pattern I was looking for was the amount of people coming and going and at what hours. I needed to know the traffic patterns of the riders in order to access my special room. I had to bring material to this room and I had to do it unnoticed. One doesn't carry a ladder into a subway station and expect this to go by as routine. Besides, it was obvious to me that I would have to make many trips in and out of the area and needed a schedule, one that wouldn't get anyone's suspicions up. I finally got out of the subway and went home. I was tired, hungry, and needed sleep. Tomorrow was another day off and I planned on spending the day at the main library on Forty-Second Street and Fifth Avenue. I figured I'll kill two birds with one stone by hanging around the Twenty-Third Street subway station on my way to the library. I needed to research the New York City Subway System from a passenger's perspective and see what the old system looked like. Perhaps I can zero in on the location of the Twenty-Third and Fifth Avenue's old system and help me pin-point just where I am to dig my gold mine. I also felt that any facts about New York's first subway system would be kept at the library. After all, New York was proud of their subway system. They don't only have books, and manuscripts, but interesting facts about this City, after all New York is a City known throughout the World and any new immigrant or tourist who would like to broaden their knowledge of this great City would come to the library to find out more. I always went to the library in disguise and used different names in case the cops are smart enough to investigate who expressed an interest in the subway system. In order to make this as untraceable as possible I spent the first few hours on Monday morning changing my appearance. The disguises I bought a few days ago at a costume shop on the West Side of the City proved to be perfect for my trip to the library. I had bought two wigs at another shop located in the Bowery, once again hoping to cover my trail as best as I can. I also felt that these purchases will be long forgotten in time as the actual deed will not take place for many months and I'm sure any library clerk will have seen hundreds of people since then. There is no room for carelessness so a little overkill will not be in vain. There were so many details that had to be covered, it was mind boggling but very exciting just to make sure this project was flawless. Without clues what could the cops do? This reconnaissance was the most important part of this project, no clues, no mistakes, no chances, and nothing to lead the cops to who may have done it. I am in no rush at all, those who keep their money in these boxes don't usually spend it too quickly and are too busy putting more in. I'll wait until everything is just right and then the deed will be done. Perfection can't be rushed and being the perfect crime requires patience. I knew I have these attributes and nothing could deter me from being patient and efficient, after all, the fruits of the deed will be enjoyed for years and years, plenty of time to savor the rewards as long as one is careful.

Before going to the library I got off the subway at the Twenty-Third Street Station and stood around for an hour or so. I wanted to see how crowded the Station got and what activity took place. The one fly in the ointment was the newspaper stand that was open all day and closed by eight in the evening. Although the stand was located before the turnstiles, it was still a look-out point for something that might be construed as unusual. The one good part was that they didn't have a view of the platform area and none at all of the short hallway to my special room. They could only present a problem when bringing in large items like a step ladder or taking out heavy bags of money. I will have to make sure I solve this problem very soon. I then took the train to Forty-Second Street and spent the day in the library reading and making notes about the subway system. I learned a great deal about the new and old systems and finally found the exact location of the old system and the tracks that I walked earlier. There it was, in a clear and detailed description, the station, the tunnels and the storage rooms. The original subway system, how proud the City of New York was, and I was the recipient of this knowledge even if it was for a different reason. I was also very lucky when I came across an article in the Daily News. It was all about the construction of a new bank and the location was exactly where I banked. It wasn't called the BNZ Bank back then as they referred to it as the First New York Subway Bank. I guess somewhere down the line they either sold it or merged with BNZ Bank. It didn't matter to me, all I cared about was the job at hand.

I now had my work cut out for me even though the trip to the library helped clarify a lot of things. One thing I did discover was, all the exits I could have used at the other end of the tunnel unfortunately were all blocked with debris and were not accessible any longer, the only way in and out was via my little hallway and the magic door, as I now call it.

I still didn't have enough information and returned to the library on the following Sunday to continue my reading. I made copious notes, no detail was too small. I did not want to visit the library too often, I thought it may arouse suspicion even though I was in a different disguise each time. By the end of my second trip I had enough information to work with. I was certain I had weeks and weeks of drawings and calculations to make and then destroy. I decided to shred all papers I work with and make sure there are no scraps left around. I placed some of the papers in incinerators in various buildings. Papers burn very easily and quickly and no traces are left behind. No laziness here, the project was far too important and I knew this wasn't going to be an easy task, but nothing worthwhile is.

My work schedule kept me busy from Tuesday through Saturday. I didn't mind this as I was able to return home after work and put in a few hours towards my project. I worked on the project while I ate my dinner. I didn't watch television at all, my project was far too important, therefore I did this each and every night non-stop. Once I felt tired I quit working on the project and hid the worksheets in case someone would come into my apartment, invited or not. I made sure that my hiding place was secure even though there wasn't any reason for someone to come into my apartment. I realized that my enthusiasm could easily take over and I could make a mistake here and there and not realize it until it might be too late so I set a schedule. I was rigid about this as I felt it was not in my best interest to make an error, and when one is tired it's easy to make one or two. It only takes one mistake to ruin the best laid plans and I was determined not to make any. I quit working each and every night at precisely nine-thirty, it didn't matter if I was tired or not. As far as I was concerned this was my discipline to make certain I didn't make any errors. The smallest of details could be the undoing of this project and I wasn't going to be defeated by something like that. I also made sure that any material I was working on was well hidden each day. If my place was broken into, no one would find any clue about my secret project. My planning was meticulous, each detail was carefully studied over and over again until I was certain it was perfect. Once I was convinced things were right I went over them again. Funny how you see something on Tuesday and on Friday it looks different.

The Project:

I HAD FINALLY PIN-POINTED THE LOCATION OF THE SAFETY deposit boxes vault. My confidence in the project soared. The area I have found in the old subway was directly under the Safe Box Room, there was no doubt about it. I now took some measurements using the information I obtained during my visits to the library. Although I was only able to walk off the measurements from the present subway platform to the area I found in the old subway section they seemed to be pretty close. I then took accurate measurements in the old tunnels and placed the exact target very near the opposite end of my new room. It was a good thing that I made a layout of my area complete with measurements, and now with that information I was able to copy from the plans I reviewed at the library, I believed I knew exactly where the mother-load was located. According to the plans I carefully perused at the library I was able to find that the safety deposit boxes were located about thirty feet into the hallway of the old subway tunnel. This helped a great deal as it was farther away from the door and will help me immensely in keeping sound from being discovered. I planned to soundproof the door as that is the only weak point and now that my starting point will be farther away, about thirty feet away from the door to be exact, I was able to breathe easier. I figured that I could get to the safe box area through the ceiling which is the floor of the vault. I can make a little noise seeing that I'll be much farther away from the door. The problem is how to drill through the concrete floor in a reasonable time. I am not sure how thick the floor is so I'll use the supposition that the thickness is six inches. I didn't know if the Bank had taken steps to add additional reinforcements when they took over the building and constructed their present bank. My guess is that they didn't, there was no need because the original floor was poured before the subway construction was begun. According to the information I was able to uncover, while at the library, was that the building was constructed two years before the subway construction crews began their project. The plans as well as information on other buildings that were constructed at that time all indicated that foundations were poured at five to six inches thick. This would be more than enough thickness to thwart any attempt to gain access to the bank through that avenue. Secondly when the bank was constructed the subway was already there and operating. It didn't seem logical to me that the Bank would take on the additional expense to reinforce the floor when the subway ran twenty-four-hours-a-day. No one could access the Bank through that area as it was never free of people and activity. Also I could not find any building permits, plans, or any information that would indicate that the bank had to close for a time due to additional construction such as reinforcement of their floors. If this type of project was performed it would have made news at that time. I further felt that the bank would not accept being saddled with this tremendous expense and would have insisted that the City of New York pay the bill. Due to the fact that none of this type of rhetoric was reported in the press it reinforced my theory that the floor was not re-done in any way. I now believed that this was the original floor and has been for over fifty years without any changes. Because of this I was convinced beyond any shadow-of-a-doubt that they have done nothing. The biggest challenge will be to maintain a quiet room while drilling away, after all this is still a subway station that caters to lots of people each day. What if one person decides to take a walk down this dark passage for any reason? Here is a perfect example, what if one guy needs to take a leak and can't wait and he wanders to a dark spot where he can relieve himself in privacy. *What if'* that is the question as *what if* could be the undoing of a masterful plan! I had a plan in place for sound proofing the door as that was the only place where sound could actually escape. Now that I had discovered the exact location of the Safety Box Vault, I decided I would use overkill and add one more layer of soundproofing. Because the area is located in the hallway and is an additional thirty feet away, I will construct another barrier across the width of the hallway as well. The hallway is four feet-six inches wide, it should not be difficult to hang a thick blanket, just like the kind movers use when they are trying to protect your furniture. I'll hang that blanket from ceiling to floor and tape the ends to the walls, this should do the trick. The method was not foolproof but it will add one more sound deadening area to my room. It's almost like constructing a permanent wall, something I couldn't do under the present circumstances, so the blankets had to do. I'll do the very same with the door and will add thick weather stripping on the bottom so no light or sound will be emitted. Once I am in the room doing the job there will be no reason to exit until the project is completed. Covering the door and all cracks in it will be essential and the additional blankets in the hallway will just about keep us as quiet as church mice. As I said, the job takes careful planning and I'm doing just that. No matter how trivial I continually go over these security issues to make certain I have not left something out. Planning for the unusual, the unexpected, and a freak mishap, is almost impossible and could be the undoing of this project, that is why reviewing these plans so often was so vital. No one can predict some unusual event, but I felt I might lessen the odds and be prepared. If I stick to that process the odds are in my favor that things will proceed as it should.

I feel I have covered every possibility so far! Every eventuality I could think of. I couldn't stop thinking about ways this project could be screwed-up. You know the old expression, *'an ounce of prevention is worth a pound of cure'* and even though it is an old cliché it was quite appropriate in this instance. I kept trying to imagine the unexpected and how to prevent it.

The next dilemma was still very much in the air, how many people I will need to assist me? If I do try to do this project alone it will take several months to complete and who knows if I can complete it at all. Drilling into six inches of concrete above one's head is not an easy task. What happens when the weight of the concrete itself becomes way more that I can handle and it comes crashing down on my head? Let's assume I have, by some miracle found my way into the Safe Box area, how do I get everything out of the area after I have opened as many boxes as I can in the time frame available? Can I even open enough boxes to make all this worthwhile on my own? My answer is no! I was convinced I would need help even though I hated to add risk to the project but I realized I could not do this alone. If I bring on one person to help, it will shorten the job somewhat, but will add the possibility of exposure. If I bring on two it will help move things along a lot quicker but once again the risk of exposure gets greater. I realized I couldn't do the job alone and will have to give in to at least two associates. In order to lessen my exposure and keep this as perfect as possible I'll have to do all the preliminary work alone. I'll get the entire project ready so when I do recruit associates I will not have to rehearse anything with them. I will not have to reveal too many details about the project. I will have to let them know that the rewards are very high. That the risk is minimal and there is no violence involved. I do not have to let them know exactly what kind of job it is, where it is located, and when it is to be done. Most of the details can remain on a need-to-know basis. Although I will always be in disguise I'll make sure that the person they will get to know will always be the same. This is like a fine movie and the main character must always be in full costume at all times. This was essential for self-preservation and is the only way I can eliminate the risk of being exposed. The smallest mistake could cause the failure of this project, therefore, I still must be very careful not to leave any clues as to my real identity. I realized that I must keep everything about the project as secret as possible, especially the job's location is and what it would entail, just in case I was dealing with an undercover cop. Yes, I realized that I must take the attitude that I cannot trust anyone especially those I may meet in bars or other questionable places. I will take my time getting the project ready and will change my routine so I may meet people and make judgments about their ability to be trusted. I will wait and see how it progresses before making any decision regarding as to who will be my associates. I'm sure that no matter how much I emphasize to my new associates about keeping one's mouth shut there will come a time when one or the other will say something they shouldn't, and that could be the undoing of the project before it begins. I wasn't worried what anyone could say after the completion of the project. It is human nature to brag when one is successful so the chances of silence being adhered to is slim. I feel we can keep the project secret before the actual deed because I won't reveal very much about it except that one could become a millionaire overnight. The lure of those riches will buy the silence required to maintain secrecy. At least that was my theory and I was sticking to it.

I made up my mind to spend every day off researching, purchasing, and reviewing the plans. I needed to do a few preliminary things to secure the room before I put the project into high gear. I placed a few things in the room as a test to see if they would be disturbed. I didn't mind if a few worthless items were stolen as that would tell me that my room was being penetrated. I would have to rethink the project if that happened. I would, most likely have to abandon the project, rather than take any risk. So far, in the past few weeks, nothing has been disturbed and in my opinion nothing will be, it was an abandoned area and everything I have seen so far proved me right. I felt if anyone was using the room as a shelter I would see the footprints in the dust and if a subway employee should wander in he would have to break or pick the new lock. I did walk the entire subway complex more than once and found nothing disturbed, I wanted to make sure there wasn't another entrance where some bum or anyone could find their way into this complex. After all, if one read the Batman comics, they would see that one of the characters used the old subway station as his headquarters. Even though that was fiction it didn't mean that some curious person wouldn't explore abandoned subway stations. These facts, although quite a remote possibilities, made me check and recheck the entire subway cavern over and over many times. I was finally convinced that I was alone in this abandoned World of years past and it was safe to proceed. This being the case I could remain with the project as planned.

I clearly understood that after the project would be completed there will be an immediate rush by the cops to investigate every angle possible. They will not have a single clue as to who did this. They will tear the tunnels apart and look for any clues possible and when they feel they are being stymied they will begin to grasp at any straws possible and would probably investigate every shop in and around the Bank. Of course, a lot of that would be routine. I'm sure they will check out everyone who has a box and that will include me. I have to maintain the same profile I have kept for the last year. Any changes could arouse suspicion and that included my asking Saturday off as that was my busiest day of the week. I realized that I must stay on as a haberdashery salesperson for at least another year before I could change my way of life.

I continued to do things in the same manner as I have always done. The only change now was that when I went to the underground room I would always be in disguise. This was an added precaution in case someone did see me and recognized me as the sales person from the store up the street. As long as I was in disguise I will never be recognized. I also thought that different disguises would be better if anyone did pay attention. They would see an older person with a mustache, some gray hair and wearing glasses. The next time they would see a different person and that alone would confuse the cops even more. When smuggling in equipment, I used a long coat as long as the weather permitted me to do so. Other times I dressed as a subway employee complete with a badge. I always made sure that my facial disguise was not too crazy as I didn't want to stand out. People will remember the guy with one leg, or a bad facial complexion or a wild looking hat. Those were things that would bring attention and I had to make sure I never did that. Of course, I could only wear the long coat while the weather was still chilly and then I had to find another way. That was when I decided to take on the subway employee disguise. What was the most inconspicuous costume of all? Of course, a subway employee. They were always doing things in the subway and it wasn't out of the ordinary and no one would pay any attention, especially a year later when the project will take place.

It took me about thirty minutes to put on my make-up thus making my time very precious as I had to be home by eleven each night so I would be ready for work the next day. This was my new schedule and kept me sharp enough for work and to continue in my quest. This required a change in my routine, but this job was first priority so I did make this sacrifice. I was getting better each time at putting on make-up, I guess when all this is over I will be able to get a job in Hollywood as a make-up man. The one thing I was very happy about was that I did change the handle on the door of my special room. By the way, just in case anyone is concerned I always wore gloves so I would not leave any fingerprints. Whenever my hand touched the handle of the door it was covered by something.

It was my day off and as usual I dressed as a subway worker and carried an identity card that looked like one the employees of the transit system used. I still had a problem and that was to enter the subway via the service door used by the workers. I didn't have a key that would allow me access via the service door so I went to the kiosk and asked the girl if I could borrow her key. I told her I will return it in a minute and showed her my identity card. She pulled out her purse and took out her key and gave it to me. I had a wax mold with me and pressed the key into it and now all I had to do was to make an exact copy. I left the gate open and ran back to the kiosk and thanked her for her key and then returned to the gate. Later that day, and using a different disguise, I went over to see a guy that I heard made copies of passports, keys and other identification papers for a price. I paid him twenty bucks to make a proper copy and now I could enter the subway through the side door next to the turnstiles as all subway workers did. The key fit all subway stations as far as I knew. I wore jeans, a shirt, and a hard hat that was in keeping with the subway worker's dress code. I had a small tag hanging from my jacket showing a picture of myself, of course, disguised and looking like any other subway worker. I had a few pieces of the plan to test out and this was the best way to do it. It was a Monday and I wanted the station to be crowded and see if I would be noticed. Most people on their way to work would probably ignore me as another subway worker which was not uncommon. I also wanted to enter the subway station without any hassle from anyone and see if I can enter my secret room from another angle. I noticed that if I turn right immediately after I have descended the stairs I can disappear into the shadows and make my way to the room unnoticed rather than going to the platform. I felt if I tried this while disguised as a subway employee I will have less hassles. If I was discovered I could just say I was on my way towards a maintenance area. The most important thing was to discover if I could enter and leave unnoticed. I just wanted to be a part of the scenery and blend right in. That may sound like I was over cautious but it was very important because of the constant movement of people. In a subway every few minutes, different people come and go. Would my exiting bring more stares or would people just continue on their way indifferent to everything else? If I went in as a subway worker and emerged as another commuter, would anyone pay any attention to me? Every few minutes another train arrived or left and a different crowd took over the station. Some people were coming in and running towards the train, their only thought was to get on that train before the doors closed. Other were getting off the train and rushing towards the exits and didn't spare a moment to see anything else. The situation remained the same train after train with some people hanging around the platform for three or four minutes and others rushing as last minute commuters. The same results in all cases, no one took a second glance, they were all too busy with their own thoughts and paid little or no attention to anything else. I tried this on two Mondays and came-up with the same results, I was satisfied with my experiment.

I now decided to try the same experiment at a later time when things would be less busy. I arrived at the subway station a little after ten. I figured that the rush hour traffic was over and the station would be less crowded. This would make being detected less likely even though I was dressed as a subway employee. I was right, the area had very few people milling about waiting for their train to appear. I went down the stairs completely unnoticed and took the right turn as planned and once again I was invisible. Not one person turned their heads to look at me. Of course, this is what a New Yorker does, most are far too busy to care about the other's actions and usually mind's his own business.

From here it was an easy walk to the room, it took me a half-hour to make sure my new handle was installed properly. I installed it a week ago but had a feeling I might not have installed it just right and I also wanted to make sure no one was tampering with it. The door handle and lock was intact and had never been touched. The room was secure and remained lost to the World. I also left a five dollar bill on the floor and it was still there, I had no doubt that this was the place, this was my gold mine and all I needed to do was to extract the treasure and I'd be rich forever. I felt better, a lot more confident in my plan now that the room was secure. I would be able to start bringing in my equipment and not concern myself with detection.

The next task was to find the electrical fuse box. I had light in the room and found one electrical outlet but I didn't know how many amps the fuse box had. I also didn't know if the fuse box serviced more than one area. These things are very important to the success of the operation. I spent another few hours searching for the fuse box and finally found a hallway in the tunnel of the old subway station. The passage must have been an original one and hasn't seen any foot traffic for years. I thought I went down this tunnel before but stopped short of this area. I knew I was the first visitor in here in a long time, it was evident to me as I was disturbing a thick layer of dust that was on the floor. My footprints showed up easily, thus my assumption of no traffic. I found another room just off the passageway that was an ancient electrical room. There were four fuse boxes and all of them seemed to be in working order. Each box was clearly marked with a room number, the problem was that I didn't know what room number I was using. I removed one of the fuses and went back to the room, wrong one. I searched above the door to see if there was a number but there wasn't. I went back and replaced the fuse I had taken out and removed another. This one turned out the lights in the electrical room. I quickly replaced that one and removed another and walked back and to my delight, the room was dark. I was in room #333 and held a fifteen amp fuse in my hand. I took the fuse so I could find a matching thirty amp fuse. These fuses were no longer in use as modern times dictated breaker fuses. All I had to do now was find a store that still had fuses of this type. It was like trying to find tubes for my old radio when now all the radios were transistors. I could not use less than thirty amps as a lesser fuse would not handle the load when using the power tools.

I had to work all week and could not get out of the store early enough to make the trip to Canal Street where I could look for these old fuses. I had no choice but to wait a full week before going out to find the fuse. I went down to Canal Street in the Bowery and began my search. Of course, I disguised myself as a janitor. I wore a faded pair of jeans and a plaid shirt and an old jacket and a hat. I had a beard and mustache and spoke with an accent that would lead someone to believe I was from a European country. I went into an electrical store, or at least that is what the sign outside said. It was literally a junk shop. *"Hello sir, would you have fuses like this."* I said as I showed the clerk the fuse I had taken from the subway electrical room.

"Yes, I think we have some lying around," he said as he went towards the back of the store. He rummaged through a counter that was filled with old radio tubes and fuses that looked like the one I showed him.

"I would need a thirty amp, maybe you have two?" I said using my best European accent.

"Here we are. I have one, let me see if there is one more. Ah there it is, we now have two, is there anything else I can help you with?" the clerk asked.

"No tanks, how much are dese?" I asked.

"One dollar and ninety-five cents each," he said.

"Maybe you can find one more, I might as well have extras," I said.

He found another and wrote out a receipt. I paid in cash and left the store. I was very pleased now that I have fuses and back-up reserves. Everything was working to perfection and I was very excited. Funny how the purchase of a few fuses can make one feel like they have just conquered the World. Well, that was how I felt and it gave me confidence that my plan wasn't just pie in the sky!

Preparations:

MY FIRST TASK WAS TO FIND A LOCATION WHERE I COULD work unnoticed. Each day I bought the papers and looked under garage for rent. I was looking for a place in the Bronx that I could rent so I could test out certain equipment for the project. I chose the Bronx because it was easier to drive there from my Upper East Side apartment. I called a number of the ads and finally hit on one that sounded pretty good. The lady I spoke with sounded like she was from Eastern Europe, her accent was very thick. She told me that her husband died a year ago and she had a garage in the back where he kept his car. The one problem was that the car hasn't been touched in over two years and she does not know how to drive. She wanted ten dollars a month for the space but didn't know what to do with the car. I told her not to worry about the car because I was also looking to buy a car and I might be able to buy hers.

I took the train to her place and introduced myself, *"I'm Harold Robinson, I called you about the garage,"* I said.

"Oh yes, come right in please," she said. *"Would you like something to drink?"*

"No thanks, can we see the garage?" I said.

She took me through the house to the back door which opened into a yard at the end of the building we were in. At the end of the yard there was another building that looked like an old wooden shack, one that was about to fall down. My first reaction was that my trip was wasted, but she was a nice old lady and I wanted to be polite so we continued to the garage. I opened the door that seemed to sag as the door opened wider and wider. The floor of the garage was just plain dirt. There was a roof and walls but the structure looked like it was about to collapse. It was a sad excuse for garage, but an old 1951 Dodge car was parked in the middle of this place.

"Vat you tink, Mr. Robinson?" the old lady asked. "It isn't a very good garage but my husband, Ivan, got sick over two years ago and not have time to fix it up. Also he don't drive the car for more than two years. Vat you tink, you can use?'"

It had electricity but no water but I spied a spigot nearby and could use a garden hose. The space was no bargain and the car made it less of an ideal place to work. If the weather was cold this place had to be colder and terribly hard to work in. During the warm season it would be okay but what will I do for the next couple of months? She looked old and sad and obviously alone. "Do you have any children?" I asked.

"No I'm all alone since my Husband left me. My name is Polina Stressky, you call me Polina, okay!" she said.

"It is a pleasure to meet you Polina. I will see what I can do with the car. The battery is probably dead and if it hasn't been used for two years who knows what is wrong with it. I'll take it to a garage and if the car works I'll give you forty dollars for it. If the car does not work I'll get rid of it for you. If that is okay with you Polina, then we can have a deal," I said because I felt a pain in my heart for this lonely old woman. She told me that she came to America over forty years ago and has always lived in this house. It wasn't a large house but it certainly served its purpose. We agreed on the deal and wrote out a bill of sale for the car to Harold Robinson and explained that if the car wasn't any good we'll tear this up, but I'll try to fix it if possible. This was not the best place for anyone who needs a garage or work space but for me this was perfect. There was no one around to bother me and it was easy to get there and

I'm sure this old lady would not interfere with me. I gave her twenty dollars to cover the next two months and thanked her for being so nice. She was thrilled with the money and gave me a big hug and a kiss on the cheek.

My first task was to get this car running. I removed the battery and found a service station a few blocks from the place and had the guy charge the battery. He told me that he doubted if it will hold the charge. He was right and sold me a new six volt battery and put it on a charge. He also volunteered to help me get the car started at no charge. Once again he doubted if it will start that easily but there is no harm in trying. The first thing he did was to remove all of the spark plugs and showed me the carbon on the ends of them. He suggested that we replace them all and that we empty the gas tank and fill it up with fresh gasoline. He also took off the oil pan after he emptied the engine oil to see if things looked okay. He put the oil pan back on and filled the engine with new oil. He installed the new spark plugs but left one out. He explained to me that it will be easier for the engine to turn over without any fire in one cylinder. It will run rough until he puts in the missing plug but that will not hurt the engine. Finally after two hours we were ready for ignition and much to my surprise the car started. He let it run for a few minutes and then installed the missing spark plug and backed the car out of the space. I was thrilled and the entire charge was twenty-four dollars. When I offered him a tip he refused and explained that he knew Mr. Stressky and serviced this car for him for five years. When he died he felt very sorry for Mrs. Stressky as she seemed so lost. He offered her fifty dollars for the car but she refused simply because she was so heartbroken with her husband's death. In time we both forgot about the car until now. *"It's sort of in the family, if you know what I mean?"* he said. *"One thing Mr. Robinson, when you get tired of the car please let me buy it from you."*

Now that the car was working I made sure I registered it. I went to DMV in the Bronx and showed them bill of sale and completed the form for new tags. I registered the car at an address in Brooklyn that corresponded to my phony driver's license. I wasn't going to screw-up my project because of some silly omission like a wrong license or something like that.

Now that I had a second car and a space to work in, I started to make runs to flea markets. The beauty of the second car was that it was registered to Harold Robinson so I was free of exposure if someone would take the license number down. I honestly didn't feel any danger that someone would remember me a year later. I was no more out of place than any other flea market buyer.

My next two Sundays were spent going to New Jersey where I found two big flea markets. I found the blankets I needed for my soundproofing even though they were dirty and smelled a little raunchy. They would do the trick perfectly because they were thick and I got them at bargain prices, like two dollars each. I took all the guy had, nine in all. I also found, at another flea market, some diamond tipped drill bits that were probably stolen or the guy didn't know the value of what he had. He asked me for two dollars for each one and I offered him seven-fifty for the six, he took it and I was thrilled once again. These bits at the hardware store would run me at least fifteen dollars each. I also bought a few rolls of masking tape and a sledge hammer that weighed ten pounds, a few screwdrivers and one crowbar and three punches and a regular hammer. Everything, except the drill bits, were used but that didn't make any difference to me. Seeing that I have a limited budget I must take advantage of every bargain I can get. One would laugh at the entire project when one thinks about the objective. Here I am, an ordinary working stiff that earns no more than one hundred and fifty dollars a week, planning a heist with a potential of millions of dollars but not having enough money to buy new equipment. I thought it was ironical to say the least.

I continued on my buying spree and was thrilled with the savings by buying used stuff for next to nothing. I found another flea market just off of route forty-six where one guy had a metal box that almost looked like an old safety deposit box. He had a key for it which didn't mean anything to me, I offered him two dollars for the box and he agreed. I wish he had a couple more, but he didn't. I also found a vendor that had an assortment of various tools, most I had no idea what they were for used for, but for five dollars it was a good deal and I was able to take a completely full toolbox and figured that I couldn't go wrong with this purchase.

Over the next few weeks I began buying the equipment I would need. I bought two electric drills, one was a regular one, and the other was a heavy duty version. I took the drills to my new workshop where I could test them out. The one problem I was facing in my new work space was the kindness of Polina. Every time I arrived she would look out the window and in a few minutes would be knocking on the garage door with a plate of food. It was her responsibility, as far as she was concerned, to make sure I was eating properly. I loved her for her genuine caring, but it did make me feel very uncomfortable. Here I was trying to hide what I was doing and this wonderful and kind lady kept right on poking her nose in my affairs. She meant no harm and I'm certain she never suspected that my motives were less than honorable. I was always in disguise as Harold Robinson so if anything did develop and she was questioned by the cops she would only know me as Harold Robinson. She was not a threat but still I was a little uncomfortable even though she didn't understand anything I was doing.

During the week I could not work in my space in the Bronx, it was too far and I finished work way too late. I made certain I visited my special room as often as possible, this was for my psyche just to see that the room remained untouched. I also moved stuff into the special room as often as I could. I went over to the room at least three times a week to make sure nothing was disturbed. Each time I entered the room and saw the five dollar bill lying on the floor I felt great. It's hard to describe the feeling but it was like I was being transported to another World each time I entered the place and nothing was disturbed. It was like I had discovered a treasure mine and had to make sure it was always there.

After a few trips I had all the nine blankets in the special room. I also decided to hook-up one of the blankets in the hallway where the drilling will be done. I placed one of the blankets at the bottom of the door to the room. I wanted to eliminate the light, although very faint, it could still be detected from the outside if one walked down the hallway. By eliminating the light no one will pay any attention to this door and will just move on. I spent a couple of evenings installing two blankets from the ceiling to the floor and securing them to the side walls. I did this so I would feel better that I have been able to cut out some of the noise. When the time for the actual project comes I'll secure the bottoms and try to keep the two blankets together using the masking tape and some thread. Most importantly was my head. When taking on a project such as this, one has to be sharp, confident, and sure of the actions they take. If I falter, I fail and that cannot be an option, thus, I'll test and re-test until every detail is perfect and all the pieces fit.

On my days off I worked in the garage. I worked late into the night because I needed to know if my plan will succeed or fail. I bought six concrete blocks twelve inches by twelve inches and two inches thick. I now had a metal container, an old steel safe that I picked up for five dollars because it had no key and the guy didn't know the combination. Of course, my interest was to see if I could drill through this piece of steel and if so a safety deposit box will be a piece of cake. On Sunday morning, as early as eight, I began drilling the concrete blocks. It took me until nine-fifteen to drill through the three blocks. That meant I would probably need one and one-half hours to drill through six inches of concrete. Perhaps longer because I'm sure there is re-bar mixed in with the concrete as a reinforcement for the floor. If I allow two hours per hole I will need about twenty-four hours to open a hole on the floor that I could fit through.

When I was at the flea markets I found some knapsacks that I was able to purchase for five dollars each. These we're originally military knapsacks and looked pretty sturdy. The one problem I felt about these was the khaki color so I bought some dye and let them soak in my apartment in a metal tub that I bought, for two days. The dye was navy blue and now these knapsacks were also navy blue. I felt it would not be as suspicious as khaki.

In the meantime I was testing the drills. I had bought three concrete blocks that were two inches thick and brought them to the garage. I also brought some of my equipment moving them piece by piece into the garage. I carefully made sure that each piece of equipment worked to perfection. If there were any mistakes to be made it had to be now and not in the middle of the job. Each piece of equipment was for a specific purpose and I had only thirty hours to complete the job. I have planned every detail to this point. I have committed myself to this deal spending every waking hour thinking about this project and most of my money as well. This was my future, everything I was doing was geared to the success of this project, as there was no room for error. People's undoing was usually the small things that were left unchecked or overlooked. I tried to be certain that I checked, and double checked, and even triple checked to make sure nothing was missed. And even though I have been so thorough I retraced all my steps to be certain I didn't miss a single thing. Sometimes it is best to walk away from your project, take a day or two off and when you return, you see things differently and can re-check to be certain you left no clues. Yes, this project has to happen without any clues, without any traces, without any idea who could have done it. This is where the project begins and ends and must leave those who investigate scratching their heads. Be thorough and be objective, no clues that is the mantra!

Once the project is started there would be no turning back and no room for errors. I have been in the safety deposit box room and now know how many boxes need to be opened. I don't know which boxes contained the most money or any at all, so I'd have to open most of them to find out. I believe that the larger boxes contain more money than the very small ones, just on size alone. But I can't let that be my guide so my plan is to open as many boxes as I can within the allotted time. I will then have to remove the money from this area and transport it to a place where it will be safely hidden. I can't go walking through the subway station with heavy bags. Someone will see me and although I'll be in disguise it will be another clue, another direction for the investigators to take. Once I leave the privacy of the hidden room the opportunity of being detected increases. Every person who makes contact with me is a potential witness that could bring down the entire project. There Is no percentage in doing the job and not making provisions, in advance, to remove the money out of the subway station. The entire subway station will become a crime scene and out of bounds to everyone. I still had a lot of work ahead of me as well as a few decisions to make. How to transport myself and the money out of the area is one of the most important things on my to-do list. The next very important decision is whether I take on another partner or two? So far I have accomplished everything I set out to do but am I being realistic? There is no way I can drill through the floor, cut open hundreds of boxes and remove the money from the building totally on my own. I don't have enough muscle to hold a drill above my head for hours on end and to drill through four to six inches of reinforced concrete. What happens when the concrete loosens enough to fall down, it would make a terrible racket and alert anyone who may be in the vicinity. I need help, there is no doubt about it. I need at least one other person, perhaps two and I must consider the time element. I would have to choose a week-end that includes a Monday holiday, as banks are not permitted to remain closed for three days in a row. If the bank was closed on Monday it would not violate this rule because they are open on Saturday. The Saturday half-day opening cuts into my working time if I chose a weekend as that leaves only thirty-six hours to work with, while a holiday weekend adds an additional twenty-four hours. If I do that I will now have close to sixty hours so the actual time of the project must be on a holiday that includes a Monday. There is no doubt I'll need one, perhaps two, additional people to assist in this project. This complicates matters as it leave me vulnerable unless I can come up with a way to maintain my anonymity. There is so much more to do, much more than I realized when I first hatched this scheme. No matter what twists and turns may arise I must achieve success. This plan has been in my mind too long and nothing can stand in the way. I have to work a little harder now that I realize how difficult this project is, especially if it is to be a perfect one without any clues at all. I just have to work within the parameters given and make sure there are no flaws.

Stage One:

THE BIGGEST PROBLEM I WAS NOW FACED WITH WAS HOW does one recruit an accomplice? I certainly cannot run an ad in the local paper, so what do I do? How do I interview the prospective partner? How do I make sure that the weakest link does not change a perfect job into a failure? No matter what the obstacles are I knew I'd find a way and shall make sure that all goes smoothly and, above all, no one gets hurt. This job has to be without violence of any kind!

There are other problems that require solutions. Let's assume I find one or two accomplices then how do I get the money out of area without being detected? Yes, there are a lot of parts in this project that need to be addressed and solutions must be found. If there is the large amount of cash in the boxes as I imagine, what do I pack it into? So many problems, so many things that can go wrong. I will tackle each problem long before the job is ready. I will find a solution and it will be solid or I will not do the job. This caper has to be perfect, there is no room for chance.

I decided it would be best to approach this project as if I was writing a book, or a play, or a great movie, a thriller. Although I am not an expert at either I have read a number of books and plays and understand the premise in all genres. There has to be a beginning, a middle, and an end. My project has to be like a very good play, movie, or book. Therefore the project must have players and each one must perform their part or the project fails. I think I must take on two more people, yes, that is the number. I'll not set a date for the project until I have everything in place. I agreed with myself that

I shall need two people, two lucky people who will benefit from this lucrative deal. I'll take my time to make sure that the ones I choose fit the part in every way, which includes my liking them as people. I will not reveal the full scope of the operation until the very last moment. By doing it this way I will avoid any possible leaks and if one of my associates decides to drop out of the project, there isn't anything they can say that will jeopardize it. I will probably be considered just another nutcase and that will be the end of it. Always keep your associates guessing until the very last moment. I will not reveal the nature of the deal except for the fact that it does not entail any violence. I will not reveal the location or the type of project it will be. No way will I be silly enough to trust two complete strangers with details that would derail this project. Rehearsals will take place in areas far away from the actual project and it will be limited to only one of the associates at a time. There will be other security measures when the time warrants it, until then, my first task is to find two helpers.

I felt I could kill two birds with one stone. I will look for my first associate and at the same time I will also look for a place where I can simulate some of the things we will have to do on the actual job. My first priority was to make sure my disguise was a perfect one. One that could be duplicated on a regular basis. If this was to be a perfect and successful project there is no need for my associates to have a clue who I really am. The weakest link is what breaks the chain and by bringing in two associates I will have doubled the possibility of being discovered. If these people knew me only as I look and sound from the very beginning they would not have any reason to suspect that I was not who I said I was. They could only describe me as what they saw each and every time. It may have seemed like a difficult way to go but it couldn't be helped. If you went to a movie and an actor played a certain part and was made to look differently you would eventually identify with him as he looks. It was very simple for me to be motivated to maintain this disguise because I couldn't trust anyone except myself. It has never entered my mind to use this disguise to cheat my new associates out of their share of the rewards, that would only make them very determined to expose me and that was not my goal. I wanted them to keep their rewards and hope that they will use them wisely. But let's take into account that people are all different and what would these two people do with a million dollars each? Would they be able to sit on it for a year or two? Would they be able to sit back and not buy a new sports car or a new home? Who knows what they would do if, for some unknown reason, they made the authorities a little curious. If the cops came by and asked them where they got the money to buy all these new toys or how did the obvious change in their lifestyles happen? Or if they, in a moment of weakness caused by liquor, or a silly confession to impress a girlfriend, would lead the cops to them. It has happened before, we have all read about how a silly remark, a fight with a loved one, silly things that become major events in the undoing of a perfect crime. What would they say or do to keep themselves out of jail? There was no telling what one will do so rather than worry about things like that, I'll maintain my disguise throughout the project and if something should happen let them describe their other associate. I have to think of what these people will do when faced with adversity and then take the steps to make sure I cannot be compromised in any way. That is what it is all about and that is what I intend to do every step of the way. There isn't any room for error, not one single one, no matter how small.

Stage Two:

I BEGAN WITH MY NEW DISGUISE, THE DISGUISE THAT WILL be with me throughout the project. I changed my appearance by wearing a dark wig. I also made sure that I had a mustache and wore glasses. I walked with a slight limp by adding some paper padding in one of my shoes. I couldn't leave my limp to chance that is why I put the paper in the shoe so I would limp without thinking about it. I made sure I spoke with a severe nasal accent and used phrases that would identify me as a guy from Brooklyn. I made sure I had a couple of suits that I had made at work during my lunchtime with extra shoulder padding and I made the pants with a wide leg so it would look like I weigh more than I really do. This would give anyone the impression that I was heavier than I really was. If a description of me would ever be given it would not match what I really look like. Most importantly was to maintain this disguise anytime I am out of my apartment and conducting project business. To add to the mystique of the new man, I rented a room for fifteen dollars a week on the Bowery. The room sucked but was perfect for my purposes.

I was now ready to begin my recruitment program. I decided that the best way to do this was to frequent a bar on a regular basis. I chose Roscoe's Bar on the corner of Ninth and Twenty-Third Street. This was a neighborhood bar, most people who spent time there were locals. My main reason for choosing Roscoe's was the two pool tables they had in the rear section of the bar. It was my belief that those tables will draw the type of person I want to meet much easier than a place that only serves booze. I set no time limit on this phase because I understood that it takes time for one to be accepted as a regular. Time was on my side and as long as I play my cards right, I will be considered a regular real soon. I decided to use the name Benny Robinson, it had a nice ring to it and people can call me Ben, most importantly it's an easy name to remember.

This was my first visit to the bar and I realized that it would be best if I say very little. I took a seat at the bar and enjoyed a beer. First step was to get to know the bartender and make sure he remembers who I am. The bar wasn't crowded at all, perhaps it was because of the time. I wasn't one who went to establishments like this, as a matter-of-fact, this is the first time I have ever been in a bar. I didn't much care for the smell and the atmosphere wasn't much better. The place was dark and eliminated any connection with the outside World, it was eerie if this was the first time one was visiting a bar like this. I have to admit that the experience of being in that bar was something very scary. There were posters on the walls and a long bar that had a jar of looked like pig's feet. There was another big jar that had hard boiled eggs in it. After a short period of time that allowed my eyes to adjust to the dark light, the place started to look better. I noticed some old guy sitting at the end of the bar, he looked like he was in another place as he stared at the mirror in front of him. I felt out of place, I didn't really fit in here at all. The smells, a strong odor of beer permeated the air and cigarette smoke hung near. There wasn't anything that made the place warm, the lighting was low, and the lack of anything cheerful was something I would have to get used to. The bar was still an exciting place for me. My excitement was in high gear as watched people come in and greet Peter the bartender. There was a friendly feeling in this bar, once you got know it. This was going to be my recruitment center and I was sure I'd find the right people in here.

I sat down at the bar and waited until the bartender came over and said, "*My name is Peter, a pleasure to meet you. What will you have?*"

"I'll have a draft please. I'm Benny Wilson, I just moved in nearby. I'm trying to meet my neighbors and figured this is the best place to do it. A pleasure to meet you Peter, I hope you don't mind if I bend your ear a little, at least until I get to know the area," I said with a smile.

"No problem Benny, welcome to Roscoe's, great to have you with us. I'm the owner/bartender of this place and am always happy to help someone get settled. Where do you hail from?" Benny said.

"I'm from Brooklyn, Brownsville area. I just moved to Manhattan to be closer to my job, I work over at Brown's Furrier on Ninth and Thirteenth, I'm the bookkeeper. It is such a hassle to take the train every day back and forth to work and Brooklyn. I decided to find a place in Manhattan, much closer to work. I just took a room on Eighth and Twelve Street, temporary of course, until I find a nice apartment I can afford. If you hear of anything that is available Peter, please let me know," I said as I sipped on my beer.

"I sure will, Benny! I'll keep my eyes open. Are you looking for a one bedroom or bigger?" Peter asked as he excused himself to serve another customer.

I hung around the bar for another hour shooting the bull with Peter. While I was there he introduced me to two regular guys and told me a little about the neighborhood. He also let me know that Friday and Saturday were the busiest days and that the pool tables were busy all day and night. He closes up at midnight and his other bartender, Ron, opens up at six in the morning most days. He has a part-time bartender, Mac, who opens on Sunday and Monday and works the Wednesday and Thursday late shift. The place is open seven days a week. The way it looked to me, it was a lot of hard work just to make a living. Peter wanted to know if I was married and, of course, I told him I wasn't. I finally picked myself up and left for the night. I said good-bye to Peter and thanked him for being so nice and kind to me.

The way I figured it, it could take me six months to find a pair of associates for my project. By being patient I will lessen the odds of getting the wrong kind of person. Time is a wonderful ally and it is my aim to use it wisely. I also wanted to establish a routine that would serve me well while planning my project.

In order to do that I went back to my room on the Bowery that I had rented a few days ago and took off my disguise and returned to my normal self. I neatly hung up the clothing I was wearing and put on my Sam West clothing. I then left my place making sure no one saw me leave and made my way to the Subway station and took the train home. I felt by coming and going from my place as myself would serve me better in the event there ever was an investigation. My theory was that my life as Benny Wilson must be different than my life as Sam West, and by keeping them separate, I was making sure the connection would not be there.

This process of going to the bar continued for the next four weeks. I went there three times a week and spent every Saturday night and Sunday evening as well. By the third week I felt I was accepted as a regular and was considered one of the guys. I met quite an assortment of people but could not safely make any decisions about who was right and who wasn't. I was placing some of those I felt might be possible associates into two categories. One was a group that I called *the most likely* and the other was a *maybe* group. I now started to do my research as best as I could to see what background information I was able to get on the guys I had met.

In order not to raise any suspicions I made careful notes of each person's name and pertinent information like where they worked, where they lived, and any habits I can detect. I kept very accurate descriptions of each person so I would not confuse anyone with another person using the same or a similar name. This was not going to be an easy job, but neither is the project so every effort to find out as much as possible will pay off in spades. When I choose someone I must be certain he is who he claims to be. There is no use in putting in all this effort and then failing because you made a mistake, a very costly one.

I needed an avenue that would allow me the ability to check out the background of the possible associates. The only thing I could do that was to run a credit check on them, and I, as an individual, could not do that. It would put me under suspicion if it ever came out and that wouldn't be good at all. I had to think of a way to accomplish this without arousing any suspicion. One day I went to my Boss and suggested that the store would increase its sales a great deal if it allowed purchases, let's say over two hundred dollars, to be financed. No different than when one purchases a car and cannot pay cash. I knew that we did not have any credit accounts in our stores and for some of our customers this would be an incentive to purchase more. We used a lay-away plan but that does not allow the customer to take possession of the suits they ordered until they paid their account in full. That didn't really help sales that much simply because when one needed a new suit he needed it now.

My suggestion was to sell the suits on a credit basis, one that the client can take with them at the time of purchase. Buy now and pay later, this will allow the customer to buy more products and not feel the pressure of the purchase. It all sounded great and my Boss loved the idea. *"We'll clean-up with this idea, this is great Ben."* Of course, the object of my suggestion was to learn how they would be able to check people out. How they verified that a person was creditworthy, what method they used to determine this person was going to make his payments. I needed this knowledge so I could have a way of checking out the guys I choose for my project. I felt that I would be able to make sure that each guy was for real, or at least not someone who just came onto the scene like myself. Most importantly I needed to learn this without making anyone suspicious, my entire project depended upon it.

My Boss loved this idea and thanked me for the suggestion and told me that he will investigate how to get this incorporated into his business operation. Things were starting to look real good, all I had to do was to wait for the store's credit plan to become a reality and I'll be all set. Much to my surprise we received a notice that a sales meeting will take place at eight in the morning next Tuesday. Deep in my heart I knew that that this was the start of my future even though no one else knew that. I was very excited and, of course, anxious and could hardly wait for the week to pass.

Stage Three:

TO ANYONE WHO MIGHT HAVE BEEN PAYING ANY attention, nothing would appear to have changed in my life. My routine remained the same as I came and went to my work place exactly as I have been doing since I began working here over two years ago. All those who knew me would not see one single thing different in my comings and goings. My visits to the bank didn't change as I continued to take my weekly check to be cashed. My savings account was growing as I continued to deposit the same amount each week. I made sure to visit my special room underneath the Bank at least three times a week. I wanted to make sure that nothing was disturbed and, of course, I was able to bring over more stuff I needed for the upcoming project.

I still frequented the bar, at least three times a week, looking for future associates. At least now I was getting into conversations with a few of the guys. I was slowly leading the discussion towards personal stuff like, where one works, are they married, stuff like that. At times I didn't even wait for an answer as I acted as if it didn't matter. I tried to be a regular guy even though I limped a little and spoke through my nose. If anyone made fun of my accent I laughed with them because I wanted to be one of the guys. Finding the right people may not be as difficult as I thought as long as I take my time and use all the resources available to me.

On Tuesday we had a special sales meeting. The staff was speculating why we had to attend this special meeting. They all had different ideas why this meeting was called. Some of those thought it was to announce the expansion of the chain while others felt it was a major shake-up of the management team. I felt it was all about the suggestion I had made, using credit as our next sales tool. The meeting got underway and the big boss, Sy Johnson himself, got up to speak. This was a rare occasion as he rarely spoke at a meeting let alone attend. He was smiling from ear to ear and one could see he was excited, the news must be really good. The announcement was that effective at once we will begin to offer our clothing on credit. *"This will open the door to a whole new customer base, a customer base that never purchased suits with us in the past. Our sales will rise and everyone will make more money,"* Sy Johnson said. He went on to explain how it will work and how we can sell more than ever before. *"There will be a form that must be completed by the customer. This form will be submitted to the Finance department and in a few minutes we will have a response along with a credit limit. H & H Finance Corp., is one of the leading lending institutions with offices all across the country,"* Sy Johnson continued.

Here is a little secret that the Boss gave us at the meeting. *"Take out the form and ask the questions directly and write them in and then, after you have completed the application ask the customer to sign it at the bottom and that will be that. Make it as painless as possible so the customer will always feel at ease."* The best part, for me that is, I now have a way to check someone's identity. The only fly in the ointment is if they should ever get caught and the cops, by some fluke, may find a connection to the store. I gave this a lot of thought and felt the odds of the connection being made was very remote. I certainly didn't think that was a big risk at all, especially that I didn't look like the guy he would describe. This was such a bonus for me, I almost burst out in joy over this new development. Things are starting to look rosier already.

I continued my working at my garage and finally reached the point where I could drill through six inches of concrete in less than two hours. Now all I had to do was to figure out how many drill holes

I must make to remove a large enough piece of concrete to allow a body to pass through. I have found that to drill out the locks on each box would take no more than five minutes or less per box. This would allow me twelve boxes per hour and I'm allowing the maximum of twenty-four hours for this part of the project. I was thrilled with the progress I was making, everything was going along quite smoothly. It was time to choose my future associates.

Stage Four:

MY VISITS TO THE BAR HAD BEEN VERY REGULAR AND I might add very rewarding. I have finally become close friends with two guys. Reggie Green was a real nice guy, soft spoken and quite handsome. He stood a little over six feet tall and weighed one-hundred and ninety pounds, all muscle I may add. In the two months I have spent with him I learned his habits and made very copious notes about him. I knew his address, his telephone number, who he lived with and how long he has lived there. The only thing I didn't know about him was his Social Security number and didn't really know how to get that. One thing about Reggie was that he didn't drink more than one beer during a visit to the bar, but he loved playing pool. I got to like him a lot and I felt he liked me as well and trusted me as a friend would. I needed his Social Security number and had to devise a way of getting it.

This was going to be a difficult task, but I'll find a way. My first try was to go through his garbage but that presented a big problem if I should ever be caught doing that. I decided to take a shot at it and dressed up as a street bum. Reggie lived in a walk-up on Eleventh Street near Ninth Avenue and his garbage cans were lined-up outside his building where the various occupants would throw their trash. Garbage pick-up was on Tuesday and Friday so I gathered that Reggie would throw out his trash the night before. He did not strike me as one who took out his trash more often than on the night before. I dressed in disguise as a street bum and hung around Reggie's place on the first Monday night. I arrived a little before seven and figured I'd hang around until I saw Reggie's light go out. Of course, while I waited I rummaged through the trash and found a bag that contained Reggie's trash. I knew this because there was an envelope with his name and address on it. I searched through his bag and found nothing with his Social Security number on it. I continued looking through other bags and suddenly I found one on the bottom that had a statement from a bank, and lo and behold, there was his Social Security number. Reggie had not made any attempt to hide it or destroy it in any way, I guess he didn't worry about it. This was just dumb luck but I'll take it, never ignore lady luck when she is being generous and this is one case she was. I placed this treasure of information safely away and left the area.

Tyrone Shelton, my next choice as an associate, was also a tall guy like Reggie except he was even more muscular. Reggie was a trainer at a health studio on Seventh Avenue and Fifty-Fifth Street and Tyrone worked in construction. I guess that was why Tyrone was more muscular than Reggie, construction is a lot harder.

I was attracted to Tyrone because he constantly complained that there wasn't any way a black man could ever get ahead. He railed on how he is being poorly paid and that the future looks bleak. He lives on Ninety-Sixth Street and Eighth Avenue because, as he said, *"a black man can't get no place to live uptown. Too many honkies just won't give a black man a break."* Perhaps I was wrong but I felt this guy was perfect for my project. It would be his doorway to a new life and because he is so bitter he couldn't be an undercover cop. I, of course, did not stop there. I will still put him through a credit check and see what comes up. I don't have his Social Security Number and I don't think I can disguise myself to look like a black man so I'll try to pass it through without one and see what happens. I certainly had enough information to complete his credit application. It is now up to me to get my team together and get this project on the road.

I chose two guys that looked like they were very strong and would be able to do some heavy lifting. Cutting through a concrete floor above one's head will require a lot of muscle. I was pleased with my choices but couldn't let them know anything about the project until the very last minute. I certainly knew how to entice them into this deal, but that will have to wait until I get back their credit reports. So far things are starting to look really good, all I have to do is be very careful and patient.

Stage Five:

THE EXCITEMENT IN THE STORE WAS ELECTRIC. EVERYONE was thrilled with our new credit plan and expected the crowds to tear the doors off once it was announced. The ad appeared in the Sunday papers along with a special offer of a men's suit for as low as ninety-nine dollars. The announcement of credit purchases took up half the ad and the hook was that the store was to remain closed until Tuesday morning when it will open at seven A.M. and the first one hundred customers will get a free necktie with their purchase. The staff was filled with anticipation as everyone expected a large crowd especially with prices as low as advertised. Now was the time for men to get their business suits at a very low price and not have to pay for it right away.

Tuesday was my day back after my two days off and when I reported for work at six A.M. there were hundreds of men standing in line outside the store. I must admit I was excited, this day was to be a great one, especially if the crowds continue like I have just seen. It was also a perfect day for me to slip my two applications into the mix. Of course, there won't be any orders with their names on it but I'll get confirmation that they are who they claim to be.

I sat down at my little desk in my section of the store and filled out two applications for credit. On Reggie's application I was able to put down the Social Security number but on Tyrone's I couldn't. I completed the applications and filled out a measurement sheet along with the proposed sales slips and attached them to the credit application. I kept each sale below seven-hundred and fifty dollars and showed an intended purchase of two suits on each order along with accessories and a free necktie. I was very excited about these turn of events, it fit right in to my plans. I was feeling great and lucky as well. My plan was moving along as I had anticipated, all I could do now was to wait for confirmation. I didn't put my two applications in until nearly eleven in the morning. I wanted to make sure that everything looked right. The only problem was that the store was very busy and so was I, so I had to be sensible, it is not possible to measure too many clients at once. When one buys a made-to-measure suit it takes a little time to take all the measurements. To be honest, I was a little concerned because I had four real customers at my station and if one took the time to calculate my workload they might say that wasn't possible. I was dealing six different clients at about the same time, not realistic, but because of the large influx of people, it could happen. In any case I muddled through and submitted two applications at a time. By eleven-thirty I had concluded my first six sales, all were approved, except Reggie's application had a notation that his credit limit was only four hundred dollars. No problem at all as I cancelled his order and wrote that Reggie's purchase was for double the amount and he didn't have enough cash to cover the difference. I cancelled Tyrone's order using the excuse his girlfriend got angry at him because he was spending too much on clothes for himself and not enough on her. I was pleased with my day's work as I had opened up nine new accounts and lost four including Reggie's and Tyrone's. The day was great and this credit deal was going to boost our store sales way up. Best of all I had my two guys and they were who they claimed to be and that was the best part of it all. The show was really on the road now and soon we'll have everything in place, I could hardly wait!

Stage Six:

THIS WAS THE TURNING POINT AND NOW IT WAS UP TO ME to put the rest of the pieces together. I worked hard every day at my job and spent the evenings in my underground location going over each and every inch. I mapped out the entire area and located where I felt the safety deposit boxes would be. I also located the spot on the concrete floor where I felt I must cut through. Now all I had to do was to start bringing in the equipment and making sure each item was clean and in perfect working order. Day after day I carried my equipment to the special room. Some pieces had to be disassembled and then assembled once again when I finally got them into the room. Other times I was forced to use my disguise as a subway worker because the equipment was too big to be hidden in any way. I could not take a ladder apart so the easy and safest way was to bring it in whole. Dressed as a transit maintenance man, badge and all, I carried the ladder as if it was part of my job. To be honest I don't think anyone gave me more than a passing glance. The best part was the fact that the project will not take place for many months, by that time no one would remember a transit employee carrying a ladder. So far so good, things were going according to plan.

On the weekend, after work, I went to my garage and worked on drilling through concrete. Over and over again until I got this part perfect, down to a science. If there was an area that could squash the entire project it was, as far as I was concerned, drilling through the floor. If it takes too long the entire project would be cut down and would have less chance of success. The one area I didn't take lightly was the fact that it was possible that they used rebar back at the turn of the century. Previously they used wooded slats and if that was the case there wasn't going to be any problem cutting through that. If it is rebar I'll need a few hacksaws and a lot of extra blades and a really lot of muscle. Opening the safety deposit boxes was a piece of cake. I estimated that it would take no more than one minute to knock out the lock on each box. I would take another minute to pull the box out and examine the contents. The keys to success were very simple, take cash only. No jewelry, no anything other than cash. Cash would not be a clue but a piece of jewelry, a bond, a stock-certificate, any item that could be traceable must be left behind. There is no sense in being greedy and being caught over a small meaningless bauble or a piece of paper that you might get ten cents on the dollar for. Once I let my associates in on the exact nature of the deal, I will stress the need for self-discipline. After all, success is predicated on one being able to control themselves and stay on course to attain their goal. Only those who can control these emotions can be successful in business or in crime. No matter what the business is we must remain on track all the time. My biggest fear was that my two associates may not have the ability to remain in control after the job is completed. There is no question that they satisfy my need for brawn but when it comes to brains I'm not so certain. Regardless of that risk I need these guys because of the heavy lifting that will take place. These are my horses and I cannot expect more from them, that is why I must always remain as Benny Wilson. I cannot ever step out of my disguise, not for one second and I always must remain vigilant and make sure I'm not being followed. It's so easy to fall into a mental trap and to let my guard down and think that I'm too smart for these associates of mine. I can just see myself holding on to the bars in a jail cell wondering where I went wrong. There can be no deviation in my plan, no loopholes and no letdown of discipline. No matter what the temptation may be I must always stay true to my plan.

Stage Seven:

IT WAS EARLY IN MARCH, WINTER WAS LEAVING AND SPRING was approaching, and so were my plans for the greatest crime ever. During the last little while I spent every available free moment preparing my skills for the actual deed itself. I was now very proficient at concrete drilling and the opening of locks that safeguard a great deal of hidden wealth. During this time I nurtured my relationship with Reggie and Tyrone. I was a regular at the bar and so were they. We played pool and drank beer every time we saw each other and I made sure we met at least three times a week. It was time to test the waters, I couldn't wait any longer, I had to approach them and see where I stood. I gave it a lot of thought and felt that I have given our friendship enough time to grow and now it was time to get started or find different partners. Although I did not set an exact date for the job, I had a few in mind. There was no reason to rush, perfection needs no haste and every detail had to be perfect. This was a one-time deal and if I screwed this up there would not be another chance, the cat would be out of the bag. As things stood now everyone responsible for security was convinced that their system was foolproof and there wasn't any reason to change their minds.

On Tuesday night I walked into the bar as usual and greeted everyone. I walked to the end of the bar where Peter had placed my beer as he usually does and picked it up and walked over to the pool table where Reggie was knocking balls around aimlessly. "Hey Reg, how are you? Man? Nice to see you," I said.

"I'm great, Ben and how are you doing?" He said.

"I'm fine man, can I buy you a beer? Let's take a booth and relax with a couple of beers," I said.

He smiled and put down the pool cue and walked over to the booth where I placed my beer. Peter brought over a pitcher of beer and two glasses. I put five dollars on the table to cover the beers and the tip and Peter casually picked up the money. Once Peter had left I leaned over the table and said to Reggie, "I wanted to ask you if you are interested in getting with me in a project that could pay a lot of bread?" I said.

"That depends on what I have to do, but tell me more, I could always use some extra bread.

"I'll be honest with you Reg, I will not reveal the entire deal just in case you choose to refuse my offer. I'm sure you can understand that I want to be protected just as you would want to be. What I have in mind, and if I may add, I have researched this every which way possible, is to grab a nice score in excess of a few million dollars. The best part of all this is that the money that is up for grabs is money that can't be reported, or at least most of it will be like that. There is no violence involved as there are no other people involved. I cannot, as I said, reveal the exact deal right now, so please trust me that what I am telling you is a real possibility. Secrecy is the key to its success and must always remain between us, there cannot be any exceptions. We will require another person to help in this project and, although I am the creator of this project, the proceeds will be split three ways. If you have no interest in the project, that will be okay with me, I will respect your decision and ask that you respect my privacy and forget we ever had this conversation. I just want you to think this over, the risk is very minimal. I cannot do the project on my own because it requires some brawn, more than I could do alone, and, of course, perfect execution. Think it over and if you want in, you let me know. I wish I could give you more details but caution prevents that at this time. Even though details are sketchy at this

time I hope you can make a decision on what I have told you. I'm sure you understand that I must be extremely careful and can't just invite anyone to share this with me. I trust you simply because I got to know you over the last few months and feel your desires are the same as mine. I hope this very confidential conversation remains private and does not impact our friendship," I said as I looked at Reggie.

"Wow, Ben that was something. I never expected that kind of conversation. I don't know if I can get any sleep tonight. My imagination has been ignited and will not rest until I come up with some kind of answer. If I take you at your word there is no use in my asking what the nature of the project is. Wow, I'm stunned with this conversation, but I promise to respect your privacy. I'm flattered that you had the faith to trust me with this information and to ask me to be a part of it. I have gotten to like you a lot Ben, and trust you, so I'll give this a lot of consideration. I will think about this and the opportunity to become a millionaire, it's very hard not to be tempted. I mean it Ben, it's very hard. I promise I'll get back to you very soon. If I don't want in, and I don't see how I wouldn't, I will forget this conversation and we will remain friends. If I go along with the deal, I sure as hell hope we will always remain friends. It's getting late Ben, I got to be at work tomorrow and need my beauty sleep. I'm so damn excited I probably won't get any sleep at all. Thanks for the confidence in me, see you soon," he said as got up and left the bar.

I wasn't sure if I did the right thing or not. Who knew what the right way was to approach this. Was I really right? I felt I had to get the ball rolling and by revealing very little I was not taking any big risk but I was wetting Reggie's appetite. I also felt very confident that Reggie was who he said he was and that he was a perfect fit for the project. If I was wrong there was little else I could have done to verify his credentials. If confronted, my comeback would be that all I did do was to make-up a fantasy tale for a book I'm planning to write. My conversation was nothing more than that. Of course, if it turned out that Reggie was indeed an undercover cop, then the entire project would have to be scrapped for now. I was very confident that Reggie was the right man for the job in every respect and I left the bar quite confident he would be on my team.

I like to refer to the entire job as a 'project', as it had a much more legitimate ring to it, and keeps words like crime, stealing, and any other explicit words that would make this whole deal sound more risky, out of it. I guess I was a little whacky to think that way, but that is the way it was. When presenting the deal to Reggie I used the word *project* as it made the proposal sound a lot more legitimate and more acceptable to him.

I left the bar a few minutes after Reggie left and went home making sure I wasn't followed. Of course, I went to Ben's home, the one room I had rented and changed out of my disguise. I then proceeded as Sam West and took the subway home leaving Ben behind. I made sure I was alone and was not being followed. I had devised a method that would help me detect anyone, no matter how good they may be, who might be following me. I took a route that I carefully planned for weeks. I made turns that gave me full view of the streets behind me so if anyone was following me they would have lost me there and then. I realized that no one should really be following me as Sam West. No one knows me as Sam so why follow? But my desire to eliminate any risk no matter how trivial overshadowed that logic. I believed that the old saying, *"an ounce of prevention is worth a pound of cure,"* fit the bill in this case.

I had made this trip three times a week for the last few months and knew every inch of the route. If something was out of place, no matter how small it was, I would detect it. I didn't let my familiarity with the area make me less attentive. No way was I allowing myself to become sloppy, no not me, there was too much riding on this project to let one small slip-up screw-up the deal. Discipline, caution, and steadfast concentration, remained my top priority at all times. I always felt I had plenty of time to rest after the project was successfully completed.

When I arrived home I took a quick shower and jumped into bed. I would have to be at work tomorrow and I don't want to be tired. This has been a long day and a lot has happened, most of it was very good. I tossed and turned for a little while as I went over and over my conversation with Reggie. I searched for any flaw that may have been said. I was especially concerned over the words I used and the way I spoke and found none. I finally fell asleep and allowed my body and mind to regenerate, tomorrow will be even better than today.

The day was very busy at work as this new credit idea seemed to catch on and has been bringing in a different group of customers. I still had my regular clients and was thrilled to see Benny Guarino. I spent an hour with Benny and enjoyed every second. He let me know that he was still bringing plenty money for his Bosses and hoped that they don't run out of available safety deposit boxes for him. He would hate to miss our regular visits as he looks forward to them. He said he liked talking to me and considered me a friend.

"Well, Benny I hope they don't run out of boxes as well because I look forward to seeing you too, and Benny, I also consider you a friend and if there is anything I can ever do for you all you have to do is ask," I said as a passing remark as I continued to take his measurements. *"By the way Benny, your measurements haven't changed in over a month. That's a good sign, you must be exercising a lot."*

"I'm very busy Sam, it's not easy running around town picking up all this bread, and it keeps me on the go all the time. Soon I'll be promoted and someone else will be doing this job. The big bosses like the way I work and trust me to always do the job right. And, thanks to you Sam, I'm always well dressed," he said with pride.

I loved having Benny around, besides giving me a lot of business, he always lifted my spirits with his tales of how much money he is secretly putting into safe boxes at the bank. He didn't know it but he did make my day every time he bought a suit or two. He was a breath of fresh air to my project each and every time. I just loved seeing him and talking especially about the money. As long as he was continually putting money in, I felt great. I was tempted to ask him if he ever takes any money out, but didn't, I thought that might cause some suspicion. It was great to see him as he seemed to always pop-up when my spirits ran a little lower than usual and by just listening to him brag, made me feel ten feet tall, yes, Benny was my strength, my inspiration to carry on with my project.

My day went by very quickly after Benny left as I went through the rest of day dreaming about the project, it was no longer just about the money, it was also a matter of pride that I can accomplish what I set out to do. Whenever Benny came by it made me feel more determined that I can complete this without leaving a single clue. Of course, the fact that, according to Benny, there was more money than I could count sitting in those boxes didn't hurt my feelings one bit. His constant trips to the Bank added fuel to the fire that was burning inside of me. I had to succeed with this project and make certain everything was in place as it should be. The fact that there was a risk involved made this even more exciting even though I realized that this project was not a game. If something went wrong I could spend more than ten years in prison and that was not something I'd like to do. I didn't spend a lot of time worrying about the down side as that would only dampen my enthusiasm. If a project was to be successful one must concentrate on the positive and eliminate the negative. I believed I would be successful and all I had to do was to stay focused and my dream will come true.

After work I went over to my special room underneath the Bank. I felt very comfortable and safe in my very special room beneath my pot-of-gold. I realized, in my excitement, that I did not take the usual steps to protect my identity. A mistake of epic proportions that I must not ever make again no matter how anxious or excited

I may be. It was very stupid of me, after all, anyone could have seen me, or I could have been stopped by a security guard. Who knows what people remember and the possibility that someone would, later on, remember seeing me, Sam the guy who works at the clothing store. I stood in the room beneath the Bank and realized what a foolish mistake this was and how stupid I was. I was actually shaking and experiencing the sweats, all because I allowed myself to do something without thinking.

I must be calm and make the best of my error and make sure I never make this mistake again, never! I decided to get out of there very carefully and just go home, tomorrow will be soon enough to come back here. Right now I must get out of here and I have to do it carefully and make sure I stay alert, no more let down. I put out the light and slowly opened the door making sure the way was clear. I walked slowly hugging the wall and keeping my head down, all I wanted to do was to blend in with the other travelers and get the hell out of there undetected. I was being overly careful as paranoia permeated my every thought. What a fool I was to jeopardize a million dollar project because of emotions. I exited the hallway and slowly made my way to the subway platform. Of course, because I was so paranoid I imagined that everyone was staring at me. All I could think of was that everyone was registering the fact that Sam West just emerged from a secret passageway. I was freaking out, all because of one simple act of stupidity. Finally I began telling myself to relax. 'Be yourself' was all I could think of as I looked around at the people on the platform. I realized that no one really cared about me, no one at all. Everyone on that platform was as anxious as I was to get home after a full day's work, they certainly didn't have time to worry about someone else. Once the train arrived and I was on my way, my heartbeat started to return to normal. I still didn't trust myself, after all, this project was my life's ambition and could have easily been fouled up forever. I finally arrived at my stop and made it home in one piece with no one following me. The one positive I took out of this screw-up was to remain calm and solve the situation with a clear and cool head. When one allows themselves to become frazzled, proper decisions cannot be made. I was thankful that I learned this lesson now and not later. Although I'm being extremely careful and am trying to cover every situation, there will be times when things happen that are beyond my control and it will be my responsibility to remain cool, together, and solve the problem. There cannot be any on-the-job-training for this eventuality.

The rest of the week went by without incident. I spent every evening at my special room making sure that all my calculations were correct. Each day I brought more equipment into my special room that I needed for the project. On the weekend I went to my garage and drilled through concrete over and over just to make sure the drill bits were right and the time allotted to drill through six inches of concrete was spot-on. I opened the safe once and could not practice on it again but lucked out with the interior. When I had the safe open there were two drawers that were locked. They mimicked a safety deposit box because they were made of metal and had very similar locks on them as my safety deposit box had. I brought my safety deposit box key with me as a hunch that it might fit and found that it did. Although my key did slide into the lock, it didn't turn, so I could not open the drawers. Of course, this was okay with me as I now get to open these two drawers as I would a safety deposit box. I was estimating that it would take me about five minutes to open each box and now I can actually find out. I tried using different tools to open the lock and none worked within the time frame I had expected. I then used my punch and a regular hammer, I covered the head of the hammer with a cloth to muffle the sound and began working on the lock. Much to my surprise the lock was punched out in less than two minutes. Once I opened the first drawer with ease and felt if I had hit the hammer a little harder it would have opened sooner. This was a great discovery and showed me that I only need some steel punches and a few hammers and I will be able to open each safety deposit box in two minutes or less. That will give three of us the ability to open sixty boxes per hour. In my calculations I figured we would be working at a rate of thirty to thirty-five minutes per hour. I allowed for rest and removing the drawers and going through the contents. This means we will be able to open every box in this vault, if everything goes as planned, in twenty-four hours. According to my calculations and the photos I took at the very start of this project there were, at a minimum, twelve hundred safety deposit boxes. I was getting more excited each day especially since I have found the solution to opening the boxes.

I was ready to start the most important phase of the project. Boot camp so to speak as I was about to begin the training program for my two accomplices. It will not be an easy task to train these guys, not easy at all. I must do so in a manner that will keep the exact project secret. I cannot reveal the location of the job or any specifics. I wasn't sure I knew how to do that, quite frankly I was winging it, but felt I would see the way as I got closer to Tyrone and Reggie. All I wanted was to make these guys happy and convince them that there is a pot-of-gold at the end of the rainbow. I can't take any risks that one should back out and have enough information to cause trouble. Caution was the key word in this project and I wasn't going to abandon that procedure now! Let the show begin, I'll be the teacher and hopefully we will be a cohesive team and together make this project pay high dividends.

It was Saturday night and usually Reggie showed up about an hour earlier than Tyrone. He liked to play pool and, as he put it, *"get a head start on the night."* I made sure I was there before he showed up so I could have a nice talk before Tyrone showed up. Reggie walked in as usual and made a bee-line directly to the pool table. I got off my stool at the bar and went over and said, *"Hi Reg, how was your week?"*

'The same as usual Ben, nothing special. How about a game my good man? Do you think you can take me?" He said with a big smile.

"No way Reg, you know you can beat my ass every time. This just isn't my game, how about if I buy you a beer? I wanted to talk to you before Tyrone gets here, can we sit down for a few minutes?" I asked.

"Reg, I have explained the deal to you and I need you to help me. If you would like to make a cool million dollars without too much risk, this is the deal of the century and I'm offering you that opportunity. I think you are like me and would like to make a lot of bread with a small risk. It's a win, win situation Reg, and I want you in," I said.

"That sounds great but I know very little about you and even less about the deal. If you can help me out with some additional information it will make my job easier," Reggie said.

"You are so right Reg, it's hard to make up your mind especially on something as important as this without proper information. Let me be honest with you Reg, I want you to be a part of this but what if you decide you don't want any part of it? What will I do once you know everything about the deal? I'm sure you can understand my position, so in order to be sure and safe I can only reveal some of the details. This is for your protection as well as mine, I know if you had a deal for me you would act the same way until the deal was complete," I said.

"You are so right Ben, what if I was an undercover cop? What if I was an informer? You really don't know shit about me and I know very little about you. So let's get the crap out of the way so we can move forward and get this deal on the road as a team. First let me assure you, I am not a cop in any form whatsoever and have never been. You are my friend that is for sure, even if we only know each other a short time. Friendships must have a beginning and no one has written a rule as to how long the beginning should be, or how long friendships last. I'm sure it depends on how the friends treat each other. Let me put your mind at rest Ben, I will say it again, I'm not a cop of any sort. I'm not undercover or above-the-cover and have never been associated with cops except if they wanted to hassle me for something. I'm what you see and what you have been seeing for the last few months. I want to make a lot of money and I'm willing to take some risks to get it. I do not want to be involved in something that can land me in jail unless the rewards are so great that I should take my chances. I have not been able to decide what size rewards qualify for that type of risk but your conversation with me has tempted me. I want to hear more and if the rewards are sufficient, I'm in. Ben, I can't be any plainer than that and hope you trust me, now let's move on and tell me all I need to hear," Reggie said.

"Thanks for that Reg, I will give you details but must warn you that they will be sketchy. I cannot jeopardize the deal in any way and seeing that we both need to get to know each other better, I'll keep certain details to myself at this time. I believe the project fits your requirements as the rewards of this deal would be at least one million dollars. That Reg, would be your share, as I would also have a reward of a similar amount. We will need one more person to assist us and their share will be an equal amount. The proceeds are to be split three ways and the total jackpot should exceed three million, and I may add, all in cash. There is no jewelry involved, no stocks, no bonds, no anything, except cash, untraceable greenbacks. The job will be done on a weekend so you will not miss a day's work and you can return to your job when it is done as if nothing happened. There are a few steps that have to be taken and I will go over them with you. Once you have agreed to be on board, we will do things as a team.

"As a team, we will choose our other associate and then, and only then will I reveal more details. I am cautious Reg, and will remain that way until the project is completed. Of course, you realize that this is very important to me and because I am so anal about precautions, everyone associated with this project will benefit. All the precautions I have in place protect all of us so don't try to breach my resolve to maintain that strict rule. Reg, this a perfect project that can and will be done to perfection. If we do follow those rules, there will not be any clues left to associate the project to us. I am covering every base, every detail no matter how minute, and will review the entire project with you and our next associate when everything is in place, and most importantly Reg, that there is a mutual trust between us. The goal is a perfect project that is done quickly and over without any repercussions. We are and always will be our own worst enemies and can only fail if we fail ourselves. We need discipline and it's a job-well-done. I think it is a simple thing to demand that we be true to ourselves or suffer the consequences. If you or anyone of us fails to follow this simple but very important step, we can bring failure to this project and that would be very stupid. We are so close to being millionaires it would be a terrible thing to fuck up because one of us couldn't keep their mouth shut or be very careful on how they live. So I believe you can understand the importance of being disciplined. The only clue that could lead the cops to us would be a sudden change in our life styles, so using everything we know to our advantage, we will remain under the radar and as long as we maintain the same way of life we'll be home free! This need only last a year or two and then this project will be history and we will all be able to use our new-found fortunes for a better life. I'd gladly give up a couple of years of living high-off-the-hog to live the rest of my years in total comfort. Be honest with me Reg, if I asked you or almost anyone to spend two years in prison and when released, a million dollars would be waiting, how many would say no? I guarantee you, very few and yet with this project there is no need to spend one day in any prison to reap the rewards offered. Do you have the discipline, the desire, the honest belief that you can commit, to this then you are in, if not you are out, it's all up to you Reg, make your choice and we can move on," I said as I signaled Marie, our waitress and ordered two more beers.

"*I told you a few minutes ago Ben, I'm in! Well let's clear the air once-and-for-all. I am in from the beginning to the end and will carry my end properly. I accept the risks that may be involved and will not hold you accountable. I agree with the few details you have released to me and accept the rules. I will not be a part of any deal that involves the use of weapons or force on another human being. If that is clear I will repeat this once again, I'm in!*" he said with a smile on his face. You would almost think Reg just received the highest reward in the land as the expression on his face said it all. I was sure he was in, and now all I had to do was to get to know him intimately. I knew where he lives and I had a credit report on him, I just needed to be one hundred percent certain that Reg was actually who he was. How to do that would be my job over the next week or two. I'll have to put the garage and our special room in the subway station aside for now and spend my time watching Reggie Green. If he is a cop he has to make contact with his handler and that is where I will find all I need to know. I hate to waste time on this type of crap but it is essential that I clear Reg of all suspicion, after all, he is an associate of mine.

I left the bar and went back to my room and decided it would best if I slept there tonight and get home early in the morning. Who knows what actions Reggie might take if he is really an undercover cop? If he has put me under surveillance it would be best if he saw me as what I said I was. Just a bookkeeper living alone and trying to get my shit together. When I went home I took a long walk so I could detect anyone who might be following me. The coast was clear and when I leave my place early tomorrow morning there will be no one on the streets so detecting any followers would be even easier. Deep down I trusted Reggie, I felt he was honest and most of all my gut feeling said he was an okay guy. One more thing fortified my reasoning about him, Mario's Bar was not a place where illegal drugs were being sold or a lot of bad apples hung out. It was a neighborhood bar and most of the people who came there were regulars. There is no way an undercover cop would be wasted in a place like this. This didn't stop me from being doubly sure, but deep down inside I felt Reggie was actually who he represented he was, a straight guy who wanted to take the chance to make his future a lot more secure, nothing more.

I changed back into my true identity and left my room at five-forty-five in the morning. The streets were deserted this Sunday morning and I was now certain that the coast was clear, no one was watching me. I took the train uptown and carefully proceeded to return to my place. No one cared, no one followed, the coast was clear and Reggie was getting better and better all the time. He was going to be a good associate that was for sure.

I felt it would be best to nurture the relationship with Reggie a lillle more, especially now that we were on a different basis. Having the discussions we had put us on a different level in the friendship department. In our minds there was no more secrets between us as we were about to embark on a partnership that required mutual respect and trust. I could almost equate us to being brothers but really couldn't because I never had any.

I met Reggie at the bar on Tuesday and could sense the difference at once. He greeted me much more warmly and wanted to discuss our future relationship in a lot more detail. The excitement and possibility of being a very rich man in the near future made him feel ten feet tall. Of course, I think it would make anyone feel that way when the prize was so high.

Nevertheless I felt great and enjoyed every second of his company now that we were on this level. We talked in general terms because I wasn't going to reveal any details that would alert him or anyone else to the exact details of the job ahead. Instead of playing pool all the time as we used to we were now having a beer alone in a rear booth and talking. No one paid any attention to us except Peter, *"Hey you guys, have you lost your moxie for pool?"* Peter said to us.

"No Pete, just unwinding from a long work day. Reggie and I thought we'd have a change of pace and just have a few beers, is that okay with you?" I said.

"Don't get your panties in an uproar Ben, I was just kidding around. I understand, so you guys relax as much as you like, just don't stop coming in here, you are family and I need my family here to make me feel better. The next round is on me," he said as I began to protest his offer he jumped right in and said, *"Hey guys, don't make a federal case out of this. I 'm just making a peace offering to show you how much I care about both of you. Now shut-up about a glass of free beer, I can buy you a round or two anytime I want to,"* he laughed and began filling to big steins.

Reggie said in a relaxed voice. *"I'm glad we are partners and even though others can't know about it, we can act like we are good friends. Don't get upset with Pete, he's a nice guy and means well. It's nice to know that someone cares about us isn't it Ben? Even though I don't have too many details I'm still very excited and can hardly wait to get started. When am I going to meet our other partner?"*

"As soon as I meet him. I haven't found that partner yet and wanted to discuss it with you. The choice of our partner will be made by both of us so be alert and if you have any suggestions I would like to hear them. Just to bring you up to date I have been watching a few people who come into the bar and feel I have found one that might be perfect. I would like you to decide which one of the regulars would you choose and then I'll tell you who I chose. I'm doing it this way Reg, so I can see if we are on the same wave length. After all this is a partnership and although it is my deal I could not do the job without your help. If you turned me down I would have to abandon my idea because it requires more than one person, and in reality, needs at least three. Well, we now have two, you and I

and all we need is one more and we can then sit down and go over details and start planning the project as a team. Take your time my friend, you let me know by Friday who you might select and then we'll talk about it. What do you think about that? It'll make the rest of the week go by quicker or at least, I hope it will," I said as our free beers arrived.

I spent the rest of evening playing a couple of games of pool with Reg and then said good-night as I left for home. I did not relax my vigilance for one second, I was careful and checked out each and every possible space where someone could try to stay out of sight. I wanted to make sure no one was following me and I was intent on following Reggie, at a safe distance, of course. I walked around the block, I knew I would not lose Reggie because he just started a game with another guy and would be at least a half-hour. I really wanted to run to my room and change into my regular dress and follow him as Ben, but could not predict how long his pool match would take. It would be foolish for me to miss this opportunity to see what he does after finding out from me that we need one more guy. If he was an undercover cop it would be logical that he would contact his handler and try to set-it-up that one of his other cops could be the additional guy. It was only logical so this must be done tonight. Of course, he could meet with his guy during the day if he wanted and I would not be the wiser. I was taking a shot even though I was convinced he was legit. But, of course, any good undercover cop would leave the impression that he is not a cop at all or else he wouldn't be an undercover cop. No proper undercover cop would blow his cover easily and Reggie, if he was one, wouldn't either.

I could not take any chances so I made my pass around the block using this to double-check that no one was following me and waited for Reggie to leave the bar. When I rounded the corner I saw Reggie leave the bar and turn west towards his place. I walked carefully at a safe distance even though he didn't look back. I guess he didn't have reason to believe that someone would be following him. I followed him directly to his place and watched him go directly to his apartment. I waited for his light to go on and then settled back to watch for the next hour or so. Thirty minutes later the lights in Reggie's apartment went off, it was now ten-thirty. Not satisfied that he went to sleep I decided to wait another half-hour in case he was going out to meet someone. I waited a full one hour watching the front door of his building as well as the lights of his apartment. Nothing happened, it was time I left and went home after all, I have to work tomorrow. I was a lot more confident that my impression of Reggie was correct and he was the first of my associates. Of course, I still had the daytime hours to worry about and felt that Reggie, if he was an undercover cop, would not really be at work as that would only be a cover.

According to his credit report he worked Vic Tanny's Gym Gym over on Forty-Fifth and Broadway. He was an instructor and according to him he was at very good at his job. It was not the best paying job but it was rewarding and the future looked bright, he wanted to open his own health studio in the future. I had all this information carefully documented simply because if he was to be my associate I wanted to know every possible detail. I didn't want to leave anything to chance, especially in a case like this, too much was riding on every decision made.

I decided to go by the gym during my lunch hour and, as Sam West, I could easily observe Reggie at work. Once again I felt if he was a cop he wouldn't be working too hard and he wouldn't know anything about me or my plan as Sam West. Nevertheless I had to be careful and not be obvious in my surveillance job. Although Reggie could possibly be questioned after the project is done and might remember a suspicious character watching him many months earlier and put two and two together, but the possibility of that was remote, even so, I took every possible precaution. I was extra careful to make sure Reggie didn't see me as I watched through an observation window as he went through his paces with a group of women who wanted to lose weight and look sexy. A mini class I thought, even though I was never in a place like this before. On one side there were a lot of people lifting weights and doing other exercises that seemed suitable for a weight loss program. On the other side there were only men who, I have to assume, were boxers or wanna-be boxers. There were two boxing rings and a lot different types of punching bags situated around the place. This section of the gym was far busier than the other and a lot noisier.

I watched Reggie work hard and, what I thought to be, efficiently. He seemed to take his job quite seriously just as I do with mine. Satisfied that my future associate passed another test and because I had to be back at work in less than twenty minutes, I had to leave. I stopped at the front desk and inquired as to when Reggie was on duty explaining that I liked how he treated his clients and would like to enroll in a class. I asked what the rates were and further explained that I work most days so my schedule would have to work out after my workday. He very obligingly gave me Reggie's complete schedule for which I thanked the young man and left. I now had his schedule and could see if it was possible to explore a little more. Something still nagged at me about Reggie, I didn't know what is was and thought, quite a few times, that I was being a little over-the-top in my investigation. Of course, reality stepped in and that special voice in my head told me that I could not possibly be too vigilant especially when it comes to a project this important. I was determined to make sure Reggie was clean and I wasn't leaving myself open for disaster. I always felt that the most difficult part of this project was going to be finding the people I need. If I was doing this on my own then I would have no worries at all, but I can't handle it on my own so I need these two associates. Once Reggie is one hundred percent clean and a bona-fide member of my team, it will be a lot easier to check out the next associate, or that is was what I thought back then.

Needless to say I was more motivated than I ever imagined I could be. This project was consuming my entire life, as a matter-of-fact, it was my entire life. I needed a break, but couldn't take one now. I was tired and perhaps my sharpness was dulled a little because of my lack of rest. I wasn't sure how I felt except that I was obsessed with this project and wanted to get to it as fast as possible. Tonight I decided I would put everything associated with this project on hold, at least for one night, and just vegetate. I needed the respite, if not for physical reasons, for mental ones for sure. I needed to start a new day with a clear head and relax a lot more. I could easily miss an obvious detail because of my zeal that added to my tiredness. I realized that I wasn't following my own advice and that was not good business sense at all. A day's rest will be just what the doctor ordered. I'll go to work and have some fun and not think about the project today. I'll see everything in a new light tomorrow when my mind has slowed to a reasonable speed and good sense has returned. One cannot be a success if they are not planning each move long into the future. Life is a chess game and in order to be successful at it, one must be patient, deliberate, and realistic. I have all these qualities plus and cannot let an over anxious moment destroy everything I have worked for. I went to sleep to rid my mind of distractions and to renew my faith in myself. Tomorrow will be a new beginning and the project will be back on track.

A New Beginning:

I WOKE UP BRIGHT AND EARLY AND FELT AS IF SOMETHING heavy has been removed from my mind. I felt good and ready to take on another day. I showered, dressed, and left for work picking up a container of coffee and a sweet roll to enjoy on this the first day of spring. I was lighter than air and could fly, or at least I felt like I could. The sun was peeking through and I knew the day was going to be a beauty. Yes, it was a new beginning and my project was once again on the right track.

My heart raced with excitement as I now felt convinced that Reggie was for real and I could move forward. When I meet with him at the bar on Thursday, I'll move forward. Although he does not know the actual nature or the mechanics of the project, I will get him involved in the recruitment of our next associate. I felt, deep in my heart, that this project was now on the road. The one big stumbling block was finding my first partner and now that it has been accomplished, I can move forward. I felt great as I sat on the train on my way to work. Yes being successful was just around the corner, I could almost taste it.

I spent the rest of the day flying through it, as if time went by as fast as I have ever experienced and each customer was a perfect distraction. I made haste to get home and change into my subway disguise and proceeded back to my special room beneath the bank. Being dressed as an employee of the City made me feel as if I was actually holding down a second job. Of course, I realized that this was nothing more than a disguise, but that didn't mean a thing when

I was in that uniform. I rode the subway back to my apartment and changed and then went back as Mr. Subway employee.

I went into my special room and once again found everything to be undisturbed. Not a speck of dust was moved, not a drop. All my equipment was in place and the entire place seemed to welcome me home. I carefully measured out the main room that was directly under the safety deposit boxes and placed a very faint X to mark to the exact center point where we will begin removing the concrete floor. Access will be easy once we get the drilling started, the key was no longer how to get into the safety deposit box area as that was the simplest part of the job, the real challenge was getting out and I believe I have that covered.

My job now is to get our second associate and then we can, as a team, start to prepare for the biggest project of our lives. Yes, I believe I have this project covered from start to finish and I know it will be done flawlessly. I could hardly wait for Saturday when I will meet Reggie meet and get started on the vetting of associate number two!

The Choosing:

I SPENT THE REST OF THE WEEK WORKING AS USUAL AND could hardly wait for Saturday to arrive. Of course, it did finally come and I, as usual, went to the bar and waited for Reggie to arrive. I waited about thirty minutes and Reggie arrived with great big smiles and an attitude that was just great. He came right over to my booth and sat down opposite me and had a big smile on his face. *"I couldn't stay at home Ben, I wanted to get here as soon as possible so we can move forward on this project. This is the most exciting thing that has ever happened to me,"* he said as he kept on smiling. I signaled to Peter to bring us two shots of bourbon and a pitcher of draft.

"I know exactly how you feel Reg, I feel the same way and can hardly wait to move on. I don't know if you have paid any attention to Tyrone? He usually comes by on Saturday nights. I chose him because he looks strong, the little I know of him he seems quite honest. Of course, he's liable to tell us to go to hell, I hope not, as I said he looks like he fits the job description to a T." I said.

"I remember him even though I didn't have too much to say to him. I played pool with him a few times and we both said very little. Tell me what you have discovered about him and we can move on from there," Reggie said.

"So far I have done a preliminary search on Tyrone. I went to his workplace to see him in action. He works at ON Construction and did not see me. I just wanted to make sure he wasn't a cop and that he really does what he says he does. That is as far as I went, now

that you and I are partners we can finalize this thing and get on our way. Of course, this doesn't mean that we should relax our strict investigation methods. I expect he should be here in a few minutes and we should lay the ground work tonight. If he has no interest in our project then we'll forget him and find someone else. What do you think, Reg?" I said.

"I agree with you, we might as well get started now. Let's not waste any more time and move forward. I will suggest one thing Ben, either you or I talk with him but not both of us. It is not his affair that we have agreed to do this project as a team. If he agrees to be part of the deal then we'll let him in on the third person, but if he opts out why should he know anything more than he must? If you would like I'll interview him or you can do it, it's up to you Ben as it is your project. I just feel it is safer this way until we are certain he is on board," Reggie said.

"I believe you are right Reg, I'll interview him while you play a game or two at the tables. Let me see where his head is at and if he wants to be part of our project I'll then introduce you to him as the third associate. I like you're thinking and am glad that you took the initiative to suggest this. He should arrive any minute now so why don't you get a game started while I prepare for my interview with Tyrone," I said to Reggie.

Reggie went over to the pool tables and within a few seconds he had a game all set-up with some other dude. Five minutes later Tyrone came into the bar and went directly to say hello to Peter and ordered a beer. I got up from my table and went over to the bar and sat down next to Tyrone and said, *"Have you got a couple of minutes, I'd like to talk to you."*

"Sure thing Ben, you wanna sit by the bar or at a booth?" Tyrone said.

"Let's grab a booth so we can be alone for a little while. Soon the place will get too crowded," I said as I picked up my beer and walked towards the booths on the other side of the bar. We sat

down and took a swig of our beers and I finally said, "*Tyrone I know I haven't gotten to know you that well but I've seen you in here every Saturday for over six months so I feel you are part of the joint, if you know what I mean! What I have to say to you is very private and should not go anywhere else once we get up from this table. I trust you will honor my request of confidentiality,*" I said.

"*No problem Ben, whatever we talk about here shall remain private, I give you my word. Now you've got me all excited and curious, what the hell is it all about?*" Tyrone said with a smile on his face.

"*Thanks for your promise of privacy. I'd like to ask you a few questions if you don't mind. I have to point out to you that if you decide not to accept my offer then this conversation never happened. For reasons of security and good sense I can only skim over the project. Complete details will follow upon your acceptance of my offer. Sorry to make it sound so mysterious but caution is very important.*

"*During the last few months I have seen you around, mostly on Saturday nights and I've heard you complain about how little money you make and that things seemed to be stacked against you. Well Tyrone, I'm here to offer you an opportunity to correct that situation. First let me point out that the rewards are high and so are the risks. I'm sure that you have heard the expression risk-reward, this is one of those opportunities. To further help you get a proper grasp on the project let me give you a head's up on the rewards. Your share of the pie should be a million dollars or more. The rewards we all get depends on what we find in the location that we are about to get into. Why I say 'about' is very simple, we know there is a lot of money located at our objective but we don't know exactly how much. Of course, what we are planning is not exactly legal, but there is one thing in our favor, the victims or shall I call them the losers, will not be able to cry for help. That is all I can say on that subject for now. There is no violence involved, as a matter-of-fact, we will not*

85

encounter any other human beings while performing this project. No weapons are required or permitted as there will not be any need for them. Of course, there is risk as the actual deed itself is not legal but if you follow the carefully laid plans that I have made, the risk will be very minimal. The most difficult part of this project will be self-discipline. Although we will complete our task of obtaining this large amount of money, we will not be able to use it freely for at least two years. Your lifestyle cannot change in that period of time because this project is foolproof if we follow the guidelines I have set for us. The only way we can be tripped up is if one of us shall start to display new found wealth. Like a new car, a new home, new suits, you know what I mean Tyrone. We will not take anything other than cash while on this project as we cannot leave any clues and taking something that is traceable is a sure fire way of leading the cops to us. This is a small sacrifice for us especially when the rewards are so good. No worries or cares about money for the rest of your life. Not such a bad deal Tyrone, not such a bad deal at all, what do you think?" I said with a smile on my face.

"How many others are involved? Do I know any of them? I'm very excited Ben and I'm in, where do we go from here?" Tyrone said.

"I can't answer those questions at this time Tyrone. Once we agree on our association, I'll introduce you to our other associate. Neither of you know that the other is being offered this deal. It is safer this way in case you decide you are not in or the other partner feels the same way. I have to be sure that you are whom you say you are. There is no way I can take any chances on a project like this by taking in the wrong person. What I would like you to do is tell me a little bit about yourself, stuff like where you live, where do you work and how long have you been at your job. I'm sure you can understand why these precautions are necessary. I would not like to put you in a position where you could be in trouble and I hope you would not ever do that to me. I feel that given the opportunity to make a lot of money with almost no risk at all should be incentive enough to be a straight shooter, unless you are not what you say you are. I want to emphasize this once again Tyrone. This project does not involve any other people. It does not require any violence at any time and no weapons are needed and none will be tolerated. This is an easy and simple project that can be done in less than forty-eight hours. Once completed you will return to normal life as it was before and no one will be the wiser. I know you said you are in but now, after I just explained all the details of what I need, are you still in?" I waited to hear Tyrone's answer.

"I am in. I am so grateful that you are allowing me in and hope I can satisfy every detail you need from me. I am not a cop! I never worked for the police department, fire department or any other department that may be associated with Police or any form of law enforcement. I was not ever a stool pigeon or an informer for any law enforcement agency or anyone else and am not one at the present time. I am not a member of any organized crime group nor do I have a criminal record. I do not do drugs and drink very conservatively and I live alone. I work for ON Construction and have been with them for three years. I tried boxing a few years ago but I didn't enjoy getting my ass kicked. Now I instruct would-be boxers on proper strength training and good eating habits as well as boxing skills. I am a better boxing coach than I was a boxer. I used to live in Harlem and now live in Brooklyn with three other roommates. My rent is one hundred dollars a month and I've been living there for two and one-half years. I am twenty-nine years old and yes, I want to make some real money and get my ass out of the shit hole I am in. Yes I can and will remain in my present lifestyle for at least two years after we complete the project. I am a solid guy who will not ever betray a friend no matter what deal is offered to me. I don't think I can add anything further to all this Ben, except here is my exact address, my phone number and my Social Security number," he said as he slid a sheet of paper over to me.

"Thanks Tyrone, you have been very above-board and I appreciate it. If I think of anything else I need answered I will get in touch, in the meantime give me a few days to digest everything. I promise I will get back to you in a few days, until then relax, and forget our little chat. Once you have cleared my security search we will be able to talk more about this project. Go have a good time and enjoy what's left of the weekend. Oh by the way Tyrone, if you live in Brooklyn why have you chosen Peter's Bar to spend Saturday night?" I asked.

"It does look funny, that is for sure. In the first place Ben, I don't visit any bars or nightclubs in the area where I live. Don't like the people who go to them and I don't like the section of Brooklyn they're in. I believe they are dangerous and I can easily get mugged or worse. Second reason is that my construction job requires volunteers to work on Saturdays. I need the money and I haven't anything else to do so I work Saturdays from twelve noon to seven every Saturday evening and this bar is only ten blocks away from the construction site. Before I started coming here I stopped in a few other bars in the area but none of them had what interested me except this one. The pool tables drew me here as it gave me a few hours of fun before going back home to my depressing digs. Once I saw the pool tables I was hooked and also the atmosphere here seemed like a nice and safe one. I don't drink a lot, as a matter-of-fact, Peter would go broke on my one beer a night, but the pool tables held me in place and now I'm glad I did hang around," he said.

"Good enough for me Tyrone, how about a game of pool, I see the end table is empty," I said as I started to walk towards the pool table.

Tyrone and I played two games of pool when Tyrone said he had to leave as he had been at it since early this morning. Tyrone left and I went over to the bar and ordered a small draft and sat down to relax a little. Reggie came over and sat next to me and asked, "How did it go Ben?"

"It went very well Reg. I believe he is our man, I like him a lot and he has all the physical attributes we need. I think we hit pay dirt with Tyrone. I'll check him out this week but I believe he will pass with flying colors. He is a good guy and I think we'll be good partners. I promised him a response no later than next Saturday. I think we have a team Reg, I have a gut feeling this is the right guy for us," I said.

We finished our beers and I bid Reggie good-night and left for my one room palace. I arrived there fifteen minutes later and changed into my Sam West persona and left through a side door and walked to the train station and rode home.

I spent the week passing by Vic Tanny's Gym just to keep checks on Reggie. I had called in on Monday and asked the receptionist if she could give me Reggie's schedule even though I already had it, and much to my surprise she gave it to me. I was checking to see if the schedule had changed. This guy worked hard and long hours as he covered a few different group sessions and also worked at being a night manager. He closed the gym four nights a week and opened the place on Sundays. It seemed to me that Reggie was their all-around guy who did just about everything except make the big bucks. I could not believe for a second that he was an undercover cop. No way possible, he just didn't have enough time. One of the girls I had dated a few times worked for the cops as a secretary. I knew she had the hots for me, or should I say for the person she thought I was. I was always in disguise as Ralph Decker and made sure there was no way she could ever associate Sam West with Ralph Decker. It was insurance if I should ever need some information from the police. Having a mole right in their midst couldn't hurt. Well the time finally arrived for me to use that connection, so I called her and asked her out to see a movie. I had a perfect excuse, or that is what I thought, as the film *The Raven* starring Peter Lorre was just being released in 3D. I knew she liked horror flicks and this one, in 3D would be what the doctor ordered.

It didn't take much persuasion and we agreed to meet at the theater on Broadway and Forty-Second tomorrow night at seven.

This was a very exciting night for me. I wanted her to check the files on Reggie Greene and see if he was ever employed as a cop or if he had criminal record. We watched the movie and she screamed many times and reached out to me to hold her close. The 3D glasses made parts of the movie jump right out of the screen and almost hit you in the face. It was quite an experience, one that I enjoyed as well. After the show we went to Lindys for a piece of their famous cheesecake that she had asked for. I decided it would be best to ask her to do me a favor and over a piece of Lindys' World famous cheesecake was the right time. Much to my surprise she didn't question me why I wanted to know. I was a little taken aback by her lack of interest but thought it best to leave it alone. I left her at the train station where she went home to Rego Park in Queens.

I called her two days later at home and she told me that there wasn't any records of Reggie Greene as an employee in any capacity and no criminal record existed matching that name and Social Security number. My heart raced as I digested this news, our team was almost set, just one more person to check out and I can move forward with my project.

I couldn't ask my contact to check on another guy so I decided to take my lunch hour by bringing a sandwich with me and walking over to Tyrone's construction site. If he was what he said he was he would be working real hard on his job. If he was an undercover he would have an easier job. Well, at least that was my logic and I thought it best if I confirmed things with my own eyes. A proper undercover situation would have all the personal information in place in case someone checked them out which, of course, I did. I passed by the site two days in a row and there was Tyrone working his ass off. When I say working, I mean, really working hard. He pushed a wheelbarrow full of earth and rocks and shoveled as if there was no tomorrow. He didn't know me as Sam West so he had no idea that I was watching him. There wasn't anything out of the ordinary and he was a hard worker. Of course, I had all the credit information on him and he checked out real good. I felt secure with him and settled the matter after my second trip to the construction site. Tyrone will be our third man, we can now get the project on the road!

The Plan:

I CANNOT FIND THE WORDS TO EXPRESS THE EXCITEMENT and the satisfaction that all my research, hard work, and preliminary planning, has finally brought us to this point. Day after day of practice to perfect the many steps that are needed to make this project successful. Days of sacrifice and the many trips to the special underground area just to prepare the area and get the project on its way. Now I am ready to move on and complete this stage of the plan and get the team ready that will help make it all successful. I felt like a new day has finally arrived and lifted all my worries off of my shoulders. Of course, there are still a lot of things that have to be done but now they will be done by the team. Now we can move forward and get this job done.

I must admit that I have been very calm, cool, and collected up to now regardless of which disguise I wore that day. This Saturday was a very special day in my quest, I was a little too excited as I brought Tyrone and Reggie together for the first time. I did not want to set-up a meeting place that was too obvious like Roscoe's Bar. If anything should happen after the project was completed and the cops should somehow connect this bar, it would be easy to piece together that three guys, who were always regulars, met here very often. They could easily find out that these three guys sat in that corner booth and had many discussions. Of course, they would not know what these discussions were about but just the mere fact that the actions of these guys stood out would be enough of a red flag to warrant further inquiries.

Let's look at another scenario, let's assume one of my associates did not follow the golden rule and didn't maintain a low-key life style. If that happened, I'm sure Peter would become one of the informants and would call the cops in the hope of his collecting a nice fat reward. If one of these guys began living high on the hog, the cops would know, *where there is smoke there is fire* will have a lot of meaning and would instigate a full-fledged investigation. In view of all those possibilities I went out on Saturday after work and rented a hotel room in a flea bag place on Eighth Avenue and Forty-First Street. I went in as a street bum and paid cash for one night. The room was on the second floor in the rear at the end of a long hallway. The only good thing about this room was that it was next to the service stairs and I could walk down one flight and open the side door and let the other guys in. I registered as Nathan Smith and paid cash. The guy at the desk couldn't really care what my name was, all he made sure was that I paid the forty bucks for the room in advance. He also let me know that this hotel likes to rent the room many times a night and would like me to let him know when I'm through using it. I promised I would drop the key off when I leave. The best part was that the clerk who will be on duty tonight will not be the same dude that will be there when I checked in.

I then carefully wrote out the address of the hotel and instructions to meet at the side fire door precisely at seven-thirty tonight and bring this note with. I went to the Bar as usual and played a game of pool with Tyrone and gave him the note along with instructions to play one game with Reggie and give him a note as well. I told Tyrone that he should leave the bar first and then Reggie should follow about ten minutes later. I left early and made sure I said good-night to Peter and gave him an excuse that I have a hot date at nine tonight and didn't want to be late. I went to my room in the Bowery and changed into my Nathan Smith disguise and went to the hotel.

Once I was in the room I changed into my Ben Wilson disguise and waited for seven-thirty before going downstairs and opening the side door. Tyrone arrived right on time and waited with me inside the doorway until we heard a faint knock on the door. Reggie stood there smiling and quite anxious about being let in. We then proceeded up the stairs to the room where we could sit and talk. There wasn't much room for us all to sit so I sat on the bed while the boys sat on the only two chairs in the room. This was it, the new team that would seek out their fortune, and it was time I revealed a few more details of our project.

The Meeting:

"I'D LIKE TO WELCOME YOU BOTH TO THE FIRST MEETING OF our little group as we set-up the plan to make a lot of money. I realize Tyrone, that you were a little surprised to see Reggie at this meeting. Well I hope the surprise is now over and we can get down to business and move forward. The next few months will be very important in planning our project. Once the project is under way there is no room for doubt and uncertainty. I will start with the ground rules as I think they are as important as the project itself. If we are to be successful we must not leave a single clue of who was involved in this project.

"The first act as a group is to settle some real important ground rules. You may have heard the expression loose lips sink ships, well this is very appropriate in our case. Small things that no one pays any attention to can result in our undoing. For example, using names is a clue that often results in the best of plans being undone. So whenever we are together in regards to our project we cannot and will not use names. I'll be one, Reggie you will be two and Tyrone you will be three. When we are doing the project if something should occur that results in anyone alerting the other all they need do is say 'one watch out' and that will suffice. There is no need to find that one of us used the other's name and now they know that a person with the name of Ben was one of the perpetrators. A simple slip of the tongue opens a very wide door and soon the cops are narrowing their investigation to anyone named Ben. Of course, there are probably millions of people named Ben but why give them a direction. It's

as simple as that so we get used to using our numbers. When we are at the bar we use our names and act as we usually do. Nothing must change for us, nothing at all. Again, I'll use an example like tonight. Usually we are at the bar on a Saturday night. When one of us doesn't appear, Peter usually asks what happened. Tonight we are all not there so if something happened over the weekend and the cops started nosing around they might hear that all of a sudden the three of us were not there as they usually are on a Saturday night. Bartenders are one of their biggest sources of information so please be careful. Perhaps it doesn't sound like a big deal, but a big enough reason for cops to ask more questions. So all our meetings will take place on days and nights that we do not frequent the bar. Let's eliminate every possible angle we can, even the simplest of things can undo the best laid plans so we make sure we cover all bases all the time. Just remember this, when a crime takes place and there aren't any clues it stops the cops in their tracks. So let's make sure they don't stumble on a clue that because of our stupidity may point them in our direction. And most of all we must make sure we don't act or do anything stupid.

"I know all this sound silly but discipline is essential. All I ask is that we make certain we use our brains and think before we act. After this is over we will all be living in the lap of luxury without a care or worry. Trust me, trust your partners and remember no matter what is ever said to you none of your associates will rat on you. Don't fall for that bullshit ever! The cops love to use the following, 'You might as well come clean, your partner has told us the entire story,' please don't fall for that bullshit, it will never happen. I don't know how to stress that point but I hope it has hit home. If we are loyal to the project and to one another, then nothing or no one can ever break that bond. Okay, now let's get down to brass tacks and learn a little about this project.

"I will not reveal the location or the time the project will take place. I am telling you this now because I don't want anyone to *feel uncomfortable or impatient. You can understand my concern, I have to make sure nothing derails this project. I have worked on this project for a very long time and cannot have anything screw it up. I have already done most of the work. I have chosen the location and have secured the proper equipment that we will need to carry out the project. I have everything in place except the people I can trust and now I have you two guys. Now we are a team and I can start planning the date and the final method of carrying the money away from the scene and putting it in a safe place. I believe that getting into the area had been solved but getting out has not. Please have patience with me as you will benefit by my meticulous planning, this I promise. If we are to be successful we must trust one another, as I said earlier, at no time will anyone of us divulge the identity of the other no matter what bullshit the cops may throw at us. Even if they use the old trick that 'Your partner has told us everything,' then you may respond simply by telling them that if my partner told you everything you certainly don't need me. We are a team and will remain so as long as there is one hundred percent trust in our group."*

"Do not use your home telephone.

Do not use any telephone near your home.

Make all calls to a designated pay phone that we will establish and only in the case of an emergency.

We do not deviate from our usual days at the bar.

We meet only on days we do not stop in at the bar.

All meets will be set-up when we are at the bar playing pool. The note passed to you must be returned to me that same night.

Do not write any notes anywhere at home, at work, or at any other place. No notes ever.

Never discuss this project with anyone.

Do not drink more than one beer at the bar and no drinking of any amount when away from the bar.

Keep a low profile in your daily life. Do not stand out. The less people who pay attention to you, the better.

"Follow these instructions to the letter. Do not deviate and never be late for a meet.

No one, and I mean, NO ONE is to know what you have planned even if it is nothing more than a joke. No girlfriend, friend, relative, landlord, NO ONE at all.

When the project is completed you are to return to your usual life. I will give you complete instructions on how to seamlessly blend into life without suspicion.

No money is to be spent for two years. The project must get cold before we can start using the gains. This is a key part of this project and must be carefully followed. The only way you will be tripped up is to become rich before your time. The only clue that can lead anyone to you is the way you spend the money. Be careful and the years ahead will be a bed of roses and your life will be one of plenty.

"I cannot emphasize enough that the money is the only clue that can reveal your part in this project. Once again, I repeat, be very careful and use it wisely. I feel that after two years you can start a new life, perhaps in California or some other great place. Always leave your friends happy by making sure your cover story is always the same and is simple. Like an uncle died and left me a few dollars. Or a dear friend passed away and left me a little money. Try not to be too fancy if and when you meet new friends. Whatever your story is make it believable, simple, and easy to understand. It's nobody's business on how much money you may have so don't make anyone suspicious by throwing money around. Never be too explicit, just enough information to satisfy your friend's curiosity and nothing more. Common sense should always prevail and your lives will be filled with wonderful things and no worries at all. I suggest it would be best if you move to another City, even another State, and start a brand new life. Do not tell anyone you came from New York, pick an easy place like New Jersey if you have to pick a place at all. Enjoy *your new life by being careful and not too much of a big-shot. Drugs and drink will be your undoing so try your best not get hooked into any of it. Remember, there will not be another project! This is a one-time shot and your career of this nature is over, don't screw it up. You will never see me again after the project is over and I won't ever see you guys. I suggest you both make sure you don't see each other again after the project. Move away from the bar and get as far as you can from Peter by using some story that you got a job in Jersey or Pennsylvania but never in the place where you intend to move to. You will have at least one million bucks in cash and it must be yours for the rest of your life. This doesn't mean you cannot get a job, you certainly can and it probably won't hurt.*

"Please do not forget these rules and as long you act carefully we will be living the lives we always wanted. Do not ever forget these things that are mentioned, they are important and will keep us safe at all times," I said.

I sat there exhausted after that-way too-long speech and looked at the guys. The expressions on their faces said it all. They looked like they were in way over their heads and that they would run out the door if they could. I was pleased because I felt the message was delivered and I believed, mostly because I wanted to believe, that they would be strong. As I sat there Reggie said, *"Wow! It's like being hit with a baseball bat even though I've never been hit with one but can imagine. Your points are well taken and I know they are meant for us all to enjoy the benefits of the project without hassles. It would be nice if we would learn what the project is. I, for one, would love to know what we are going to do. How about it Ben, it's time you let us in on the deal!"*

"Yeah," Tyrone said, *'I think we deserve a little more information. You would not have gone this far if you didn't have faith in us. So open up Ben, and let us in on the sixty-four dollar question."*

The Project:

"*I THINK YOU ARE RIGHT, IT'S TIME I LET YOU IN ON THE project. Please understand that certain details will be left out because it is not wise to discuss those yet. We trust each other, there is no doubt about that, but anything can happen between now and D-Day. Just be patient and everything will be very clear. If you have any questions please save them until I finish and I'll be glad to answer them.*

"*I realize that this sounds quite easy here in this room but let me assure you it isn't. I thought I could do this project on my own but I couldn't because I need assistance simply because of the many things that have to be done. As you realize the room that contains these boxes is heavily fortified and in order to gain access one needs some brawn. In our case I cannot move thick pieces of concrete on my own and it would take me hours to drill through thick concrete reinforced with steel. Once I would gain access, how much money would I be able to carry? What would I gain by doing this alone except the fact that no one could rat on me. Needless to say I may not succeed at all if I went at this alone, therefore, I chose two of the best partners I could find. You are both strong and eager to become millionaires so you fit the bill perfectly. Are you disciplined enough? Only time will tell, but I believe that once you see the color of the money, discipline will be an easy task.*

"*We will take care of this project on a holiday when the building where these boxes are held is closed and there are no people there. This will give us about forty-eight or more hours to complete the* project. As I said earlier I will give you the exact location when the time is right and not one second before. You may ask me any questions you wish but none about the exact date and location of the project," I said.

Reggie stood up and said, "I understand why there isn't any violence involved. There won't be any people around except us. Isn't that right number one?"

"Yes. There will not be any weapons required and certainly no violence or interactions with any other human beings," I said. "The only people we will see are those people who are going places just as we will be doing and they will be far too busy to pay any attention to us."

"Is this location here in the City? Do we have to travel anywhere out of the City? What equipment do we require to do our parts?" Tyrone said.

"There is no need to bring any equipment with you. I have bought and obtained all the equipment we will need. You will have to bring a few things with you but those will be very simple items and I'll explain each one of them to you. As far as location, yes, it is in the City. We will not have to leave this City to do this," I said.

"Hold on number one, I understand everything up to a point, but would like to clarify how we will carry away one million bucks each. That is a lot of bread and some of it will be in small bills thus adding to the weight and space needed. I have never seen one million but would imagine that it is heavy and bulky. If we are opening safety deposit boxes we certainly will find a lot of cash in many denominations, wouldn't that create a problem of logistics? I'm not trying to throw a monkey wrench into the project but we might as well think of every angle. We may be in trouble because of the sheer volume of cash. When we leave the scene we will, without doubt, face some other people who might notice three guys pulling large sacks of stuff around in the middle of the night or possibly in the middle of the day. I think that is a very legitimate scenario, number one," Reggie said.

"You are quite right two, but I believe I have solved that problem. Please address me as one and not number one. The word number is not needed here guys, I'm sure we are aware of who is who on this project. I did not want to go into that right now but I do have a plan that will solve our transportation concerns, both of the money as well as our personal well-being. The solution depends on the time of the project as that will also play a big role in this plan. If we choose a weekend like Labor Day, July fourth, Memorial Day, etc., we gain the Monday and we can also use the holiday to help us cart away our piles of cash. I really didn't want to go onto detail at this time, but seeing that you brought it up I shall do so.

"Let's use Memorial Day as an example. If we all dressed as if we were folks who had a long weekend to enjoy nature we would solve two problems. One, we would look like any other camper or hiker who went away for the long weekend and was now returning home as the holiday ends. As a matter of fact we would look like many hikers who love camping and use the subway. We would be wearing and carrying one of those large double backpacks with some external gear showing on the outside, like a sleeping bag rolled up and sitting on top of the backpack. Anything that would make us look like real campers including facial growth that was a few days old. We'd be beyond suspicion because it would be the end of a holiday and what do hikers do, they return home so they can resume their normal lives after the holiday. There is very little chance that anyone would know that stuffed into that backpack was a million or more dollars? It is so innocuous that you could even use public transportation without fear. I would remind you that we have not decided on an actual escape plan but this is one that allows us the easy way of taking away our cash. Using the backpack method as the way to transport the cash will be fine. I caution you to remember that greed is a negative factor so please don't try carry a backpack that would be too big and make someone suspicious. It would be terrible to get caught or create suspicion over a few dollars, believe me it's not worth it. Earlier I pointed out some rules that we should follow and stated that common sense was one of them and here is a perfect example of that. I would hate to say that we were undone because of the unusual size or look of the backpack, one that seems way too big for that hiker. It might make a good detective novel very much like a *Perry Mason Mystery* with a title of The Overstuffed Backpack Case, but would not do us any good when the cops are told about the hikers with overstuffed backpacks. Be smart and do things that would not make us stand-out from the crowd, let's just blend in and become very rich guys with no worries," I said.

"All I can say it's a brilliant idea and yes, I agree with you, we must use common sense and this will be successful. I had my doubts about all this until you explained this to us. I am in, all the way, no more doubts from me, that's for sure. You don't have to reveal anything more to me at this time. It doesn't matter if you don't want to tell me more, I'm in all the way and it's your baby and your timeline. Just tell me when and I'm there and thanks for inviting me in on this project," Tyrone said.

"I second that, one, I'm in hook-line-and-sinker. Just give me the final instructions and I'll be there at your side. Thanks for taking me in as well," Reggie said.

I was very pleased with the result of our meeting and was quite satisfied that this project was now on the road to success. I felt that these two guys were deeply committed and that they actually were not cops. I couldn't vouch for their ability to remain strong and well-disciplined after the project but that was not a big concern to me. Once the project was over I will never see these two people again. I will disappear and Benny Wilson will be gone forever regardless of their ability to remain quiet and well-disciplined. I was happy with the way things were going and could hardly wait to complete the project.

Now I must choose a date, a date that will fit into the schedule perfectly. Not only must I find a date that will allow us enough time to complete the project but one that will make our escape easy and non-conspicuous. Taking the money out of the boxes will be easy, taking the money out of the area and hiding it will be the hardest thing of all. I know I must plan the exact escape route and hope that my associates follow it to the letter but I also must find a proper and safe place to hide the money. I have the perfect place in mind and will begin to prepare it in the next few weeks. To say I was excited was an understatement, I was ecstatic and had to tell myself to calm down, now was not the time to get carried away.

The Hiding Place:

I HAD SPENT THE LAST FEW DAYS RACKING MY BRAIN HOW
to find a secure spot where I will be able to hide a lot of money for
an extended period of time. I was looking at all possibilities and
found that this task was not as easy as I thought. I figured, even
though I felt the possibility was remote, that the cops would for
some unknown reason suspect me? Well, if they did they would
certainly search my apartment and it isn't big enough to hide a
stash that big. If I went out and secured another safety deposit box,
there is a chance that they could locate it. So where the hell can I
hide that much money and know it will be safe as well as keeping
me off the radar? I finally decided to use the piece of land I have in
Adirondacks Mountains.

My Dad bought this piece of land many years ago with the
thought that we'd go there during the summer. Unfortunately that
never happened because he got sick and was not able to build
the cabin he always dreamt about. He did build a small cabin so
we would have some place to sleep when we visited there but he
never was able to complete the full size house he dreamt about.
Three years later, when I was just eleven years old, my Dad died of
tuberculosis. He left a will even though he didn't have much and left
the nine acres of undeveloped land to me. My Mother was shocked
that he left a small boy a piece of land but being old fashioned and
very much in love with my Dad, she made sure that when I turned
twenty-one she signed the land over to me. I was not that pleased
as it was of no use to me, but because my Dad thought so much of

it and my Mother held on to it for over ten years just to give it to me, I felt I had to accept it and see how I can make it useful and fun.

The piece of land was located near the towns of Lake Placid and Lake George. It was accessible via a dirt road that was rarely maintained. The only saving grace was the fact that two other houses existed higher than my piece of land thus forcing someone into keeping the road open all year around. During the last two years I had spent about one week at the cabin. It was an escape for me but was very isolated as the cabin didn't have any electricity or running water. Actually the cabin was nothing more than a shelter from the elements and had no value in winter. Yet this isolated property was the ideal place to hide the money. I decided to drive up there in a few weeks or as soon as all the snow melts. Spring was upon us and the snow was melting quite quickly on the lower levels, but up on high where my piece of land was, it was a process that took a little longer. The temperature at that level seemed to be a little cooler even though the sunshine seemed brighter than anywhere else I have ever been. The area is so large that even if the cops, by some remote set of reasoning, would search the entire nine acres they would never find a reasonably secure hiding place. Nevertheless I made up my mind that this would be the ideal place to stash the money. I would, over the next few weeks, find a suitable place and take all the necessary steps to make sure it was a secure spot. I decided that I would find that safe place and make sure that every other step was rehearsed and tested over and over again.

My next step was to create a plan that will stand all of us in good stead. This project cannot succeed if we do not have a strong plan in every respect and that is what I was putting together. Hiding the cash was very important and so was how we act when go to the project site and how we act when leaving the project. If we do not create the right impressions we won't need to hide the cash because we will be caught before we even have time to squirrel the money away. In order to keep to the type of impression I wanted to make I felt we should make a few trail runs. I also felt it would be best if both Reggie and Tyrone participate in the trial runs as well. During the trial runs the knapsacks will be filled with clothing and other items that would be found in any hiker's bag. I'll make sure that this simulation will be as close to the real thing as possible. My real goal is to see how many people actually pay any attention to us and can we get from point A to point B without problems. This will be the real test and I'm pretty confident I'll not have any problems at all. Most importantly was that we used the public transportation system so we can see if things will go smoothly. Although I never told my associates that our escape plan was to use the subway system I felt it best to use it now and see what happens.

The Test Run:

FINALLY THE MEMORIAL DAY WEEKEND ARRIVED AND although it didn't give me any additional days off it would suffice for the purpose of my test. I dressed up as Benny Wilson and added a few touches like I was a real hiker. I filled my backpack with clothes and had a sleeping bag attached to the outside of the backpack. I looked a little scruffy as if I had been in the outdoors for a few days and went out to the subway station. Today, being a Monday and the last day of the holiday the crowds were light. I walked around the subway platform while I waited for a train and watched very carefully to see if people looked at me as I was a suspicious character. No one actually bothered with me except for one kid who was about fifteen. I could see it in his eyes, he was looking at me with that envious look. I could read his mind, *'If I could go hiking like that guy I'd be so very happy,'* it was as if he wanted to yell out to me and ask me where I went camping. I felt pleased that my presence in the station and on the train created no bad vibes at all. I got off at the Forty-Second Street station and met up with Reggie and Tyrone. They were both dressed to look like hikers coming home from a long weekend of hiking. We greeted each other and talked about where they were and where I went camping. I was convinced that this was the best method to use to make our clean get-away and that backpacks had to be the answer to carry the cash. I realized that there would not be any special news event that might jog one's memory on the night, we would have completed the project. The conditions would be the very same because we will be doing our project on a holiday just like the one we are experiencing now and the subway would be just about the same. The more I saw the more I was convinced that this was the prefect way and the only logical method of removing the cash safely. Will someone remember three suspicious characters the day after and connect them to a bank robbery? No, I didn't believe anyone would associate these guys with any Bank robbery that happened days before. I believed it was a stretch to think that people paid that much attention and would relate three hikers to a bank heist. Needless to say this heist will make headlines and when the police reach out to New Yorkers and ask if anyone was at that particular subway station on that day or a day close to the date the project took place. I'll bet my bottom dollar that no one, or very few would associate the hikers with that robbery. In the first instance most people would think that any robbers would use a vehicle to make their escape especially when carrying so much cash. Will it be construed as a coincidence that three hikers appeared in a subway station adjacent to the actual crime scene? Maybe, but not provable and New Yorkers usually mind their own business and don't have time to associate one person to an event as obscure as a benign bank robbery. And I'll bet there will be other hikers as well on that very day. The only difference from today's test run would be that we will not gather as a group and will take the train individually and in different directions. I was counting on New Yorkers going to where they must go and doing so without concern about others. I also felt that anyone who would think about a bank robbery would associate an event like this with the perpetrators running to a get-away car and speeding down Fifth Avenue. After all that is the way you would read about it if it made the news, a car chase. And best of all was the fact that most bank robberies seen in Hollywood movies ended in the thieves using a get-away-car. Preconceived thoughts would easily rule the day in this case. But three guys, three hikers all appearing at once in such close proximity to the crime! No, not a good idea at all, as it would arouse suspicion and perhaps make someone notice and try to identify one or all of us. Although the idea of hikers serves the purpose we must make sure that we leave the scene separately in order to avoid detection.

I decided to rest my overworked brain for a day or two and revisit the escape plan another day. I felt it would be best if I cleansed my brain of all thoughts and looked at the project in a fresh light. I gave myself a rest and for two days and did not think about the project at all. I worked and sold suits and accessories and just left the project somewhere else. I must admit that when it came time for me to fall asleep I could not eliminate the thought of the escape plan.

On Thursday, after work, while I was changing into my Ben disguise, it came to me. In the first instance when I went to the subway station as a single hiker no one took notice. Just another different New Yorker on his way home after a holiday weekend. But add two more hikers and I was certain there were those that took a second and third look. The answer was to have only one of us to use the subway at a time. One will not arouse any suspicion at all, especially when it is revealed that many safety boxes have been opened and cleaned out. The cops and newspapers will figure that more than one person must have planned and committed this act, so one hiker would not arouse any suspicion and although it still contained an element of risk it was nowhere near the risks involved in the original plan. The answer was right there, staring at me. Use only one in the subway while another could use a City bus that can be caught on Fifth Avenue and Twenty-Third Street. The other will walk toward the East side of the City along Twenty-Third Street and take a train at Lexington and Twenty-Third Street. Of course, those are only preliminary thoughts and cannot be taken as the final way. The best part of using the subway is that every few minutes there is a new crowd on the platform. So if one hiker takes a train and then in another ten minutes another train comes along and then the last one gets on in an additional ten minutes, I think we have eliminated any risk at all. I like that scene better than walking along any streets with a heavy backpack filled with a million dollars of cash. The weight alone might cause some type of problem after a while. On the train the hiker can take the backpack off and place it on the floor by his feet, nothing unusual, quite innocent as anyone who carried such a backpack would do! I decided it would be best if I examined each one of these routes in the next few days to make sure I am on the right path. Perhaps Sunday would be a good day to test out these escape routes. I have come this far and have checked most things out so why not this one as well. The escape route is as important as getting into the safety deposit box area and must be taken lightly. I made up my mind that I'll walk these routes on Sunday and while doing so I'll also take a few subway trips. I wanted to mimic the actual event as closely as I could. I also decided to test it all in my hiker disguise so I could see what reaction people have when they see me walking a City Street and taking a subway. Yes, Sunday will do as it is close to a holiday and the traffic will be almost the same. I was very pleased with my decisions and proved to myself that taking a day or two off from the grind was the right thing to do. My mind worked better and solutions were a lot clearer.

I met with Reggie at the bar as usual and played a few games of pool and asked him to meet me at the same hotel on Friday night at seven. I then called Tyrone at the gym and asked him to meet at the same place as well on Friday. Both agreed that it would be okay and I suggested we use the same method to gain entry, the side door! I would change into my disguise as Nathan Smith during lunch time on Friday when I run over to rent the room. I will make sure I have this disguise in my room so I may go there right after work and change. I was pleased with myself, things were starting to work out exactly as planned. 'Keep it intact Sam,' is what I told myself many times over and over just to make sure I didn't forget that discipline was the most important ingredient needed to succeed. I constantly told myself to take it slow and careful and things will run as smooth as silk. I needed to constantly remind myself especially after I screwed-up when I went to my special room as Sam West. As long as I always remember to be disciplined and calculating, this will be the sweetest deal ever and I'll be set for life.

It was noon on Friday and I had to get to my one roomer and over to the hotel and back to the room and back to work. There will not be any time for lunch and it'll be a stretch to make it to work. I went over to my Boss and said, *"I have to stop at the dentist during my lunch hour to get this tooth fixed. I might be a few minutes late, I hope it is alright?"*

"Of course, Ben, take all the time you need, I'll cover for you," he said with a big smile.

This made my task a lot easier but I still wanted to get back to work as quickly as possible. Somehow I always felt very secure when I was at work. It was like the work place was my sanctuary where I could feel safe from any prying eyes. Here in this place my secrets were safe and so was I.

I completed everything I had to do in a little over one hour and arrived back fifteen minutes late. My Boss was pleased to see me and I was happy to be back in my safe and secure environment. Life was good and was only going to get better.

The Start:

THE BOYS ARRIVED ON TIME AND I LET THEM IN THROUGH the side door. We walked up one flight of stairs and went into the same room as we had used before. *"I'm so glad you guys could make it, please relax and enjoy a minute of rest. I want you to be sharp because what I am going to say is very important to all of us and a successful project.*

"I realize you still do not know the location of the actual project and I will not tell you where it is until the very day of job. This is for security reasons and for your safety as well as mine. I will now tell you the nature of the project and how we are going to go about it. Please listen very carefully and ask any questions at any time. Do not take notes as nothing may be written down, ever. I will review all details one more time before the actual date of the project and will give you the coordinates then. Now please pay close attention and be alert.

"Our project, as I detailed in our last meeting hasn't changed so please forgive me if it seems like I'm being repetitive. I feel it is very important that I emphasize the importance of discipline as this is the key to success. Our project is to break into a set of safety deposit boxes located in the heart of the City. These boxes should contain a great deal of wealth in many forms. Jewels, stocks, bonds, and many other valuable but traceable items. They will also contain a lot of cash. That is our target, cash and only cash. We will not take anything other than cash because it is untraceable. Most people who keep large sums of money are actually hiding the cash from

someone including the IRS. In most cases the cash is not reportable so we will not have a lot of problems because no one, including the cops, will know how much was actually taken. Least of all the box holders do not want any authorities to know how much cash they have hoarded away and where they got it. If there wasn't any reason to keep it secret they would keep it in their bank accounts. Needless to say it is our job to remove as much of this cash as we can possibly carry but not to allow greed to foil a perfect project. When I say this I mean it very sincerely and you will understand my meaning in a moment. There are many problems associated with this project and I believe I have covered most of them long before I met you guys. I'll start from the very beginning with details even if you think they are boring and I've said it all before, and slowly work my way to the end of the project. In this manner I will be able to review the entire project with you. In reviewing the project we will hear the problems and we'll hear the solutions, please feel free to point any flaw you may feel exists. This project has to be perfect in every way, after all, our freedom is at stake.

"Now to begin, we must find a way to get into the vault area. One could blast the main door open with some sort of explosive but that would cause a lot of problems. One of the main problems would be the noise factor. The others are quite obvious and, perhaps I forgot to mention, the main entrance would be alarmed and this would alert the cops. So that method had been eliminated and other avenues of access were found. One of the best ways to gain entrance to a vault of this nature is through the roof, or the floor, or through an outside wall. Our method will be through the floor as I have discovered an access underneath the structure although the floor is about four to six inches thick of hardened concrete. Nevertheless I have discovered how to cut through this thick layer of concrete and gain entrance into the vault area. Over the last few months I have cut through concrete blocks that were six inches thick and discovered the method and the time it takes to do that. I have

purchased all the equipment we will need to do that little chore and have no idea if the floor that we will be cutting through has rebar or not. This floor was poured back at the turn of the century and perhaps they didn't use rebar at that time. All my research did not give me the answer and I couldn't find anyone who could tell the answer. To be completely honest, I didn't try very hard to find out because I didn't want anyone to suspect what my plan was. Perhaps you might know the answer Tyrone seeing that you are in construction. Once we gain access to the vault area we will have many hours of uninterrupted time to open the many safety deposit boxes. All this takes proper tools and specialized equipment which we have in place as we speak. I spent the last year obtaining and testing the right equipment for this job and have since placed that equipment on or near the project site. What I needed most was manpower and that is where you guys came in. It can't be easy to lower a piece of concrete from a height of about eight feet and gently place it on the floor. As a team we can do it and there is no doubt we will do it.

"We will have about thirty-six hours to complete our job and make a clean getaway. Some of the rules will be as follows. No name shall be spoken except the number system we have created. You should arrive at our designated place in disguise and your disguise does not have to be elaborate, it has to be convincing so you are not easily recognized. I'll get back to the actual disguise shortly. You must carry no identification with you and only a few dollars to cover subway and bus fares. During the time that the project is in progress you will not be able to eat as there will not be any food available. You must bring with an empty jar that is capable of containing your urine for the full period of time we are on our project. The jar is to be leak proof and should fit in your backpack easily. The jar is to be taken with you and thrown away when you are at a safe distance from the jobsite. Make sure the jar is wiped clean of fingerprints. It would be best if you could empty the contents into the sewer

system and throw the jar into a garbage receptacle. You may ask why urine and the answer is very simple. We want to leave as little forensic clues as possible and body waste might be one clue that may lead them to us. I've heard about cases where the cops found the crooks because one left his chewing gum behind. I also read in one of those detective novels how people are caught and so many of the ways are simple stupidity. I want to be certain we leave nothing behind and make their job almost impossible. By doing this we cover our asses. We must also bring along a towel. The towel does not have to be large but has to be able to absorb any sweat that may gather on your skin. We'll take the towel with us when we leave the area. Things like this may sound silly but we cannot take any unnecessary risks especially ones that may help them connect us with this project. During this period of time you will need water so each of us will carry a canteen that will come and go with us, nothing unusual for a hiker. Fill the canteen with drinking water and attach it to your backpack. Make sure it is on the outside of backpack as we need to leave space for the cash. A canteen, once again, is not unusual when one goes camping. Each one of us will wear hiking or work boots with steel toes and scruff them up so they look like they have seen many previous hikes. I suggest you get the boots now and wear them just to make sure they do not hurt your feet. Wear them so they get worn in and they get good and dirty. Hikers do not have brand new shiny boots, especially after a hike, and neither shall you. It is essential that you look the part when you are disguised as a hiker and the boots will come in handy if a piece of concrete should fall on your foot.

"Once we have made our way into the vault area we will be able to open the safe boxes. Each box should take no more than one minute to open. It will probably take another minute or two to sort through the contents of the box removing the cash. And once again I mention this, cash only, nothing else. No weapons are to be carried by us and none are to be taken from anyone's vault. If

you see one leave it where it lies, who knows where that weapon was or what someone did with it. Temptation is a strong motivator, eliminate that from your mind for this project and the trail to your door will remain ice cold.

"In regards to the money, let me tell you how it will work. When we first met I told you that the project should be worth about a million to each of us. To be honest with you I really don't know how much will be in those boxes, but judging by things I have learned, I would estimate there is much more than I estimated. It is not our job to worry about how much there is, our job is to take all we can safely carry. The key word here is 'SAFELY', please remember that. You are to wear a backpack to look like a hiker's and, most importantly and known only to us, to carry the cash away from the project site. The size of the backpack should be reasonable so anyone who may see you will not think you are anything else but a hiker out for a weekend trip. Remember we have two exposures with the backpacks in plain sight. One is when we arrive at the project site and the other is when we leave. When coming to the project your backpack should be stuffed with newspapers to make it look full. Start saving the newspapers now so you will have enough to test it and finally fill it. You must have one that will not arouse any suspicion when you are on your way to the project and when you leave the project site and move among the public. Please, I emphasize this as it is so very important, don't let greed blind you to caution. I'd much rather have a million than to try and stuff in more and find that people would think I'm carrying something different than my underwear. Be disciplined and you will reap rewards beyond your wildest imagination. Be foolish and you'll suffer more than you could possible imagine. Cops and banks don't like to be fooled and if they should stumble into you it would not be pleasant at all. Nothing like this can ever happen if you maintain discipline, never ever forget that!

"Once you get away from the project it is over and when you have safely reached your final place you must hide the cash and get rid of the backpack. I suggest you make arrangements now as to where you will hide this money. Don't leave it for the last moment and make sure you are placing it in a safe place. If you are hiding it in a place that is exposed to the elements you will need proper storing containers and proper wrappings so the cash will not rot when exposed. Remember, you should not be using those funds for at least two years so hide it carefully and safely. Remember, once the cash is hidden you should forget you even have it any longer. Put it out of your mind and go about your life as usual. If you decide to move away, don't tell anyone about it, especially because you have a lot of cash to take with you. After you have hidden your wealth take your backpack and cut it up and throw it away and make sure when you do throw it away, it is far from where you live. Do not leave anything to chance and do not leave anything in your home that would serve as a clue. Just because we made a safe get-away this does not mean we are out of the woods just yet. We cannot afford to become sloppy. We cannot be sloppy, every step must be taken to insure your safety, and make sure you are clean. Please, and I say this once again, please be careful and forget you have this cash for two years. The new cars can wait, the new suits can wait, and everything can wait for the coast to be clear and then get the hell out of Dodge and start a new life. If you want to keep a few thousand dollars on hand for spending money that is fine, but not more than ten thousand and spend it very quietly.

"Back to our safe box area and the money. If you remember when I talked to you at the very start I said we would split everything three ways. Equal splits as partners should do. Well that has changed and I'll explain what I feel is right for us all and much more expedient. Each one of us will fill our backpack to the most comfortable level possible and that is all the cash you should take. If we do it this way there is no need to spend time, especially time we don't have, to count the cash. Just be sensible and when our backpacks are full, we shall leave. If we complete our project before the allotted time, so be it, we leave and that is that. No stuffing one's pockets or trying to put in more than the backpack can handle. Any of that stuff will bring us down and we will not be able to enjoy one penny of our new found wealth. Be careful, be thankful, and eliminate greed and you will have years and years of happiness and security. Who knows how much money your backpack can hold, but I believe it can hold more than a million dollars if you leave the small denominations behind. Hundreds and ones take up the same amount of room so take the hundreds and leave the ones behind.

"After the job is over you should stop going to the bar but do it very carefully. If you decide to continue your regular routine for a little while and then one by one we can stop going to the bar. Once that happens we will not see each other again. I will not stop by the bar ever again after the job and hope that you will, if asked, say that I took a job in New Jersey and started it already. I will make sure I tell Peter, a few weeks before the project, that I have accepted a new position in New Jersey and will not be at the bar anymore. I feel that once I am away from the bar Peter will forget about me and that is good for all of us. After a few weeks you should figure out a good story to prepare Peter. The possibility anyone will ever ask him about either one us is remote, but in his mind he may think that something is fishy especially that the cops have placed a price on information about the recent bank robbery. It would be wise for both of you to go your separate ways as soon as possible but do it very carefully. If we do this right Peter will forget all about us and never associate us with any suspicion and the Bank job will not be part of his thoughts. I did mention this before and I'll repeat it once again. The cops use bartenders, doormen, waiters and waitresses, and many others as informers and pay them a finder's fee for good leads. They are wicked people and listen to everything one says just to collect this reward. Be careful and get away from him as soon as possible. When going to a new bar or club be very careful what you say and do not ever drink too much. Loose lips sink ships and our ship can't afford to be sunk. Stay calm and disciplined and we will all be happy for many years.

"During the next two years you should not change your lifestyle too much. No new cars, no fancy clothes, nothing that will alert anyone to your new found wealth. You can use some of the money but be sure it is not to buy anything that is noticeable. For example you can go out for a nice meal or buy a new pairs of jeans but no other extravagant things. Please follow that rule, I know it will not be easy, but it is a must if you are going to get away with this deal. The cops have all the time in the World and will wait until they see someone living beyond their means and then they will pounce and no matter how much you lie, you will not be able to prove where you got the money. Be careful and, as I said before, you will enjoy a wonderful life of freedom. If you decide to move to a new place, make your move quietly and start your new life and you will be able to spend your money any way you want. The cops in other cities will not be looking for you, they won't be looking for anyone. The future is in your hands so take my advice and be smart and life will be good for you.

"I want to point out the most important thing once again. The money! Find a place to hide it and that is safe from all prying eyes. Remember you don't have to get to it for two years so if you hide it away real good, it will be out of your mind and you will rest easy. In order to make things easy on yourself when your backpack is full and you are ready to leave the project area pick-up a bunch of the small bills and stuff them into your pocket. Once again try to pick-up twenties as they are much better than singles. That will be your extra money to spend very carefully over the next two years. Your pockets will be empty so why not fill them again but not that will bulge. It will help you look pleased that you did enjoy your *hike to the fullest. Once again I emphasize, no greed, just sensible decisions and life will great.*

"Well guys, that is the project, and I'm sure you will agree with me that it is exciting and rewarding. Be vigilant and remember your future depends on your ability to be very careful for a couple of years. If it was up to me I'd move to Hawaii or some other place in a couple of years and start a whole new life and keep your mouth shut. Enjoy your hard earned cash and enjoy life," I said.

"I'm absolutely blown away," Reggie said, "truly blown away. I'm sorry I didn't ask any questions at the time, but I do have a few now."

"Go right ahead and ask away," I said.

"I realize you didn't disclose the location but at least we understand it is here in the City. Now you asked us to disguise ourselves as hikers. I think I understand what you want but if you could elaborate I would appreciate it. I would also like a little more clarity on the backpack. I can easily find a very big backpack and make sure I can pack a lot of cash in it. What is the best one to use so we don't arouse too much suspicion?" Reggie asked.

"In the first instance your disguise should be one that makes it very hard for someone to describe your features. For example if a witness should come forward and tell the cops that he remembers a hiker who was on the platform and he was six feet tall and had a beard and wore a red hat that is almost like saying I didn't get a look at him. Well, that will be a great description that will get the cops nowhere and when they have their artist do a sketch of the guy it will be so far away from your actual looks that you will be very safe and beyond suspicion. Use your imagination, the boots should add a couple of inches to your height and the actual change in your facial appearance should be subtle enough to look quite natural. Remember, you are a hiker returning from a weekend of camping in the wild. You have to look a little wild and that should throw anyone off your trail. As far as the backpack is concerned let's not be stupid about it and eliminate greed. Get a reasonable backpack

that will hold a lot of cash. Remember that when you are going to the location of our project, your backpack has to appear full. Stuff it with newspapers and make sure it is not a paper from that day, try to gather some newspapers early and save them for the right time. That will make any investigator find nothing more than crumpled-up newspapers thus throwing them farther off your trail. I'm pretty sure the cops will look at the crumpled newspapers and try to make some kind of story out of them. For example they might look at the date and think that is a clue or they'll see that all the papers are New York Times and then start searching through the files of Time's subscribers. Make sure the paper has no indication of what newsstand or who it may had been delivered to. We do not want the cops to zero in on a neighborhood. Who knows how they think but let's make their theories send them in the wrong directions. Make sure that when you crumple-up the newspapers to wear gloves. I am not sure if fingerprints are retrievable from a newspaper, but I'd rather you use caution by wearing gloves. The newspapers will be left behind at the scene as we will replace it with cash. I realize that some of these precautions seem like overkill but I honestly believe that they are not and will serve us best in the end. Just remember this, we have spent many months planning and rehearsing this project. The rewards are great, the penalties are severe, so take that extra precaution and don't pooh-paw the cautious approach taken. Follow the plan and all will be successful and we will enjoy riches for many years to come," I said.

"I am black and that will be hard to disguise. Not that I can't change my features but I can't really change my skin color. What do you suggest I do?" Tyrone said.

"I realize that you have to be a little more creative than we do because of that. My suggestion, and remember, this is only a suggestion, wear gloves. That will cover your hands and make sure you have a beard in place as that will cover a great deal of your face. Wear long pants and a long sleeve shirt and a hat while walking in public. The best disguise is to cover up as much as you can and I believe people who see you would not be able to decide if you are white, black, yellow, or whatever. Let's use common sense and cut down the possibilities as best we can. Your exposure should not last more than an hour and after that you can return to your normal self and act accordingly. I'll bet that any witness who may have remembered seeing you will not be able to say definitely if you were white or black. They couldn't identify you or anyone of us because their look would only be for a few seconds and they are gone. Remember you are on a subway train and going somewhere fast and so is the person who may see you. They may see you for a minute or an hour but if you act normal they'll not associate you with anything at all. Use common sense once again and we will walk away from this without any problems.

"I hate to be repetitive but I must say it again. Leave no clues, do not take anything traceable, only cash no matter how much something seems the right thing to take. Your freedom, your ability to enjoy the rest of your life in the lap of luxury rests upon following this rule. Cash only! The last thing you want to hear is that 'I should have listened to Ben,' it will be too late then. I trust you guys and hope the same goes when it comes to me but remember, the cops have a lot of time, they can wait until you make a mistake so don't make any and time will be your best friend. I know I sound like a broken record but it is so important not to make any mistakes, especially foolish ones that can be our undoing.

"Any more questions? All I ask is that you stay in shape, keep your mouth shut, no talking, bragging, to anyone. The time is drawing near and I'll give you the date now. I think we should do it on Labor Day weekend. It will give us most of Saturday, all day Sunday and Monday. I feel we can complete the project by noon Monday and be back at home by two or three in the afternoon. That will give you a few hours to get rid of your disguise, backpack and hide your share of the wealth. It will allow you ample time to *get yourself together so you can be back at work on Tuesday as if nothing unusual happened. I will not give you the location ever. I will tell you where to meet me on the Saturday of the project and I'll take you to the actual place. I do this because it is essential that security be maintained at all times and it also eliminates either one of you slipping up and revealing our plans. I am taking this precaution for your protection as much as mine. Believe me guys, I have thought of everything, at least I hope I did, and it is all for our protection and a successful completion of this project. If there aren't any hitches, if there aren't any screw-ups we will all be rich for the rest of our lives,"* I said and sat back down on the edge of the bed. I was tired, it seems this little session had drained me, even though the thought of the project finally coming to fruition excited me to no end.

I let the guys out through the back door and I went back to the room and wiped it down as best I could. I was sure I was wasting my time as this room will be used many times between now and a week from now so the fact that someone rented it would never be relevant. I still went about wiping everything down and then changed into my Sam West persona and I left for home.

Two weeks have passed since our last meeting and we were getting closer to our target date. I instructed the guys to meet on the Friday of the Labor Day Weekend. That will give the guys one day to meet me at the designated locations and get the project started. I set the meeting for the same hotel and used the same entrance to the room that we usually used when we met there. Labor Day was approaching, it was just a week away and it was time to give my guys their final instructions. I was very excited and very cautious as the time drew near.

I had made two trips to my cabin during the last two off days in search of a hiding place. I had found a perfect spot to hide the cash and had spent the first trip preparing the hole. I then returned the next week and brought with four containers that I bought at a hardware store. These containers were made of metal and would hold the cash nicely. I also bought a tarpaulin that I cut into pieces and lined the metal boxes. I then bought, at an Army Navy Surplus store, three rubber ground sheets that I will use to cover the boxes before I place the earth over them and let them sit underground for the next two years. I also bought heavy duty oil wrap paper so I can wrap the money into bundles that will be further protected from all the elements especially moisture. I also bought a bolt of material that I make into pouches so I can place the bundles of cash in them. I will make bundles of $10K and after placing them in the pouches I will wrap the bundle in wax paper so the oil from the sheets will not affect the cash and when I want to use the money all I will have to do is to remove one bundle or two or as many as I choose and I'll have enough money for whatever I need. Once this was done I will place the pouches containing the cash in the metal containers that will be lined with rubber sheets and covered on the outside with the tarpaulin material and place them in the earth for at least the next two years. I think I thought about everything and made sure that all this stuff was safely stored in my cabin where it will be ready for immediate use when I arrive with my share of cash. The pouches were already cut and ready to receive the cash and the containers now contained some newspapers as a test. I placed everything into the ground and covered the area as if I would on final day. My thought was that I would kill two birds with one test. I'll leave the containers and boxes filled with the newspapers under the ground for the next week or so and when I return with the cash I'll be able to see if this method worked. If the newspapers were wet then there was a problem and I'd have to fix that. If not then all I have to do is place the cash into the pouches and then into the containers and voila- the cash was well hidden, just like a pirate's treasure.

I stopped in at the bar on Thursday and reminded the guys that we are to meet tomorrow at the usual place. While I was there I told

Peter that I accepted a new job in New Jersey and will be starting the day after Labor Day. I told him that I would be moving over the weekend so I won't be here and said my good-byes. He wished me good-luck and hoped I'd stop by any time I'm in the City. I was pleased that my trips to the bar were over and Peter will not be part of my life any longer. Although he was a reasonably nice guy, he was still a bartender that was looking to make an extra buck at all times as a snitch for the cops.

Friday finally came and working through the day was most difficult for me. The anxiety and excitement was really very hard to contain deep inside of me. I left the office at precisely five and went to my room on the Bowery to change into my Nathan Smith disguise. I then stopped in at the hotel and paid for the room once again. I had called ahead and reserved the room, something they said never had happened before. As the desk clerk said to me, *"We are not the type of hotel that takes reservations. We are not the type that usually rent our rooms for the entire night. You get my drift Mr. Smith?"* I slipped him an extra twenty and told him I'd be out of hotel by eleven and he can rent the room after that as often as he likes. He smiled and thanked me as he handed me the key.

At precisely seven, I opened the side door of the hotel and let Reggie and Tyrone in for our final meeting before the project. The Labor Day Weekend was about to start along with my vacation. I had requested this Labor Day Weekend off as part of my vacation and would return to work on Wednesday. According to my boss I would be using up half my vacation time by doing it this way, and if I choose another Holiday period like this one I'll complete this year's vacation and still have had a few additional days off left as well. I needed the time because of the planned project and the things I had to do after. I didn't want to rush anything and the extra day will work out just fine.

"Okay guys I want to give you final instructions. No notes please! You will have to remember these instructions so please pay

attention. First I'd like to know if you have made all the preparations we had discussed." I said.

"Yes, I have the backpack and my complete outfit is ready. As a-matter-of-fact I feel like I am going on a real hike. Everything is in order except where to go, so give me the news and I'll be there. I know it's going to be great, I can hardly wait," Tyrone said.

"I must admit I'm very excited and ready for action. I have everything in order and feel like Tyrone, It's funny but I feel like we are really going on a real hike, now where to go?" Reggie said.

"Okay guys here are your instructions. Please follow them exactly as they are a very important part of the project. I want you to take the subway to Forty-Second Street and then take the Lexington train to the Fourteenth Street Station. Then take the train to the Twenty-Third Street Station and I will expect you to arrive at precisely four-fifteen. I will meet you on the Eastside platform and we will proceed from there to our destination. I will allow fifteen minutes in case the train is late or there is some delay. If either one of you arrive later than the four-thirty time, it will be too late, you will no longer be a part of this project. If that happens I'll be gone and the project will be cancelled and you will never see me again. Now please allow yourselves plenty of time to arrive on the proper time. Try not to make eye contact with anyone while you are on the trains and don't talk to anyone. If you do meet up while on the train, do not engage in conversation with each other. Try to stay at the opposite ends of the car if possible. You are two hikers on your way to a great weekend hike. Be casual but alert and act as if you are really going on a hike. When arriving at the Twenty-Third Street Station look around as if you are meeting others. This is to make you look quite normal when you do meet up with both of us. Don't think about the project, think only about the hike that lays ahead and all will be perfect. Now get on your way and I'll see you tomorrow. I'd say good-luck but feel we will not need luck, all we'll need is perfect execution and this project will be a piece of cake," I said.

The Project:

SATURDAY MORNING ARRIVED AND I ONCE AGAIN WENT through my entire apartment to make sure I had removed every single piece of equipment, disguises, and all material that might serve as a clue. I made sure that no trace of my photography hobby remained as I scoured the place for clues that may compromise the mission and of course, me. Although I had gotten rid of the developing equipment many weeks ago I still found a bottle of developing fluid that would have caused me a lot of problems if it was found in my apartment. I emptied the jar down the drain and placed the empty bottle in the trash that I will get rid of in the next hour or so. I spent the rest of the morning changing into my disguise as Benny Wilson and getting my hiking equipment ready for the project. I also packed an additional backpack and folded it carefully and placed it on the bottom of my main backpack. The extra backpack will fit underneath the main one and is a lot smaller and would not look out of place. I fixed the sleeping bag to the side of my backpack and made sure that the entire look was scuffed-up and looked used, including my boots that I had bought a few weeks ago. I wore these boots on my land in the mountains to break them in and now I was wearing them again and they looked worn. Overall I was very satisfied with my hiker's look and felt this was perfect.

I was now ready for the project. My heart was racing simply because of the excitement that was filling my head. So many months of planning, so many months of preparing and sacrificing half my pay to buy material for this purpose. Yes, the time was here, and I was ready for action. I went over every detail once again, I wanted to be certain I left nothing out as I prepared to leave. It was nearly twelve noon when I was ready to leave my place and take up my vigil at the Fourteenth Street subway station. The associates in my project have all been chosen and I hope I chose well. Benny Guarino was the driving force behind my insane desire to find my pot-of-gold. He bragged constantly about his briefcases filled with cash and how they trusted him to put it away in the Bank. If not for him I would not have ever felt the desire to take on a project of this nature. But my mind went into a super-imagination-mode like finding the proverbial pot-of-gold at the end of the rainbow. I chose Reggie and Tyrone because I needed physical help lowering the heavy concrete from the ceiling to the floor, as well as, some heavy lifting inside the safety deposit box area. I believe I have chosen well but have some doubts about Reggie. Deep down I feel he is what he claims to be and says things, from time to time, without thinking. But some of those things he said made me suspicious therefore I am not taking any chances when it comes to him. So I will keep an eye on him and if there is anything out of place the entire project will not happen. I'm the only one that knows where the project is to take place and all the other details about it, so it is safe and can wait until I find a replacement. Of course, that is only if there is a good reason to do that.

My plan was to leave early and wait at the Fourteenth Street Station until Reggie and Tyrone arrive. I will watch what they do while at the station. If they are alerting any others I will be able to sort that out as the station will not be that busy and any actions out of the ordinary will be easily detected. They will take the train to Twenty-Third Street and I will get on the same train but in a different car and get off at Twenty-Third Street where I am supposed to meet him and Tyrone. I will watch, from a distance to see if they make contact with anyone else. I will also be able to detect if anyone is following them. If either one is indeed working with the cops, they'll be nearby and I'll see them as I'm not expected to meet him until the final stop at the Twenty-Third Street Station. I realized that the cops could have set-up a surveillance force at the Twenty-Third Street Station a lot earlier in order to remain hidden. I understand all that but believe that I can and will detect them when I'm there watching carefully. The slightest nod, a blink of an eye, a signal that otherwise would go undetected, will all be under my radar and I'll catch it. I didn't expect this to happen but had to satisfy my paranoia and I felt secure that my little plan will find Reggie to be straight and a good partner.

I left my apartment at two and made my way to the subway station. I looked like any other hiker on his way to a weekend of mountain climbing or some other outdoor activity. I arrived at the Fourteenth Street Station at three-thirty and took up a position where I could keep watch on the entire platform and could see every train that arrives. I realized I had quite a wait but that didn't bother me as it allowed me time to check out the entire area. I brought with a pair of binoculars so I could stay back and check-out the entire area. If there is any contact between any one of the guys and some unknown people I will abort the project at once. I could not believe that these guys were anything else other than what they represented to me. Nevertheless, caution was called for and that is what I was doing here at this time. If there were cops hanging around this or any other station they would still be there as each train departs. I planned it that at least four and maybe five trains will arrive and depart before the guys arrive and if there are any people who stay there all that time then I'll accept the fact that the project has been compromised. If all is in order I'll repeat the process at the Twenty-Third Street Station as well.

A little after four Reggie arrived and stepped out of his train car and looked around for Tyrone. He did not act strange in any way at all, I could not detect any signals being given and during the time I had spent waiting for these guys to arrive I could not find anyone who remained in the station. If anyone was going to work with others there had to be a few guys hanging out in the station and there was none. I was the only one who remained there while trains came and went. When the next train arrived Tyrone got off and looked around for Reggie and once again did not do anything to alert any other folks. I moved out of my position and put myself near the front of the train while these guys got on at the end.

The train arrived at the Twenty-Third Street Station and I got off and immediately went to the platform where I would meet the boys. I kept my vision in their direction at all times to see if I could see anything unusual but nothing happened to warrant my aborting the mission. I met the guys and signaled for them to follow me. We walked down my special passageway and in less than thirty seconds we arrived at my door. I unlocked the door quickly and said, *"Inside, don't say a word."* I closed the door at once and found ourselves in a very dark room. I turned on my flashlight and grabbed some material that was lying next to the door. I placed this material near the door so I could install it at once. Once I placed this material around the door jamb and made sure all crevices were now covered I went over to the light switch and turned on the lights. Once the lights were on, we all took off our backpacks and placed them on the floor while we silently installed a sound proofing sheet over the door. It was essential that we shut out all light and sound. We had to be certain that nothing escapes from this room and alerts anyone. Once all this was done we made our way towards the main room where I had drawn lines on the ceiling with a large X on multiple spots. These spots indicated where we should start drilling based on the photos I took and some measurements I had calculated.

"Okay two and three, listen to me carefully, this very important. Please do not drill any longer than ten minutes and let the drill rest for thirty minutes. If we do not follow this procedure the drills will burn out and we might as well go home. As you can see we have three drills each and each one is equipped with a diamond drill bit.

Use one drill and put it aside after ten minutes. Your arms will also get tired so I've calculated that you need a little rest as well, so the schedule should be as follows. Drills every ten minutes, rest yourself every twenty minutes for at least ten minutes. I have brought along three clocks, one for each of you so there will not be any doubt to how many minutes have passed. We cannot deviate from that rule as we cannot leave this room until the job is completed. It has taken me a long time to prepare this place for our use and we cannot have the luxury of coming back again. We must be as quiet as we can be and be extremely careful. If you need help just ask and it will be there, no heroics please, we are here to work and get out of here safely. Now let's get to work. You will notice the lines and the X that I have marked. That is where you should start drilling and once you have reached the inside of the safety deposit room, start again, so we can cut a hole large enough for us to get through and to carry our backpacks back out. Remember the backpacks will be a little larger because they will be filled with cash. Drink water conservatively and don't overwork, remember there will be no sleep for the next forty-eight hours, so take things easy. Any questions?" I asked.

"One more job that is very important. We want to make sure that no noise leaves this room that is why I have these blankets. We must hang these across the room so any sounds in this area will be muffled and thus lessen the chance that it can escape and alert someone," I said as I lifted one blanket and found the hooks I had prepared previously and stood on the ladder and began screwing the hook into the ceiling. We did this every six inches as there were grommet holes for the hooks and we hung the blanket from ceiling to floor. We then taped the bottom of the blankets to the floor to make this a confined space and hopefully keep most of the drilling noise in this room only. We now have the door and this room sealed as best as possible under these circumstances. This done we began our main job, to gain entry to our pot-of-gold.

They both shook their heads in agreement that the instructions were understood and moved towards a spot that they would start drilling. I set my clock and began drilling as well. Much to my surprise my drill went into the concrete as if it was butter. I was a little concerned over this and wondered why. They would not have such a secure area built over an area that contains such soft concrete. I kept on drilling and when the clock hit the alarm which I had deadened I stopped and put down my drill. I didn't realize how tired my arms were. Holding a drill above my head for ten minutes felt like I was holding a weight heavier than I ever held before. After a few minutes the drill itself started to get heavier and heavier. When the ten minute signal came I was relieved to put my arms down as well as the drill. I had taken the alarm clocks apart when I bought them and eliminated the bell. I felt it was unwise to have bells ringing even though no sound should be heard outside. I placed a piece of cardboard in each bell so when the hammer hit the bell it would sound like a thud, just enough sound to alert us to stop drilling and rest.

I had abandoned the spot I started with because I felt I was not under the safety box area and must be in an area where water may have been or was present. Perhaps a bathroom or something like that so I moved to a different location. We had been drilling for six hours and so far we have penetrated the ceiling and now were able to feel that we were in an open space. We felt that we have reached the inside of the room, or should I say what we thought was the room. We'd be pretty disappointed if we came up in the middle of the bank or anywhere else other than our expected destination. We were exhausted and had to take a much longer break than originally planned. We needed to get our strength back or we wouldn't be able to continue. I had practiced drilling, but I'd never done it with the concrete above my head. I then knew that the work was not going to be a cake walk, it was back- breaking to say the least.

We had arrived in the special room at five on Saturday afternoon and we were now reaching five Sunday morning. Twelve hours and we are not in the vault area yet. Twelve hours of back breaking work and the target seemed like it was just as far as when we started. All I could think of was that our target was out of reach. There was no doubt that we have been able to drill through the floor, we could see the beam of our flashlights but could not make out what kind of area we were at. We were tired but believed that we were in the right spot. To help things along, Reggie and I abandoned our drill areas and started to work with Tyrone because it seemed that his holes were in the center of our target area. Now that we each drilled for ten minutes we were able to give ourselves enough rest to work more efficiently. Each hole added to our excitement and gave us renewed strength to carry on. By nine Sunday morning we felt we were able to remove a large piece of concrete and peer into the room. We carefully drilled through and made headway as a piece of concrete about fifteen inches in diameter was finally ready to fall down. We discontinued drilling for a few minutes and placed an army blanket made of very heavy wool under this section of the ceiling. The blanket there to muffle any sound of falling debris. If concrete fell on a concrete floor we would hear a pretty loud bang and that was unacceptable. The blanket would catch any pieces of concrete that may fall thus eliminating the noise of stone hitting stone as the concrete pieces might do when hitting the floor.

We had the blanket cushioned by placing our sleeping bags on the floor and filling them with the crumpled newspapers thus making a reasonable cushion. We then placed the blanket on top of this make-shift cushion and now felt we had eliminated the possibility of any serious noise. Once this was in place we returned to the task at hand, removing the concrete and enlarging the opening. We were now able to shine a light into the safe box room to make certain we were on the right track. To our great delight we were in the exact middle of the room and had nothing in our way, we would be in an open space. No matter how tired we were this sight gave us all renewed energy and satisfied any lingering doubts I may have had. It was now just a matter of time until we could dislodge enough concrete so we could get in and out of the room. I could see the excitement on the faces of my associates, there was no longer any doubt that this was not a figment of my imagination and was, in fact, the real thing. There were millions of dollars waiting for us only a few feet away. The drilling was now a serious affair, I could imagined that it would be like experiencing the finding of the pot-of-gold at the end of the rainbow. What a feeling we had as the excitement ran through our minds. I took a minute out and said to the guys, *"Take a deep breath and relax. Let's keep our excitement in check so we can complete our job properly. Now is not the time to make any mistakes. We are almost home guys, so let's get to it."*

The drill bits lasted a lot longer that I originally thought as we only lost three of them. The drill themselves withstood the workload in fine fashion. The plan to allow them to rest every ten minutes seemed to work quite well and the fact that we also took some time to rest allowed us to remain focused on our target and now we are very close to our target. It was now Sunday afternoon, we have been at it for twenty-four hours and have finally reached the mother-load. I had figured it would take about eighteen hours to cut through and was off by six hours, not bad, not bad at all.

6 P.M. Sunday

REGGIE PUT DOWN HIS DRILL AND SAID, *"I BELIEVE THE opening is big enough for us to get through and to get back out with our backpacks. I'm exhausted but ready for action now that we are this close. Let's get to it guys, let's do it now!"* he said.

Silently we moved our ladder over and placed it under the opening. Tyrone was the first one to climb up and enter the inner-sanctum. Of course, the realization set-in that it will not be as simple as taking water out of a well. What faced us now was a wall of safety Deposit Boxes. Each one a shiny looking wall of steel and they looked like they were as safe as they claim to be. I believe that as we sat there we were awed by the very look of the room. This sterile room looked impenetrable, and now it was our job to open each one of these and remove the booty.

I went back down into our room and retrieved the tools we would need to open each one of these boxes. I handed them to Reggie who then handed them to Tyrone who placed them neatly on the floor. The last items I passed to my associates were the backpacks. I then climbed the ladder and joined them in the room that I had visited so many times as a client. Now, here I was in the middle of my dream, I was so happy I could have shouted with joy. I didn't because I knew it was not even close to being over just yet. We had a big job ahead of us and time was ticking away.

"Alright guys, please pay attention. The best way to open these boxes is with a punch and a hammer. It should take no more than one minute to pop the locks of the box. There are two locks as you

can see and I believe that we have to pop-out both of them. I have no experience with these boxes except what I used as a reasonable facsimile when practicing and those only had one lock. If it opens with one lock knocked out, then great for us, but I think both have to go. Once the door swings open you must remove the box in order to open it as it has a lid and cannot be lifted while in the slot. Once you have removed the box, remove the cash and make sure you place only the large bills in your backpack. Don't waste your time counting or gloating over it, we don't have the luxury to celebrate while we are here. Place the remainder of the cash on the floor to your left. Do not throw it around, just place it there as neatly as you can. We will come back to that pile of money later. Nothing will make me feel better than to have three backpacks filled with one hundred dollars bills. Our only dilemma should be, is that, we have too much bread. One more time, do not take anything else from those boxes. Now let's get to it and try not to get too excited, there will be plenty of time to do that after we are long gone from here.

"We will divide the room into three sections and we'll each take one and fill our backpacks. If anyone of us fills their backpack before the other we will help that person fill theirs. Do not take anything else, leave it where it is as it is only going to take up space in your backpack and it will prove to be worthless and lessen the amount of cash you may take with. Please, guys, please follow this procedure and it will end perfectly in our favor. Now please pay attention as I open one box in my sector and then you can easily do the same," I said.

Their eyes lit-up when I said I would open a box. They were now captivated, I could see the concentration in their faces, they were ready and so was I. I took a punch and a hammer that I had wrapped the end with a piece of cloth in order to keep the noise factor to a minimum. I went over to a small box that was situated near the top row of the boxes. It took me about thirty seconds to knock out one lock. Then tried to open the door but it would not budge, I then knocked out the second lock and hooked my finger into one of holes and there it was, the door opened and inside was a gray drawer with a handle on the front. I pulled out my tray and opened the cover and discovered some cash as well as other items including jewelry. I removed the cash and placed it into Reggie's bag and moved on to the next box.

The boys moved to their sections and began to work in silence. I could hear the thud of the hammer and the noise they were making when they were disappointed with the contents of the box. I could not remain quiet any longer and said, *"Two and Three please put the boxes down carefully no matter what you find it contains. We cover the hammer to make sure we don't make noise so why do you think it is okay to throw the boxes around? Quiet please, that is the rule, so please take care. We've gotten this far by being careful so please continue being quiet and careful, let's not get fuck-up now. Please try to follow a simple rule."*

I went back to work and attacked the big boxes first. I was convinced that these were Benny's boxes and would find millions in them. I opened my first big box and was very disappointed it was empty, absolutely empty. I opened the second one and my confidence was restored. It was filled to the very top with cash. I could not imagine how much was in this box but it was a lot that was for sure. It took me longer to empty it than it took me to open it. Placing all this cash in my backpack was the most time consuming feat of all. I looked over at Reggie who must have watched me packing this pile of cash and he was opening one of the big boxes and his was also filled with cash. He was thrilled and had to take a deep breath just to relax a little and start packing the cash into his backpack. In the last hour all of our backpacks were being filled with cash. The boys were about to scream with joy as they found boxes of cash, some filled to the very top and others only half filled. Everyone was pleased beyond their wildest dreams, you could see the look on their faces, it was an exciting time.

3 A.M. Monday

WE WERE STILL AT IT. OUR BACKPACKS WERE MORE THAN three quarters full. None of us had any idea how much cash we had but we were happy with what we found so far. Whenever I found bills lower than a fifty, I placed them aside because they took up too much room and their values did not justify losing the space. The floor was strewn with one, five, ten, and twenty dollar bills, what a shame but we could not use it. By this hour we only opened about fifty-percent of the boxes and soon will be out of space in our backpacks.

7 A.M. Monday

MY BACKPACK WAS FINALLY FULL AND WHEN I TRIED TO lift it I realized how heavy it was. I could not put another dollar in that bag. I had three auxiliary bags that I had folded into my sleeping bag with me. I had to go down the ladder to get them so I declared to the guys that my backpack is full and I'm going to place it down below and asked Tyrone to please hand it to me when I get on the ladder. I went through the hole and went down the ladder and then Tyrone handed it down to me. It was heavy but not too heavy to carry on my back. I placed the backpack on the floor near the door and went back-up the ladder with the extra small backpacks. In order to avoid any complaints about my being greedy, I had brought with two additional bags and gave each guy one and said, *"I brought this along in case you want to take a little more with you. You can place this bag in your sleeping bag and attach it to your main backpack and no one will think anything about it as it will look like a regular hiker's pack with a sleeping bag attached. No more after that guys, because we have to get out of here. We are lucky that we are able to get out of here early as that will give more time to hide this stuff long before they discover what has happened here. The only sad part is all the cash we have to leave behind. I suggest we take another two hours and open as many boxes as we can and only pack one hundred dollars bills in our smaller bag. We will leave here about nine, seeing that it is a holiday the platform should be fairly quiet. I suggest that two, you take the train, and be very careful by not acting any other way except like one returning from a*

Holiday weekend would. Three, you wait about ten minutes and take the next train and do the same. I'll leave about ten minutes after you three and I'll make sure the lights are out and we didn't leave anything behind. Don't forget to empty your urine jars down the sewer and throw away the jar properly. Wipe it down before you get rid of it. Get rid of your clothes, boots and all. Keep nothing in your home that you wore and used while here. Take a nice hot shower and make sure your backpack is destroyed and gone forever. If you want to keep a few dollars for immediate spending make sure you keep no more than a thousand bucks. Nothing that would look out of place and spend it quietly. If you need to change a bill into smaller ones do so at a bank or at a supermarket like A & P. Don't do it in a small retailer because the guy will remember you because not too many people throw around one hundred dollar bills. These are a few of the precautions I can suggest now, just use your common sense and things will be great. Be prepared to see the Tuesday's evening papers with headlines about this project. Don't save the paper and don't try to give out your opinion to anyone. Let it all die a natural death and you'll realize that we are home safe and sound. Good luck guys," I said.

9 A.M. Monday

BOTH BAGS WERE FILLED WITH ONE HUNDRED DOLLAR bills. The smaller bag was stuffed into the sleeping bag and the bag was rolled up and attached to the large backpack. It now looked like we all had sleeping bags with pillows inside them and this was all attached to the sides of our backpacks. We all pitched in and helped each other make our packs look real good and readied ourselves for our departure. The mess in the safety deposit box area was unbelievable. It looked like a million safe boxes were lying all over the floor along with a lot of papers and many jewels. There was also a ton of cash lying all over the place consisting of smaller bills that we did not want in our backpacks. I was feeling great and decided because the boys did such a terrific job and we were ahead of schedule that I will suggest that the guys, me included, pick-up as much cash as you can put it in your pockets. I told them to make sure it isn't bulging in their pants pockets and that they should try to take the larger bills if possible. I instructed them to use this money over the next two years and leave the rest untouched. I felt that given a two year span, the heat will have subsided and things should be pretty clear for us all. They looked at me as if I was Santa Claus and placed the ladder back under our entrance hole and happily went up and began scooping up wads of cash.

We drew straws to see who would leave first and Tyrone got the nod to start our escape first. He left first while Reggie and I waited for ten minutes and then Reggie said, *"Thanks One, I really appreciate you allowing me in on this, I'll never forget you, so long."*

He was gone in a flash and I was left all alone in this room. I had been here hundreds of times over the long period of preparation and loved being here, but now I didn't feel quite the same and was anxious to get the hell out of this place. Before I left I went over the room very carefully and made sure there was nothing left behind that would incriminate us in any way. I then put out all the lights and carefully opened the door and left with a heavy backpack filled with my future. I walked out on the platform and at that very moment a train arrived, I got on the last car and sat down and placed my heavy backpack on the floor by my feet and held my breath. I was anxious for the train to depart and when the doors finally closed and the train began to move, I let out a sigh of relief and began to relax. Of course, I knew I couldn't really relax until this bag of cash is safely stored away and no trace of Benny Wilson remained.

11.15 A. M. Monday

I ARRIVED NEAR MY APARTMENT AND WENT DIRECTLY TO my car where I opened the trunk and placed my backpack in it and closed it again and walked home. On my way home I emptied my urine jar in a drain by the curb and found a metal garbage can where I put the empty jar and replaced the lid. I could hardly wait to get out of my disguise and get out of town. I changed into my usual self and Samuel West was back in the real World. All the other characters will no longer appear anywhere and all things used by them will be destroyed.

It took me another half hour to pack-up my clothes and my disguises. I then re-checked the apartment once again. I made myself a peanut butter sandwich and left the apartment taking with me all my old clothes and disguises and got into my car and took off for my cabin. I was floating on air as I drove along the thruway towards Lake George. I did it, I beat the odds and got into the Bank and emptied the safety deposit boxes as planned. I wish I could have emptied all of them but that would have been impossible. Yet, as I look back, I can see that things worked-out exactly as planned and our escape plan came off without a hitch. We could have spent another couple of hours and opened the balance of the boxes, but how would we transport the cash? Well, I decided that I can't dwell on the past, as a matter-of-fact it would be best if I could erase the past from my memory permanently. These were some of the thoughts that ran through my head while on the drive to the cabin. I felt good and very satisfied with our few day's work, the job was well planned and came off as predicted. I kept on thinking how the two other guys will handle their success. I only hope they will be careful and follow the advice I gave them. If not, the future will be harsh for them in many respects. If they have loose lips and just can't contain their spending habits, their money will bring them a great deal of sorrow. Once the cops get their hands on them, they will not stop until they recover the money and get them to talk as to who else was in on the deal. I was not worried in the least that I would be connected because they didn't know me as Samuel West. As-a-matter-of-fact they have never heard of me in any respect whatsoever, so they won't be able to rat on me. The only people they may injure would be themselves and in the end they may spend a lot of years in prison all because they couldn't stay quiet for a couple of years. Once they realize the alternative as they while away their days in prison, they'll probably die or go insane because they would realize how close they were to enjoying a life of wealth and freedom. I hope they understand all that and follow the guidelines, if so, they have nothing to worry about.

As I drove along I was fortified with the thought of how smart I was to maintain my disguise as Benny Wilson throughout the entire time I visited the bar and met with these guys. All they know is that some guy named Benny Wilson, who spoke through his nose, limped because one bad left leg, and who always was a little weird, was their partner. They don't know where Benny Wilson lived or worked except that he just started a new job in New Jersey and lives out there now. They'll tell the cops that he is from Brooklyn and moved to Manhattan a little while ago. They will even be able to tell the cops that Peter, the owner of the bar, can verify who Benny Wilson was. I wish I would be a fly on the wall when and if they get into that kind of mess. On the other hand they could easily follow my instructions and nothing will ever happen. I hope that will be the case for everyone's sake.

Allan Barrie

You'd be surprised how fast time goes by when you are engrossed in thought as I was. Before I knew it, I was in Albany and it felt like I just left Manhattan a few minutes ago. I arrived at the cabin just before six and it was still light. I didn't have any electrical power in the cabin but had a couple of gas lanterns as well as two heavy duty flashlights. I was glad I brought with the peanut butter and jelly sandwiches. I didn't want to leave the cabin because I had so much work to do and I wouldn't leave the bag of money in the cabin unattended so having something to eat was just what I needed. I was also pleased that I had the smarts to take that extra day off, I'll certainly need it. I had a big job in front of me and I had to get it done overnight. The sooner I got this money out of here the sooner I'll sleep better. All this cash makes me feel very uncomfortable, all I want to do is hide the cash and get the hell out of here.

6 P.M. Monday

I BEGAN THE JOB OF REMOVING THE CASH FROM MY backpack and making bundles of ten thousand dollars. I had bought plenty of wax paper to make sure I would not run out as I wrapped each bundle. I did not know how much money I had in the backpack but my estimate was that I had at least one million in cash. I then wrapped each bundle in a special tar-paper and then placed it aside. I had researched this at the New York Library because I was concerned with deterioration. I had containers made out of metal that will hold the bundles and when I have all the containers filled I'll bury them in a place I already dug out and cover each box with a rubber tarpaulin. I wanted to make sure I still had the cash after two years in the ground. Water, cold weather, warm weather, all the elements nature can throw at a cache of this type needed as much protection as possible and I was going to make sure it was all safe. I opened the hole and checked the newspaper and, much to my satisfaction, was dry as a bone.

10 P.M. Monday

I HAD JUST COMPLETED MY LAST BUNDLE AND WAS exhausted. I had counted an amazing amount of two million one hundred and fifty thousand dollars not including the small backpack. I was tired but a very happy tired and decided to count the cash in the auxiliary backpack. I wanted to know exactly how much cash I had and move on. I think I'll sleep soundly tonight knowing that I have so much cash to keep me nice and warm for years to come. After about an hour I had twenty-nine additional bundles ready for burial. I still had another six thousand dollars that I kept for expenses. I placed that money in my auxiliary backpack and placed that in my sleeping bag to act as my pillow for the night. I then retrieved my metal containers and placed the bundles of cash in them. I must have had some kind of sixth-sense because it seems that my metal containers were perfect and, believe-it-or-not, I could not put another dollar in any of them. I then took the containers and placed them in the hole I had prepared and made sure the boxes sat deep enough. I covered each box with the tarpaulin and covered the hole with earth. I then smoothed out the ground and covered it with leaves and other fallen tree branches and a few loose stones. I had to move some sizeable boulders over the freshly prepared area but decided to let that wait until tomorrow morning. I went back to the cabin and went to sleep and although I had thought my sleep would be a deep one, it wasn't. I kept on waking-up and checking out the surroundings. Even though the place was quiet I was concerned that someone would stop by. Of course, I realized that I was naturally paranoid after such a big project and found it easy to invent all kinds of disasters. In the last two years that I had been coming to this place, not one single person came to see me or just wandered onto the area. Why would they start now? I needed sleep and finally did get some rest but none that was continuous.

7 A.M. Tuesday

THE SUN WAS COMING UP AND I WAS ANXIOUS TO CHECK-out my burial ground. It looked real good and now that I was able to place my boulders in my selected strategic spots over the area, it looked like the rest of the mountain. I also figured that because fall was around the corner the falling leaves will cover the ground perfectly. I had picked-up many fallen branches and had saved two garbage bags of fallen leaves so I could spread them over the freshly disturbed earth. No one usually comes onto this piece of land but just to make sure I wanted as much of this area covered as possible without creating anything suspicious. I was pleased with my stash and pleased with the success I had with the project. As far as I was concerned everything was over and we were home free and I was dancing on air.

2 P.M. Tuesday

EVERYTHING WAS IN ORDER. I HAD CUT UP THE BACKPACKS and put the pieces in the trunk of my car. I thought I'd get rid of the cut-up pieces and closed the cabin. I would not be back here at the cabin until springtime although I'd worry a little about my stash. I now had to return to my old life and try to enjoy it until the time comes that I can enjoy the rewards of a successful project. I had one more job to do and changed into my Harold Robinson disguise and drove to the Bronx on my way home. I stopped in at the garage and sold the car for one hundred dollars to the owner of the garage. I signed over the title and wrote out a bill of sale. He was thrilled and so was I. I then stopped in to see Mrs. Polina Stressky and explained that I will not need the garage any longer and she can have all the tools and equipment I am leaving in the garage. I also gave her two hundred dollars as a bonus for the use of her place and thanked her for all the nice things she had done. The money was perfect for her, she loved every penny and didn't ask about where I was going. I was pleased to leave without leaving any ill will behind and making sure that this part of my plan will never ever come to light.

7 P.M. Tuesday

I ARRIVED HOME AND PARKED THE CAR AND WALKED OVER to a newsstand on the corner and picked up a Daily News and The Post. I wanted to see what the papers were writing about the Bank heist. I was pretty sure it made the papers simply because it was on 1010 WINS and if it had the news about the bank job then the papers would also have it but in much more detail. According to the radio, the cops were not revealing too much information about the robbery but promised that a press conference will take place at nine tonight. The station revealed that through an anonymous source, they learned that at least six people pulled-off this clever heist and perhaps more were involved. The papers revealed that the thieves gained entry into the Bank through an abandoned Subway station that hadn't been used for over thirty years. The papers claimed that the amount of the robbery is still unknown as police and FBI sort through the robbery scene. The papers claimed that through an anonymous source they were told that some very valuable jewelry was taken in this robbery. The radio report said that further details will be revealed at the news conference at nine tonight. For me it was absolutely thrilling to listen to all this knowing the truth about the project. I was convinced that we had made a clean getaway and that the cops had no clue who did this and what was taken. Most likely, I figured, they wouldn't know for a very long time.

9 P.M. Tuesday

I WAITED ON PINS AND NEEDLES FOR THE NEWS conference. I wanted to hear the news broadcast and listen to the police spokesperson reveal what they knew about the robbery. As far as I was concerned I didn't think they learned anything, but I still wanted to know what they would reveal to the public. I turned on the radio and listened to the following broadcast, *'We are pleased to have our reporters at police headquarters where Police Captain, Martin Strobel, will bring us up to date on the Bank robbery at the BNZ Bank that took place over the Labor Day weekend.'*

"Thank you Chief Britain and thank you 1010 Wins for being on top of the news at all times" Captain Martin Strobel said, *"unfortunately I have very little news to report regarding the brazen robbery that took place at the BNZ Bank during this past Labor Day holiday. The thieves must have been very knowledgeable about the layout of the Bank. It is our opinion that someone in the Bank helped them pull-off this robbery. So far our investigation, which is ongoing, revealed that there were at least six people involved in the robbery. We do not know, at this time, what was taken or how much was stolen from the safety deposit boxes at the bank, as we are still compiling a report from the actual safe box owners. This procedure will take days as some of those owners are not in town and most probably are not aware that a robbery took place. We are asking the public to please call in if they were in the vicinity of Twenty-Third and Fifth Avenue anytime during the Labor Day weekend and especially on Monday. Please call us at 212-345-5566*

and remember all calls will remain confidential. You do not have to leave your name. All calls will be treated confidentially and your safety will never be comprised. In order for your police force to solve this crime, we need your help. We are here to protect the public but need your help as well. If you saw anything, no matter how trivial, please call 212-345-5566. As this is an ongoing investigation we cannot reveal any other details at this time. We will keep the public informed as our investigation moves forward and promise you that we are certain we will apprehend these thieves very soon."

I switched off the newscast and sat back in my chair satisfied that all went as planned and now the only danger was ourselves. I prayed that my associates would remain calm and follow the instructions I gave them. Low key, please guys, low key!

The Aftermath:

I HAD GONE BACK TO WORK ON WEDNESDAY AND, OF course, the scuttle bug was all about the robbery. My Boss came in to my little cubicle and inquired about my vacation and then began his recap of the robbery. *"What do you think about the robbery? Amazing isn't it Sam? While you were away from all this, the Bank next door was being cleaned out. Isn't that where you Bank, Sam? Well anyway, I think it's very exciting that people would work so hard to get into a bank. I guess the reason is simple, that is where the money is! Pretty funny isn't it Sam? Well, welcome back and let's hope this affair at the Bank will not affect our business adversely. It would be nice if it helps us do a lot more business, heaven knows we could use it,"* he said.

I went about my work for the rest of the week and when Friday came I did what I usually do at lunchtime. I went to the Bank to deposit my check and take out a few dollars for my cash expenses. I then asked Terry, the usual lady that handles the safety Deposit Boxes and stuff, if I can access my box, *"I read all about the robbery in the papers. Is everything okay now and can I go to my box?"* I said.

"I'm sorry Mr. West but your box was one of the boxes that was broken into. I have a claim form that you should complete and we'll try to make sure that we replace anything we can if it was stolen. There is a lot of stuff that was not taken but it is impossible for us to know who these things belong to. Of course, if there are any papers, documents, or other valuables that can be identified as your property we will make sure they are returned to you without

too much delay. The claim form will help us identify many unmarked items. Please complete the form as quickly as possible and return it to me. While you are here Mr. West, do you have a few minutes to talk with Special FBI Agent Mario Talbot?" she said.

"I have to get to work, but can spare a few minutes if it won't take too long!" I said.

"I'm sure it won't take too long, let me ask Mr.Talbot if he has time to see you now." She said as she walked into an adjacent office and came back out very quickly and said, "He can see you right now. Please follow me."

I followed Terry into a small office and was immediately struck by the size of the man standing behind the desk. He looked as if he was seven feet tall with broad shoulders and a very strong looking face. Perhaps I was intimidated by the sheer size of him but he did look exceptionally strong. I was certain I didn't want to tangle with him. "Welcome Mr. West, thank you for taking the time to have this little chat," he said as he extended a hand that covered my hand up to my elbow.

"It is my pleasure Mr. Talbot, I am on my lunch break and have about fifteen minutes left before I must return to work. How can I help you, Sir?" I said.

"I'm sure you are aware of the robbery that took place over the long weekend? It has been on all the newscasts and being a customer there is no way you could have missed all the hype. I hope Terry has given you a claim form? It is essential you complete it as quickly as possible as every drop of information will help apprehend those responsible much quicker. I see here that you have an account with the bank and a safety deposit box, I hope you didn't lose too much? If you don't mind me asking Mr. West, where were you this past weekend?" He said in a very cordial and soft tone.

"I was away in Lake George. This was my vacation week and because of Labor Day I was able to get an extra day to myself. I got back home on Tuesday evening and heard about the robbery on 1010 *Wins* news while driving. I work just down the road at Sy Johnsons and bank right here. I come in every Friday and deposit my paycheck and visit my safety deposit box once in a while to place an important paper in it or squirrel away a few vacation dollars. I like to save for my vacation and if I leave it in my bank account, I usually spent it on something I probably don't need, so I take a few bucks out of my pay every now and then and put it in the safety deposit box. I can't spend it while it is in there and it helps me save for that vacation that I need. There was about five hundred dollars in my box and some papers like my birth certificate and copy of my car registration and a couple of personal letters. I'll fill out the form and list what was in it in detail," I said.

"Thanks Mr. West, I appreciate you're stopping in, please get the claim form back to me as soon as possible. If I should have any further questions I will get in touch. Have a nice day," he said as he extended his hand.

I left the Bank feeling quite proud of myself that things went very smoothly. I was a little upset with myself because I realized that I was not following my own advice. When one is questioned they should not volunteer any answers, they should remain quiet and only answer the question they are asked and nothing more. I was far too chatty with the inspector and should have followed what I preached. No harm done because, lucky me, I didn't say anything that would cause him to suspect that I was anything else other than the guy I said I was. I told myself to keep my big mouth shut if I wanted to remain free.

Another week passed and the Bank robbery disappeared from the newspapers as well as the radio. I was happy not to hear any more news about the robbery, even though a part of me wanted to know what progress they were making. The lack of news to the public meant that things were cooling off and fading away, at least from the public view. I did drop off my claim form with Terry at the Bank and received a letter a few days later from the Bank assuring me that my loss will be covered by the Bank's insurance carrier and I should receive a check within three weeks. Of course, they also apologized for the unfortunate event that happened on that fateful Labor Day Weekend. I did learn that the bank does have a responsibility to safeguard my valuables and could be held liable for my losses. Of course, I learned that from a couple of lawyers who called me at my office telling me that I needed an attorney to sue the Bank. They informed me if I had valuables in my safety deposit box that I could prove were mine they would have to replace or pay the claim. I was feeling great as time moved on and I started to feel the whole deal was all is over. Time seems to work wonders especially in cases like this. Soon this robbery will be a thing of the past, a memory of a job well done.

Five weeks have passed and things were looking real good. No news was good news and that is what was happening to me. I was thrilled as fall brought cooler weather, and more time has passed since the project. I had received a check from the insurance company for five hundred dollars to cover my lost cash as a result of the robbery and had to sign a release for the Bank and the insurance carrier. What a deal, I took a lot of money from them and they paid me an additional five hundred to boot. America, what a wonderful Country!

A Turn of Events:

SO FAR THINGS HAVE GONE AS PLANNED, THE PROJECT was history and there wasn't a mention of the Bank robbery in any news service whatsoever. This didn't mean that the cops have stopped trying to find the people responsible for the robbery at the Bank. I was sure that the cops were still trying to find the people responsible except they didn't know who they were. Since I, as Benny WIlson, told Peter at the bar that I was moving to New Jersey I have not visited the bar and didn't concern myself with it at all. Before the robbery I think I made a good move by telling Peter that I found a new job in New Jersey and would be moving there so there was no reason for him to think that my absence was anything strange.

Thanksgiving came and went as the entire City seemed to come alive with Christmas decorations and lights everywhere putting the City in a holiday mood. We geared ourselves for the Christmas rush and, as usual, dealing with those who wanted their suits ready in a day or two. Office parties and other holiday festivities dictated rush jobs and we were here to make sure we could accommodate all our clients.

A week before Christmas one of my best clients finally showed up. Benny Guarino came into the shop and needed two new suits and wanted them no later than tomorrow. I was thrilled to see him simply because he was my inspiration for the project and he also gave me a lot of business. *"Welcome Benny, it's been a long time since I've seen you. It's so nice to see you again. I was getting* worried about you because you were away for such a long time. You're here now and it real nice to see you, please don't stay away so long again," I said and smiled.

"I love coming in to see you Sam, you are one of my joys in life. I'm sure you have heard about the Bank robbery that happened back a few months ago? Well, my friend, we took a real bath and lost at least a half million K. That ain't chicken feed Sam, and my Boss was mad as hell. Thank goodness the cops don't know what the hell they are doing, they don't have a clue how to catch these guys. Really Sam, we will find them and when we do, we know how to make them talk, they'll tell us where the fucking money is. We got every place in the City wired and all it takes is for one wrong word to be said. Or some asshole spending too much bread and we'll be there to get ours back. Just in case you don't know Sam, there is a reward of fifty big ones for any information anyone may know. So if you happen to come across something suspicious you know where to get in touch. Like, keep your eyes and ears open, and then call me and I'll handle it from there. It would be nice to get that kind of bread Sam, wouldn't it?' Benny said.

"I'll keep my eyes and ears open Benny. I guess if anyone can find those people, you guys sure can. I never thought about you Benny when I heard the news about the robbery. I'll be sure to let you know if I hear anything at all," I said as I swallowed hard and tried not to show my emotions.

I spent another hour with Benny measuring him for his new suits and just shooting the breeze. No matter how hard I tried to keep our conversation away from the Bank robbery, Benny kept on returning to it. There was no doubt in my mind that he was on the hot-seat and the Mob was hell-bent on finding the people that did it. He told me that his boys are checking every bar in Manhattan and have hundreds of others looking out for the robbers. I was relieved when Benny left and I was able to sit back and take a deep breath. I always thought that the cops would search as best they could and in time they would put the case on the back-burner without any success. I never gave it a single thought that the Mob would be involved even though I knew a lot of the cash was theirs. Now it was obvious to me that we have to be extra careful because the Mob would look under every stone to find out who ripped them off of their hard earned cash. Naturally I was extremely nervous because the Mob was reputed to be very vicious and if they did, for one reason or another, locate one of the guys their lives would be worthless. This situation made me very nervous, it was something I never figured on when planning this project. Of course, what could I have done if I did think about it? I would have expressed how ruthless the Mob is and that probably would have sunk in a lot more than the threat of the cops. I realized that the Mob was ruthless and given the slightest clue they will be on it like flies on shit. They will be relentless in their zeal to make someone talk. I wonder how many innocent people will be roughed up by the Mob because they said something they shouldn't have, even if it was in jest. I wasn't afraid for myself as I was convinced beyond a shadow-of-a-doubt that I was safe and beyond the grasp of the Mob or anyone else. No one will ever associate Ben Wilson with Sam West, not in a million years. Of course, I know I shouldn't be so damn convinced but I feel I have taken every step to keep my true identity secret. But the other two could be in for a rough time if they make a mistake. I didn't trust them to follow my advice for a period of two years and, from what I have read, the Mob had as much patience as the cops and would wait, no matter how long, for someone to screw-up. My two associates had very little discipline and could easily get themselves into some serious trouble. I wish I could alert them but that was impossible. I could not take a chance to have myself exposed.

On my way home I couldn't get Benny's visit out of my mind. I kept playing with the idea that I should alert the other two guys. I could not believe that they had enough brains to remain quiet and all shall pass. I could not justify that the Mob will get tired after a little while. Finally I reconciled the situation within myself and decided that I should make an anonymous phone call to these guys using the voice of Benny Wilson. I felt that if I didn't take some action I was not being fair and I was taking a coward's way out? I could easily observe and help, from a distance, and hope that these guys take my warnings seriously. I wouldn't expose myself and would feel better that I tried to warn them. Hell, its holiday time and a little good cheer won't put me in any danger. I decided to call these guys and wish them a Merry Christmas and a Happy New Year.

I decided to call these guys using my Benny Wilson accent and staying on the line for no more than two minutes. If the warning isn't heeded then there is nothing more I could do.

My first call was to Tyrone, *"Hey Tyrone how are you? I thought I would give you a call to wish you a very happy holiday. I came into town from Jersey and am leaving in about ten minutes. I wanted to pass along a few little things that I think are very important,"* I said.

"Merry Christmas to you as well Benny. How is your new job? Things are going along real well," he said.

"My job is great and I love living in New Jersey. There is a lot less stress and less rushing around. Tyrone, I wanted to warn you about something, it is very important that you listen. You know that I have never misled you and I don't plan to now. When we did the project we had no clue whose money might be involved. I have learned, through some very reliable sources that a lot of those proceeds came from the Mob. Of course, they have no clue who did what and we have to keep it that way. They're looking everywhere and are not very successful but we cannot underestimate their resolve. They have every bartender and doorman as well as every other person they deal with to keep their eyes and ears open for anyone who displays unusual spending habits. Please remember the two year rule and follow it. I wouldn't like to see the Mob get hold of you or anyone

else that they think might have been part of that project, their lives would be worthless. Please be careful what you say to anyone and do not do things that would compromise your good health. These guys don't fuck around so be extra careful. I don't have time to call Reggie, my bus is leaving in a few minutes, so would you please get in touch with him and pass this message along to him as well. I didn't have to call you, but I did feel a little uncomfortable and in view of the holiday I wanted you to be forewarned. Please be careful and once again, *Merry Christmas and Happy New Year,*" I said and hung up the phone and left the phone booth and hurried home.

Welcome to Hell:

SPRING HAD COME AND SOON I'LL BE ABLE TO PLAN A VISIT to my cabin to check-up on my stash and see that everything was still intact. So far the winter had come and gone without any hassles and no news about the Bank robbery. I was convinced that my phone call did wonders and the two guys must have decided to take my advice. As far as I was concerned the deal was over and all we had to do was to remain patient and time will be our best friend. I didn't want to go to the cabin too soon, I thought it was best to let all the snow melt and allow the ground to dry out. I was anxious to get up there but had to convince myself that it would be best to wait. I told myself that I've waited this long a few more weeks won't kill me. Once we have had some steady good weather I will make a trip to the cabin and check things out.

I soon learned that things were not as calm as I thought. After the phone call I made to Tyrone I swore I wouldn't get in touch with either Reggie or Tyrone ever again, and I was determined to keep that pledge. I had to remain anonymous no matter what may happen. Needless to say I was concerned for the two guys and could only hope and pray that they continued to sit back and display patience. I knew how hard it was for me because I felt I had a lot more discipline than the guys, but I still had the desire to go see my stash. I also wanted to get up and leave New York. I didn't want to wait any longer, but had the willpower to wait and do nothing until the two years have passed. Did they have the same strength? I didn't want them to fall into the hands of the Mob or the cops. If that happened their lives will be toast, although it would be better to be caught by the cops, at least with the cops they would remain alive. Even that thought was scary because I have read books and heard stories about the Mob and how they can find out information even if one is in prison. I read where they got to people they wanted rubbed-out even when they were protected by the cops. As far as I was concerned no one was safe no matter where you were. The cops had plenty of corrupt guys that would tell the Mob where the suspected Bank robbers were being held and because they had so much clout they could easily get to the boys. Money buys a lot of favors and the Mob knew how to use that weapon better than anyone. I didn't believe, not for one moment, that Reggie and Tyrone could stand up to the Mob's torture methods if they were caught. As far as I was concerned the future looked bleak for these guys if they didn't watch their step. I really didn't know what to do, but felt it would be best, for me at least, to stay far away from anything that may have to do with the Bank robbery and my two associates. I had to go about my business and make sure I kept it my business no matter how tempted I was to tell someone. Believe me it isn't easy to keep one's mouth shut at times. I vowed that I'd rather bite my tongue off than ever bring up the subject to anyone.

My heart sank when Benny stopped in to buy two new suits for the Easter Holiday and told me that his boys have an idea who was responsible for that bank robbery. He was proud of the fact as he said, "*No one escapes my people Sam, and no one fucks us and gets away with it, no one. My boys have a guy under their radar and will soon make a move. He has been throwing around much too much money for an ordinary guy. I can't tell you everything Sam, because it has to be kept confidential and I don't know all the details, but I trust you, so please keep this between us. I really shouldn't be telling you this but as I said, I trust you.*"

"Benny, you don't have to worry, I'll keep it all between us. No one will hear anything from me, you can be sure of that. I hope you catch the people who did this, I really hope so," I said.

"Thanks Sam, I'll let you know how things turn out," Benny said.

I never figured that the Mob would get involved but they are. Everyone knows they are relentless and ruthless. The biggest amount of cash was taken from their boxes and they certainly didn't like that. Reggie and Tyrone had nothing to fear as long as they remained quiet and that included not throwing money around. But if they become foolish and uncontrollable the fate that awaits them will be disastrous. This was a dilemma of major proportions, one that was tearing me apart. I could sit back and do nothing and let them walk right into the lion's den. I can also intervene as a human being with compassion and warn them. The risk of warning them was great but I'm sure I can devise a way that will protect my anonymity. This was a major decision for me and was tearing me apart. I may sound like I was a hardened criminal, but deep down I really didn't like doing anything dishonest. My justification for the Bank job was that I was stealing from crooks and that wasn't bad. I realized that the justification to take on the project was not really very good. Now I was faced with a moral dilemma and could not, in all good conscience, let the two guys be faced with the horrors that the Mob will inflict upon them. I'm in the clear because there is no way either of them could identify me but that didn't seem to make me feel better at all.

I gave it a lot of thought and finally decided it would be best if I called them from a pay phone using the voice of Benny Wilson. I figured I'd be running very little risk by doing it that way and if I warn them, once again, of the dangers that lie ahead they might listen and act accordingly. If they didn't take the call seriously there was nothing further I could do, but at least I will have tried. As I thought about it I started to get very conflicted about the possible dangers to me. My mind was working overtime, constantly asking myself what I should do. I didn't have the luxury to discuss this with someone else and get their opinion. On one hand I thought it would be the right thing to call them and warn them. I have no justification not to help them no matter what reasons I may tell myself. I said to myself, '*Sam, if you warn these guys and they should still get caught by the Mob they could possibly tell them that Benny Wilson called them to warn them. If Benny Guarino is around or his guys tell Benny that these guys were forewarned he could possibly put two and two together and connect Sam West. It is risky but still I feel I have an obligation and must take a chance to warn them. They can tell the Mob that Benny Wilson was the mastermind and send them on a search for him. It was easy to allow my imagination run away with myself, yet I asked myself how much of this is imagination? Where and when do you cut the tie and keep still? After careful thought, I felt I had to warn them or I could not live with myself.*' There was no valid reason to keep the information from my two associates and not warning them of the dangers that lay ahead.

This was a dilemma of major proportions. I wish Benny hadn't said a word to me because now I was on the hot seat. He knew what he told me and if he told others then I was okay, but if he didn't, I was walking right into a trap. No matter how I sliced it, it always came out as extremely dangerous to me. I could not correct the dangers these two guys have brought upon themselves. Their reckless actions have spawned a disastrous road and I just didn't know how to get them off the path of destruction. I didn't want to see them hurt even though I felt I was safe. I was out of reach of the Mob and the cops and didn't have to worry about being identified by anyone. After all I did take the time and efforts to maintain my disguise throughout the many months I spent planning and recruiting these guys. I did all this for obvious reasons and tried to instill the importance of remaining on the quiet side of life for a couple of years. Because they now surfaced they have jeopardized the entire project without regard for my safety, so why expose myself now? Sure I want to warn these guys but Benny knows that he revealed his deepest secrets to me Sam West and how long will it take him to wake up and connect me to the robbery. With the Mob there is no way that I could just deny any knowledge of the robbery. The Mob doesn't care about anything other than the fact that what they believe to be true is true. They'd kick the shit out of me and in the end cut my balls off. No way can I send out any warnings to these guys. They'll have to fend for themselves just as they have screwed things up by alerting the Mob by their actions. It won't take the Mob long to get the boys to start talking so I'll take the right course of action and remain mute. My final decision was to do nothing and perhaps this situation will blow over without any repercussions. I didn't honestly believe it but it was necessary to convince myself to close my mind to this dilemma. If I was to be the smart person I believed I was, I must look at this from all angles and after doing that I was convinced that my decision was the correct one. No contact, no more exposing myself, if these guys cannot understand what caution must be taken, especially after I warned them, then there is nothing more I can do except remain unknown to all.

The Nightmare:

ANOTHER MONTH HAS PASSED AND I WAS BUSY AT WORK as usual. I didn't give the Bank robbery a second thought. It was now late April and the weather was warming up, the plants were starting to bloom. The lilacs were in full bloom and gave off a smell that was like perfume, it was like a magic elixir that made one's mind feel good. The air was filled with wonderful smells and the plants were growing, each day a new color was introduced. It was a great time of year when everything was fresh and clean. We also had one of the driest Springs ever making the land dry, but not too dry and easy to work with.

Last weekend I finally took a trip to my cabin and found the snow had gone. The ground was still a little damp but nothing too bad. Winter was kind to the mountain and didn't disturb my special spot where my fortune was stashed. I checked the area out and nothing was disturbed, or at least there wasn't anything amiss, and the best part was that the grass was starting to grow over the spots where I dug-up the earth last fall. In another few weeks this area will blend in perfectly and no one will be the wiser. I was very happy with my discovery and enjoyed every moment up at the mountain. It took every ounce of willpower to just stand there and look at the area where my stash was hidden. I wanted to dig up one area just to make sure my stash was safely there and intact. Yet my brain said not to do it and so I left everything intact. I finally came to understand that it would be in my best interest to leave it alone, if it was gone there was nothing I could do about it now. If the cash was rotted I couldn't resurrect it either so what would I accomplish? Not a single thing! I left it all as it was and made my mind up that I would not think negatively about it. It was much easier to live another year with the anticipation that soon I'll be very rich rather than to lament on a fortune lost. The spring air and the warmth of sun made me feel great and very confident that my pot-of-gold was there waiting for me.

It was Thursday afternoon when Benny came into the store. He said he stopped by because he needs a new suit for a wedding. One of his bosses' Daughters was getting married and he wanted to look his best. He wanted me to fit him with a tuxedo so he will stand out. He wanted to create an impression as a strong person with the personality that could place him in a crowd with anyone and he could hold his own. Benny was convinced that he could mix with people from all walks-of-life and not be categorized as a Mob guy. Most importantly Benny wanted to be someone in the pecking order of his Mob. He wanted his boss to take notice and, he felt by showing a lot more class he felt he could do it. This wedding was his opportunity to shine and his stepping stone to a better position.

As I took his updated measurements, Benny as usual, thought he would engage me in conversation. He was now the Benny from the street side as he related to me what has been taking place in the last few weeks. "*Sam, you'd never believe it, but we found one of the guys who pulled off the robbery. You know, the one at the Bank where we kept some of our money. This asshole couldn't help himself, he had to spend bucks and blow-off his mouth at a bar on Ninth and Twenty-Second Street. The bartender and owner of the bar called it in and we were on top of this asshole like flies on shit. It didn't take long for this asshole to really get crazy, last week he drove up to the bar in brand new Cadillac convertible. Now, where the hell does Reggie who works in a gym get that kind of bucks? Peter, the bartender, called us and told us about this guy. He also told us that he has been coming to this bar for over a year and* always hung out with two other guys. The other guys haven't been back in the bar for a long time but this guy has never missed a Saturday. We watched the guy when he came to the bar the next Saturday and followed him home. We didn't want to grab the wrong guy so we took our time and watched him closely for a couple of weeks. After-all Sam, he could've been a pimp. If he was that would answer where he got his bread from and we would leave him alone, but after watching him for a while he didn't act like a pimp. Finally we were convinced that he wasn't anything else but a health trainer and unless he had a rich relative or someone just died and left him a bundle, he was one of the guys who pulled off the bank job. We decided to pick-up this guy and get some information out of him and find out if he really was involved or not. Last Saturday, when he came to the bar, we confronted him and asked him if he wouldn't mind answering a few questions. Our guys acted as if they were cops and could see that this guy was seriously afraid. They sat down with him in the back of the bar and asked him straight out where he got the money to buy a new car. He told them that an uncle died and left him a few thousand dollars. My guys thought this was a load of bullshit as the guy was obviously very nervous. Once again they asked him to think it over before they come crashing down on him. Acting as cops they said they would check out his story and if it was true he would not be in any trouble. They went on to tell him that it would be easier on him if he tells them the truth now. They said they knew he was in on the Bank robbery and if he comes clean they will make sure he goes free. One of our guys acted as bad cop and the other acted like a good cop. The good cop told him that the first one to speak and help them with their investigation would be given immunity and would not serve anytime. The others will get thirty years or more. The bad cop kept on telling the other guy to take Tyrone downtown and fuck him over, no deal. Of course this asshole thought these guys were real cops and finally started to cry and saying he didn't know what they were talking about. All they wanted to know was the names of the others and where the money is. Once again this guy came back with the same story and one of the guys gave him a serious smack in the stomach. He doubled over and couldn't catch his breath and this guy was scared out of his wits. My guys figured it would be best if they picked him up and carried him outside. Anyone who might be watching would think he had too much to drink and that will be that. They were sitting in the rear of the bar near the pool table area. There was a back door right near their table so they picked him up on a side and carried him outside into the alley. The good cop told him that this was his last chance to come clean and walk away for all this. Reggie said nothing!

"They took the guy to a warehouse and explained to him that they were not cops. They told him that the bread they stole was their money and no one fucks with the Mob and gets away with it. If he wants to live he'd better tell them everything, and gave him another whack in stomach. The guy was so afraid he pissed in his pants and began to cry. It took less than a half-hour to get him to admit he was in on the robbery. He gave us a couple of names and descriptions and best of all, he took us to his place and hidden in his mattress was about half the money. We told him that we would have to keep him with us for a little while, or at least until we find the other guys. He swore he didn't know their addresses, he only knew their names and the description. We verified with the bartender that the two guys he described to us were the same two guys that came into the bar on a regular basis and the description Peter gave us matched with Tyrone's. The bartender also told us that one of the guys went to live in New Jersey, his name was Benny Robinson, or that is what the guy told the bartender and the other guy was named Tyrone," he said.

I could not believe my ears. What the hell was I hearing? I did not flinch as Benny recited this yarn. I realized that I was safe as long as I didn't do something foolish. The one thing that bothered me a lot was why Benny would tell me all this. Was he suspicious of me? Did he have some information I didn't have? I was nervous about the whole thing and wished that Benny hadn't told this to me. Nevertheless it was time to take a deep breath and act as I have always acted. I said to Benny, *"That's great news Benny, I hope you catch these guys. When do you need the tuxedo for?"* I was hoping that the switch of topics would make things right again and calm me down.

"Can you get it to me for next Wednesday? The Wedding is a week Saturday and I want to make sure it fits just right. Do you think you can do it, my man?" he said as he slipped me a twenty.

"No problem Benny, I'll get right on it and you'll have it. Have I ever let you down? Of course not, and I won't this time either," I said. We spent another half-hour bullshitting until Benny said he had to go and warned me not to ever repeat anything he just told me. I told him that I wouldn't and consider myself his friend and would always support him. I juiced him up pretty good because I wanted to be kept in the loop and to do that, I needed Benny on my side.

After Benny had left I sat down and thought about everything Benny had told me. I didn't feel anything for Reggie, nothing at all except contempt. He was told not to show-off his new found wealth. He was instructed to wait at least two years, not two weeks, and he didn't follow those very important messages. Now he would be lucky to get out of this alive and he'll have no money to enjoy. I cannot believe how stupid people can be, especially after it was demonstrated that everything that I told him was true. The money was where I said it was and the project was real. I begged both of them to make sure they didn't change their life styles and did he listen? Of course not, not for a moment and now where is he? I cannot do anything for him because he violated our agreement at least two fold. One, he didn't pay attention to the warning about spending the money and two, he didn't remain silent when confronted with danger. I realize that everyone has a breaking point and can be made to talk. I'm sure I would be as vulnerable as Reggie or anyone else as there is a maximum threshold of pain one can handle. But I would not return the money and I would not tell them who my partners were, I'd give them some other names. Based on what Benny told me Reggie didn't give up all the money. He gave them about half and perhaps he will get to spend the other half even though I highly doubt it. Two things the Mob is good at and getting rid of the body is one of them. The other is placing the fear of God into anyone who is accused of crossing them. Needless to say Reggie has stepped over the line and is standing very precariously near the end of his existence. There is nothing I can do for him and, to be honest, nothing I want to do to help. He brought it upon himself and will have to find a way to get out of it. I don't think he can so the end of Reggie is near. I'm also sure that the Mob will tear his place apart looking for any additional money and clues that would lead them to the other two guys. The lucky thing for Tyrone was the fact that he did not stop by the bar any longer. I'm sure he would be in deep shit if he did. Peter would not waste a minute to call the Mob and they'd be on him right away. I only hoped and prayed that he stayed away and let the folly of Reggie be forgotten and life can move on. My biggest fear for Tyrone was the fact that Reggie knew his real name which was Tyrone. These guys didn't think ahead and used aliases and now it may come back to haunt them. The good part was that Reggie didn't know Tyrone's last name, where he lived and what he did for work. I felt that I could not warn Tyrone to get out of town now while the getting may be good without jeopardizing myself. Then I sit back and allow common sense to take over and lo and behold, I ask myself if I'm being set-up by Benny once again. There is no way anyone could warn Tyrone unless they knew that Reggie was grabbed and the only one who knows that is yours truly. Now I had an aching suspicion that Benny really suspected that I had something to do with that robbery. Too many coincidences have taken place between Benny and myself. I was very nervous over this and now I started to take it all a lot more seriously. Yes, I was convinced that I was being tested by Benny, otherwise, why would he confide details to me that were very private? Something was very fishy, and that complicated matters in regards to my warning Tyrone. Logic dictates that I remain mute and hope that Tyrone doesn't get caught because of greed in the story that Reggie told these guys. No matter what I will sit tight and say nothing and do nothing and hope that this will blow over real soon.

Wednesday finally arrived and Benny's suit was ready for him as promised. I had no way how to get in touch with him directly. All I had was a phone number he gave me to use in case I heard or saw anything unusual, so all I could do was wait. This day was a tough day for me because I wanted to know more about Reggie even though I knew I couldn't ask. I'll have to wait and see if Benny feels inclined to tell me anything about it. It was nearing two o'clock when Benny walked in and was all smiles. We talked for a minute or two about nothing important as I brought out his new tuxedo. He went into the changing room and emerged looking like the president of a major corporation. *"Benny, you look great, that tux fits you like it was meant for you and you alone. You are a very handsome guy and will be the hit of the wedding. One word of advice, leave the heater at home, it makes a bulge in your side and might be noticeable. I suggest if you have to carry it with you, tuck it into your pants at the small of your back, the jacket hangs loose enough to hide it there. It would be a shame to spoil the great look you have with a bulge in the front. By the way Benny, do you have patent leather shoes? If you don't I suggest you get a pair as they will compliment your suit and will add to your overall appearance, we do carry a few pairs,"* I said with a smile. He looked at me and then came over and hugged me and placed a kiss on each cheek and said, *"Thanks Sam, you have made me feel great. Let's look at the shoes and if they are as nice as you say, I'll take two pairs."*

I took Benny over to our shoe department and showed him the patent leather shoes. They were shinning so bright he could see himself in them and when he tried it on with the tux he looked like Beau Brummel. Benny, even though he was a Mob guy, looked absolutely smashing and would fit in anywhere. He was a happy guy when he left the store and I was a very unhappy guy because he didn't mention one word on what was happening. I could not get the thought out of my head about Reggie and what may have happened to him. I only hope that Tyrone has more sense than Reggie and stays quiet. My deepest fear was that Reggie would give up Tyrone and that would be the end of him. Once again I was torn with this dilemma weighing heavily on my mind. Calling Tyrone might be the answer but once again if he is caught, what will it do to me? The safest and best way is to sit back and see what happens. I decided that I couldn't take the risk to call Tyrone, it was far too dangerous for me. Of course, I realized that because I was in disguise every time I went to the bar and always maintained my disguise neither of the guys could identify me. I would remain free because I was careful enough not to ever reveal my true identity. My best bet was to remain silent and hope for the best. The only one who could nail me was Benny because he told me enough but not all the facts of what was going on with Reggie. It was an easy problem to solve as far as I was concerned. Benny told me many times about the money he was carrying to be deposited in the bank. He even showed me some of it when he was bragging. To add to that, he has kept me informed about the Mob's efforts to track down the people who pulled this off. He has kept me informed on their apprehension of Reggie and what they are doing to recover their money. I have been spoon fed with information by Benny and I was convinced that he did all this because he suspected me. He can't quite find anything to connect me with the robbery because none of the descriptions of the three guys fits me. He has dropped enough details on my lap for me to take the bait and screw-up, lucky for me, I haven't fallen for this yet and most certainly won't.

If only the cops had nailed Reggie instead of the Mob. At least he would not face death with them. Deep down I felt Reggie didn't have a chance of surviving, but you never know there is always that exception. The one thing that I was glad to hear was that the money Reggie gave up seemed to repay Benny and his associates in full or close to it.

Three weeks have come and gone since Benny was in the store last. He walked in looking real dapper and came over to where I was sitting in my little office and said, *"How are you Sam? I was just on my way to the Bank with some more of that stuff,"* he said as he laughed at the saying he just made.

"I'm fine Benny and thanks for asking. I guess everything in the Bank has been resolved by now?" I said.

"I guess so, all I know is that they told me I can start using the safety boxes I have. We took quite a beating but the one guy we caught gave us back more than half of what we lost. Beside that Sam, he gave us the description of his other partners so in a few more weeks, we'll find the others and get back all our bread and maybe a few bucks ahead for our trouble, who knows?" Benny said with a smirk.

"I'm glad to hear that Benny, it's always nice to hear a happy ending to a story. By the way, what happened to the guy in the end?" I asked.

"Nothing, he told us everything and returned the bread he had taken and now we let him go. What kind of people do you think we are Sam?" Benny said with a very straight face.

"Hey Benny, I was only curious I didn't mean anything by it. You know when you read a mystery book you want to read the last few pages because you're so anxious to know how it all ended, well Benny, that's the same way with this story. It seems hard to believe that someone could be so stupid as to go out and throw around money, more money than he ever spent before, but it takes all kinds and this World is full of them. So you let the guy go and follow him

with the hope he will lead you to the others? It's just like the movies, isn't that right Benny?" I said.

"You guessed right Sam. He can't do us any harm and as you know, most people are scared shitless of us so we have no concerns. And Sam, what can this asshole do? He can't go the cops, what would he say? 'The Mob is after me because I was in on the Bank Job and I need your protection,' he said as he started to laugh.

"What's so funny Benny?" I said.

'I was just thinking about this guy and if he did go the cops. It's just funny to think how stupid people are sometimes. We'd never know about this guy if he didn't start to show off, but I guess that is what makes the World go around. But you never know what people might do at any time, especially when they are worried about being whacked," Benny said as he continued to laugh.

"I see what you mean, I guess you are right Benny. What could he say to the cops without incriminating himself? If you don't mind me saying this Benny, this would make a great story, maybe I'll take-up writing," I said as I laughed aloud.

"Sam, you must never tell anyone about this, please man, please," Benny said. "I shouldn't tell you anything about this, but I trust you with my life, so please keep it all to yourself. I just wanted to spend a little time together and say hello and tell you that the wedding went very well and I looked great, thanks to you. My Bosses were very impressed and I'm sure I'm going to get the next promotion. Thanks for all your help Sam, you and your suits helped me a lot. See you next week and take a look at the new styles for summer."

Benny left and I felt quite sick for Reggie. Why was he so impatient to use his funds? He certainly was warned often enough about the dangers that awaited and look at what he has done. I feel very responsible about one thing, that I didn't take the Mob into account. I should have known that they would be as unhappy as anyone who had their money in safety deposit boxes. After all I started this project because Benny kept stopping in and was always carrying a briefcase filled with cash. He told me that he had to rent more boxes because the present ones were filled. This was my basis for the project in the first place, so I should have warned the guys that the Mob will also be a force to reckon with. I didn't and now we are facing a dilemma of epic proportions. The cops chase leads and they do not, as a rule, beat the shit out of a person unless it was one of their own that was maligned or killed. I was too busy covering what I thought was every base. Now I realize I left out an important detail, The Mob! How could I have been so stupid and what can I do about it now? The right thing to do is to alert Tyrone somehow, but because I have taken steps to remain anonymous, I can't do that.

The big problem here is that Reggie will be killed. That is for sure simply because they always need that example. The Mob doesn't care about human flesh, they only care about their reputation even though money is an important factor. I spent the next two days tearing myself apart. I was feeling guilty about this but after two days of back and forth inner conflict I finally made, what I thought, the right decision.

The Decision:

I DECIDED TO MAKE AN ANONYMOUS PHONE CALL TO THE cops and tell them that one of the perpetrators of the Bank job was Reggie Green. I decided that Reggie would be safer in the hands of the cops than he would be with the Mob. If Reggie had any smarts he would tell the cops that he was part of the crime and he was sorry for it. He should also tell them about the Mob's involvement and the reason he has no more money is that he gave it all to the Mob to save his ass, Reggie may get a few years in prison but that is a lot better than being killed. Also if he is smart, and it doesn't seem like he is, he will still have the cash he didn't tell them about and it will be waiting for him at the end of the prison term. He could also agree to testify against the others as well. I was not concerned that he could identify me as I felt that was impossible. He could and would point the finger at Tyrone and tidy-up some loose ends.

I must admit I don't like doing this. Calling in a tip on one of my associates is not right. It's not what I ever thought about and I felt I was betraying them. On the other hand I also felt this was the best way to save their lives and what was more important, the money or their lives? As you can see I opted to save their lives and the hell with the money. I only hoped that Reggie had enough sense to hide his remaining cash properly, so when his time in prison is over, the cash will be there. I thought long and hard about this and finally went to a pay phone far away from my workplace and made the call.

I asked to speak to the detective in charge of the BNZ Bank robbery. I waited a few minutes and was told that Detective Andrew

Fellows was in charge and would be with me in a moment. *"Detective Fellows here. How can I help you?"* he said.

"I'm calling about the BNZ Bank robbery. I know one of the guys who was in the job. His name is Tyrone Shelton and he lives here in Manhattan. I was at a bar and he had too much to drink and started to mouth off that he ripped off the BNZ Bank and has plenty of bread. I don't know where he lives or anything about him except that he is a black dude and acted like he was smarter than anyone," I said in my best Brooklyn accent and hung up.

I felt shitty all over because of this call but felt it had to be done. I could not do any more to save Tyrone and Reggie. Of course, I was banking on Reggie telling the cops that his accomplices were Tyrone and Benny. My biggest concern was that Reggie would be protected and not get killed by the Mob. I wasn't worried that someone would find Reggie's stash because the Mob had already searched his place from top to bottom. I guess life is not as simple as we would like it to be, this project was supposed to be foolproof and now this snafu? I thought I had taken everything into account but didn't account for the weird and strange things to happen. What are the odds? Too late now, all I can do is to make sure I stay far away from all of this.

Lucky for me I have Benny as a confidant, otherwise, I would never know what is going on and would remain in the dark. I certainly can't ask the cops what their investigation has revealed even though I would love to. The irony of all this is that I can't call Benny and ask him what is going on either. I am on very shaky grounds and can be tripped up easily if I'm not careful. I can't ever let Benny think that I'm anxious to get the information about the Bank robbery. I was bothered by Benny's friendly attitude. The more I thought about it, the more I was convinced that Benny had a suspicion that I was involved in the robbery. Sure I sold him suits, was very nice to him, but I'm sure he has put two and two together and figured that I have a bigger interest in this deal than meets the eye. I had a nagging feeling that Benny figured that he fucked-up by bragging about the cash and because of that, I concocted the Bank job. Now I was convinced that he was trying to set me up and somehow trap me into a slip-up. I knew I had to be extra careful around him and around everyone I knew. Benny, like any other Mob guy, would try to use every method possible to find out if I was involved with the bank job. Perhaps he felt I didn't actually do the job but because of his free flowing tongue he set the job in motion and I told someone else. There were so many possibilities that it made my mind go off in so many directions, not in the least a direction that could spell doom for me. I knew I had to be very careful especially when going up to the mountains. If Benny and his crew decided to follow me I would be toast way out at my place in the middle of nowhere. It was isolated and no one would look there for a long, long time. I had to keep my mouth shut and watch my step every day and stay as many steps ahead of Benny as possible. So far I was ahead of him because I didn't take the bait and warn the guys as he thought I would. So far Benny has his suspicions because of his big mouth but has no other reason to suspect me except for the fact that he told me way too much information before the robbery. I don't even come close to looking like one of the guys Reggie described, nevertheless I felt that Benny had a nagging suspicion. His one confliction was that he liked me a lot and, unlike other cases, he didn't want to screw up a relationship especially if he was wrong. He had doubts, something a Mob guy doesn't usually have. If you think someone did you over you whack them and if you are wrong you chalk it up to a mistake, but you don't vacillate. I can't let my guard down for one minute and if I follow my schedule I'm certain these Mob guys will quit watching me. I had time on my hands and so did they and if I play my cards right they'll get tired first.

Another month has since passed since all this has taken place. I have not seen Benny and nothing appeared in the newspapers about the Bank robbery. I felt that something was wrong but there was nothing I could do except wait for Benny to appear or see some news in the papers. Today was Saturday and I was looking forward to the weekend at the cabin. All the snows were gone and the weather was very mild as it was late June. I left that Saturday night and drove to the cabin. I was very careful to make sure I wasn't being followed, instead of taking three hours to get there, it took me over four. I stopped and then started again and waited until traffic was much lighter and when I finally reached the road to the cabin I was able to make certain if anyone was following me. This road was deserted and any car that would be following would be detected easily, the mountain was as quiet as could be and from my vantage point I could see about a mile down the mountain. Because of the winding road it was impossible to navigate without the headlights on and they would be a beacon that would be detectable for a long, long way. I still took extra precautions by stopping on my lonely mountain road and parking in a blind and waiting to see if another car would come along with its lights off, a risky task to say the least. If anyone was following me this was where they would be caught. I waited a half-hour and nothing came by. I continued to the cabin where I made myself comfortable for the night.

I spent the next two days at the cabin, I had brought with enough food to last for the two days as well as my portable radio and a couple of good books. Not having electricity didn't bother me at all as I was happy to get some rest and get to sleep early. I stayed at the cabin for two days not ever leaving, just enjoying the safety and quiet of isolation. While I was there I decided it was time I added electricity to this place. I said I would call a few electricians to come by and give me an estimate. I figured it couldn't cost too much because my cabin was very small, only one room so how much power could it take! I would tell the electrician that I will be back next Monday and would like a quotation at that time. I checked on my stash and was pleased that nothing was disturbed and things looked great. I then started back to New York, rejuvenated and ready to resume another week of work. My trip back to the City was uneventful even though I was very careful all the way and watched each car to make sure I wasn't followed. I even left the highway and took the Jersey side and then crossed back into the City on the George Washington Bridge just to see if anyone was following me. The coast was clear and I went home and once again made sure no one was waiting for me. I didn't need any unexpected guests and wondered what I would do if they were waiting for me at my place! I am thankful that I didn't have to make any decisions in that regard as no one seemed to be around at my place. I checked the apartment to make sure there wasn't any sign of entry while I was away. I had left a few items around that someone would move if they entered the place. I also made sure I had placed a few hairs on drawers and by the rear door as well to further detect an intruder. Nothing was touched or out of place which made me feel a lot better. I began to think I was being overly paranoid over this deal, but soon told myself not to relax my concerns. Better be careful at all times and be safe than to allow a moment of weakness become my Waterloo. An ounce of prevention is worth a pound of cure, perhaps an old cliché but very appropriate, especially in this case.

I was pleased that I had taken the precautions I did and was very happy with myself as I settled down for a week's work and tried to keep my thoughts about the project to a minimum. To me it was a thing of the past, yet, deep in my mind, I couldn't help wondering what was going on if anything at all. On Thursday morning I opened the Daily News and there it was on page three, an article that the New York Police Department and the FBI have arrested a suspect in the BNZ Bank job. The article goes on to describe the robbery but really does not give any new details or identify the person that they have under arrest. Details were sketchy and didn't reveal where they have him or what they have found. I was very pleased to see the article because it made me feel that Reggie's life was safe for now and my call made it possible. I felt better and satisfied that I didn't just sit idly by as he was slaughtered.

On the following Sunday I went to my cabin and met with two of the electricians who gave me quotations on the electricity installation. I finally agreed with one of the contractors to go ahead and gave him a five hundred dollar deposit. The entire job was twenty-nine hundred dollars because they had to run a wire a quarter mile from the dirt road to my cabin. The electric company was charging about half of the cost because of that long line. I was happy to know I would have some electricity in the cabin so I could enjoy the nights as well as the days. Of course, my small cabin will have to be expanded and I'll have to get some running water. Right now I don't even have a bathroom other than what nature provides. I realized that it would be foolish to do anything that would be too elaborate and cause someone to ask where I was getting the money to do all this. Having the electricity installed will not arouse anyone's suspicion, especially because the amount was not very much and it would not have any basis to make one think that I had to rob a bank to do this.

I was back at work and glad to be there, it was my safe haven for the time being. I checked the newspapers each day to see if there was anything about the Bank robbery. So far no more news since the article I read a few of weeks ago.

I was sitting at my desk when Benny came in and as usual, carried his trusty briefcase. *"How are you Benny?"* I said, *"It's nice to see you. What's going on my good man?"*

"I'm great and on my way to the Bank to drop off another load of greenbacks. I just wanted to stop in and chat with you a bit. By the way Sam, remember I talked to you about this guy we found who was involved in the Bank Robbery. Well, guess what Sam?" he said with a smile on his face.

"He dropped dead. You found all the money. Gee Benny, I really am guessing, clue me in please," I said.

"Well Sam, you won't believe it, that's for sure! Sometimes stranger things happen in life, stranger than fiction. Remember I told you we found one of the guys and he returned most of our money so we let him go. Next thing I find out is that he is picked-up by the cops and have held him for three weeks and they haven't charged him with anything. One of my sources tells me this guy is singing like a canary and trying to make a deal with the Feds. Did you know that if you rob a bank, it is Federal offense? I didn't know that until now, it seems banks fall under the jurisdiction of the FBI and not the New York cops. Anyway I hear he is their star witness and they are looking for two other guys. What they don't know is, that he gave us the same information when we talked with him. So far we have not been able to find the other two guys but we have all our people on alert. We've got descriptions of them and have made sure all our contacts have this information. No one escapes us Sam, it's just a matter of time. By the way Sam, let me give you their description as well just in case either one comes in for a new suit.

"There is one guy who is about fifty years old and talks through his nose. He is about six foot tall with deep black hair, blue eyes and, as I said, he talks through his nose and walks with a limp. He won't be hard to recognize at all and his name is Benny Robinson. The other guy is about six foot two or three with wavy black hair and some serious muscles. He has a heart shaped tattoo on left arm that says, 'Love you Sue,' it can't be missed unless he is wearing a long sleeve shirt. His name is Tyrone Shelton and he lives somewhere here in Manhattan, so keep your eyes open Sam. If you should spot any of these two guys call me at this number, they are worth five grand each Sam, so give me a call if it happens. Otherwise things are going on as they always did except I am now getting my own territory and will have bunch of soldiers working for me. You won't see me coming in with my briefcase anymore, but Sam, I'll still be coming by to see you and buy all my suits from you. I got this promotion because I looked so good at the wedding," he said as he laughed. "No kidding Sam, you have made me into a real person and I will always remember you for it. If you ever need something that I can get for you or someone is hassling you, just call me and I'll take care of it. Friends are hard to come by so let's stay in touch. I'm off to the bank, see you later," he said as he went out of the store.

I sat at my desk for a while thinking how ironical it all is. Here I am sitting with the very guy that gave me the information for this big score and he tells me we are best friends. Life sure is funny at times. My day ended as usual and I took the train home as I usually do. While riding on the train I looked around as I always do because I like to study people's faces especially after a day's work and I'm no more than six feet away from Tyrone. Of course, he doesn't recognize me but I know it's him. I wanted to go over to him and tell him to get out of town because the cops and the Mob are looking for him. I knew where he lived and wondered why he was on this train going uptown when he lived downtown? Where was he going? Or maybe he moved to a new place? I decided to try and follow him although I'm not much good at it. He doesn't know who I am so it is safe to watch him. I decided not to stay too close because he will become aware of me and that could prove to be something I may not be able to handle.

The train stopped at Eighty-Sixth Street and Eighth Avenue and Tyrone got off and so did I. I was curious and realized that I couldn't do or say anything to him without revealing my true identity and this I wasn't prepared to do. I followed him as he walked along Eighth Avenue until he reached Ninety-Fourth Street where he turned west and walked another half a block and went into a building. I walked by the front door to see if I could catch a glimpse of him but he was gone. I jotted down the address and walked back towards the train station. I decided to walk home and not concern myself with Tyrone. As I walked along Eighth Avenue, I had a feeling that someone was following me. I looked around and couldn't see anyone behind me but still had a feeling that someone was there. I walked at the same leisurely pace until I came to Ninety-First Street and took a right turn and jumped into an alley and waited. A minute later Tyrone came walking by, it was easy to see the disappointment on his face as he strained his eyes looking for me. It was now dark so he couldn't see that far ahead as the street lights didn't give off sufficient light. I had crouched down behind a row of garbage cans and waited, if he came down the alley I would sit on the ground with my head in my hands as if I was asleep and was living on the street. It wasn't the best way to hide from him but time was not on my side, I couldn't find any alternative. Reggie stood by the alley and looked everywhere, I could see him straining his eyes to see if there is any movement in the alley. Finally he left he left the alley entrance where I was hiding and walked down the street, constantly looking back. I walked to the edge of the alley and looked down the street and saw him walking east. I estimated that he was two blocks away so I left the alley and retraced my steps and when I reach Eighth Avenue I hailed a cab, and had him take me home. I was in a complete sweat as I sat in the cab, all I could think of was, how stupid I was to follow him. Why was it necessary to do that? I could not answer and felt that I had let myself down and nearly got caught. If he moved to a new place then I should be applauding it and minding my own business, not trying to discover his motives and inadvertently leaving myself vulnerable. I swore I wouldn't do this again and shall remain anonymous. Why the hell did I use a disguise for so many months? Easy answer, to remain an unknown person and now I am jeopardizing all that. How foolish one can be, simple mistakes like this can undo the best plans a person can make. I walked home from the train station and made sure I was not being followed. When I was in my apartment I breathed a sigh of relief and threw myself on my bed and took a deep breath. I remained on my bed thinking of what a fool I was and once again told myself never, never again.

The right decision is to remain mute at all times and let each person find their own way. If they screw-up then it's their own fault. Silence and remaining in the background at all times is the only solution and shall be from now on!

A Turn of Events:

IT'S HARD TO BELIEVE BUT LABOR DAY WAS UPON US ONCE again. The only news I have been able to gather was that Reggie was in custody and the cops were looking for two other people in connection with the robbery. I was thrilled with the passage of time as it made me feel better and my theory seems to be right, time is our ally and soon the waiting will be over and I will be able to enjoy the rewards of my very well planned project. I was clearly out of the picture based on the things that my friend Benny has told me. By the way, Benny was now a big shot in the hierarchy of the Mob. He no longer talks about the famous Bank robbery, instead, he complains how hard it is maintaining his position. As he explained to me, "*Sam I thought I'd be so happy being made into a real Mob Boss. No way Sam, now its pressure all the time. I have quotas to reach and have to keep my territory running like a well- greased machine. I have a crew that works for me and I have to worry that they don't fuck-up. My Bosses don't want to hear any excuses ever, all they want is the cash every week or else. I'm sorry Sam, I shouldn't complain about it because I make a lot more money and I don't have to do any dirty stuff myself. Of course Sam, if one of my crew screws-up, I have to take care of it or someone will take care of me,*" he said.

"*I understand Benny, but with every promotion comes a new set of responsibilities and I'm sure your bosses would say that's why you get the big bucks. I'm sure you can handle it and if you need my help, just call me,*" I said as I laughed about that last remark. I was a tad nervous with that last remark but was relieved when Benny laughed along with me.

My course of action was to mix out of the lives of Tyrone and Reggie. If they get caught they only have themselves to blame. In the case of Reggie I read in the papers where he made a plea bargain with the cops and received a two year sentence. The article that I read was in the Daily News and it went along these lines, because of Reggie's cooperation with the authorities the presiding judge, Arnold Winston, suspended his sentence and placed him on probation. I knew that Reggie didn't have a criminal record, so the odds were in his favor that they would go easy on him. I was thrilled for him because, as far as I was concerned, Reggie made a good deal for himself but still had to watch out for the Mob. I learned from Benny, a while back, that although he returned the money there was still a few dollars missing. I also felt that Reggie must have kept about half of his money simply because no one really knew how much cash was actually stolen. Many of the people who had safety deposit boxes that were opened didn't want to admit to large sums of cash. They took the best way out by staying silent thus making the total loss a lot less than the actual sum taken. I know that because I knew how much I took out of there and because we all had backpacks of similar sizes therefore the amounts should have been pretty equal. I estimated that the amount taken was in excess of five million. My theory that most people would not report their losses proved to be right and made the reported loss a lot smaller. As a matter-of-fact, the bank estimated the loss to be less than a half million. As far as I was concerned this turn of events seemed to close the affair. I felt that Tyrone and I were safe and could make some moves to leave New York, when I read in the papers that the FBI arrested a second suspect in the Labor Day robbery of 1956 at the BNZ Bank.

I was shocked because I thought the whole affair was closed, but I was wrong. It seems that the FBI had been looking for Tyrone for over a year and never caught up with him. All Tyrone did was move from his old digs to a new place in upper Manhattan and didn't use his real name. His big mistake, like mine, was assuming that the case was just about closed because so much time had passed. Once he felt they were not looking for him, he went out and bought a new car, a convertible to boot. Of course, Tyrone being Tyrone wanted a white car with red upholstery and a Ford fit the bill. He also paid for it in cash, not such a terrible deed except he brought with a bag of money that contained far more cash than he needed. I guessed Reggie got his jollies off by acting like he was a rich guy. What he forgot was the fact that he was still a young guy and that most very rich people don't walk around with wads of cash. Add to all that is the fact that he made sure the salesman at the car dealer knew he was a rich kid. He didn't take into account my warning about the cops. I said when we went into this project that they have all the time in the World and will be happy to wait it out so don't make any foolish moves. Tyrone made one fatal foolish move and that resulted in his capture at his new place.

A few days later there was another piece in the Daily News about how stupid crooks can be and one of the examples was Tyrone's stupidity. Why would anyone who knew he was wanted by the cops go out and buy a car on his name? Why would anyone give the DMV his correct name and new address? Why people are so stupid when all Tyrone had to do was to move to another State and buy his car there under an assumed name? Paying cash for a car is not unusual but showing the salesman how much cash you actually have is a no, no! All I could say to myself was how foolish Tyrone was. Oh by the way the article also alluded to the fact that when the cops raided Tyrone's apartment they found close to one hundred K in cash. I knew from that article that at least he was smart enough to hide the rest somewhere else where they couldn't find it. The amount reported coincided with the money they got from Reggie so the cops assumed that the most the thieves got away with was about three hundred thousand. There wasn't any way to prove differently so that was the number the cops accepted. Of course, the FBI, in an interview with the paper's reporter, claimed that they are close to finding the third person involved in the robbery. The FBI agent who gave the interview also threw in that they always get their man regardless of how long it takes. I hoped that they were wrong and continued on with my regular routine.

Passage of Time:

CHRISTMAS WAS UPON US ONCE AGAIN, ANOTHER YEAR would end and it helped me feel a lot better about the Bank project. The more time between the actual robbery and me made me feel a lot more secure and closer to my goal. I was still working at the same place and still measuring the same old clients, as well as some new ones for suits, jackets, pants, shirts, and a bunch of other items. A year and a half has passed and there has not been a peep in the paper since Tyrone was sentenced to two years. The judge issued a strong rebuke and because Tyrone cooperated with the authorities, he gave him this lenient sentence. He would serve his time in a Federal Penitentiary because a crime against a Bank falls under the Fed's jurisdiction. The FBI would continue to look for the third man and were very frustrated, I assumed. I made my assumption based on the fact that two people, Reggie and Tyrone, both described Benny Robinson pretty much the same. They knew the guy's name and had him living in Manhattan and then moving to New Jersey and losing track of him there. Of course, they will never find Benny Robinson because he doesn't exist. All the items they found in the room beneath the Bank didn't help the investigators as they were unable to trace who bought them and from where. As far as I was concerned I was home free and had committed the perfect crime or the next to the perfect one. My time schedule was as I predicted and all I had to do was to wait a few more months and then put my plan into action. The only area I was concerned about was the involvement of the Mob and that worried me immensely.

I learned from Benny that the Mob was okay with Reggie and that they got back about ninety percent of their money. Of course, I did not know if that was true or just Benny bragging in order not to lose face. I also didn't know if Benny was smarter than I gave him credit for! After all Benny told me all about the money as he was bringing it to the Bank. Perhaps Benny realized that he shot off his mouth and told me too much and now he was trying to trap me into admitting I was the brains behind the robbery. I knew I could not be certain of what was going through his head so I opted to just stay quiet and do my job. I couldn't be sure if he was barking up the wrong tree or was he actually suspicious. On the other hand he could be clueless about my involvement. My dilemma was to decide what was true and what was false. I asked myself why does Benny come by so often? He doesn't bring the cash to the Bank any longer and doesn't buy suits every time he comes by, so why is doing this? My conclusion was that, if I maintain my lifestyle in time, he'll go away. That was my feelings about the situation and there was very little I could do about it.

The best part was the fact that I recently met a beautiful girl by the name of Jenny Lasko. I have taken her out three times since I met her in the store last month. She came in with her Dad and helped him, along with my kind assistance, find a nice wardrobe as he was just promoted to a new position in the company he worked for. She was about twenty-three years old and had sort of, dirty blond hair with beautiful blue eyes. She was petite as she was no more than five foot tall and must have weighed about one hundred pounds. We hit it off the moment we saw each other and she enjoyed every minute with me. Since then I have taken her out three times and must admit was head-over-heels in love with her. On our fourth date, I decided to get serious and tell her how much I cared for her.

It was Saturday and I had asked Jenny if she would have dinner with me. She said she would and that was, as far as I was concerned, the most important date of my life. She lived in Forest Hills, Queens, in a small house on Van Horne Street.

I went home after work and took my car out the parking garage and got ready for the big date. This was an important move for me as I was very much in love with this woman. This was the first time I have felt this way about anyone and I didn't want to screw-it-up. I made a reservation at a fine restaurant located on Queens Blvd, called Ristorante Luigi. I picked her up right on time and was blown away on how beautiful she looked. She was wearing a beautiful white dress that made her look like a princess. I was breathless as my heart beat a tune of desire and true love. We left her place and I informed her that we were eating at Luigi's. She said she loved Italian food and had always wanted to go to Luigi's.

We arrived at Luigi's, the place was mobbed with people. I told the hostess that we had a reservation and within a minute or two she asked us to follow her to our table. It's hard to describe the rest of evening as I was floating on a cloud and all I could see was this beautiful woman sitting across from me. We ordered a bottle of wine and began a wonderful conversation that allowed us to get to know each other more intimately. After having a wonderful meal and feeling a little giddy because of the wine, and having this beautiful woman so near to me, I said to her, *"Jenny, I love you and hope you would consider being my Wife. I know we have only known each other a few short months but I know in my heart you are the one I want to spend the rest of my life with. I didn't buy you a ring just yet but I promise you a life filled with joy, and love for all time."*

"Oh Sam, I'm so happy with you and yes I feel the same way you do. I'd be honored to be your wife, and Sam, I don't need a ring to prove how much you care. I can see it on your face and feel it with your touch. Yes Sam, I want to marry you and give you lots of children. I love you Sweetheart," she said.

I felt like I was ten feet tall, well, that was how I felt at that moment. My every dream has come true and Jenny was the best

I could ever have. I loved her so much and didn't care who knew. I got up from my seat and went over to her and pulled her out of her chair and held her in my arms. I was in love and didn't care who knew it. I sat back down at the table and signaled the waiter for our check. I was in another World, nothing could dampen my happiness or take this moment away from me. She looked radiant and very happy as we raised our glasses in a toast to the future.

My World came tumbling down in that split-second. It happened so fast, no one in the restaurant saw anything coming. All of a sudden people were shrieking and I heard a loud pop and shouting. *"Don't move and no one will get hurt. This is a robbery, cooperate and this will be over very fast. Empty your pockets and throw the contents into the bag that is being passed around. Don't fuck with us if you want to stay alive,"* A tall black man said from behind his mask.

All of a sudden one woman shrieked and fell on the floor. The thieves were taken by surprise and the world came tumbling down as shots rang out and people were shouting, *"Everyone on the floor, get back in your seats or you're all going to die motherfuckers,"* and then there was noise and bullets flying everywhere.

People were screaming and there was blood everywhere, it was complete chaos. I turned to grab Jenny and she wasn't there. I looked down and there she was lying in a pool of blood. I started shouting, *"I need a doctor, I need a doctor, she's badly hurt, somebody help us,"* when something hit me in the leg just above the knee. I fell to the floor, I couldn't get up. I tried to stand, but I couldn't. I wanted to help her, she needed me and as I started crawling towards her, I felt a stab on my side and all I could do was to fall over and cry out in pain. The blood was gushing out of my leg and I was sure my time was up and I was going to die. I moved slowly on the floor towards Jenny, all I could think of was to help her, but she didn't move at all. I was bleeding and hurt all over but I dragged myself along the floor to get to Jenny when someone grabbed the tablecloth and tied it around the wound on my leg. I continued moving towards Jenny and then everything went black. I regained consciousness momentarily and started shouting, *"Jenny, where are you? Jenny I love you, please don't die, I love you more than anything."* The next thing I remember is some people in white uniforms telling me to, *"Calm down young man, everything is under control. Now let me look at those wounds,"* he said to me. It was all a blur to me as I must have fainted because I didn't remember anything at all.

I was now lying in a bed with white sheets and white walls and no one else around. I tried to get my bearings and looked around and saw something that looked like a door, things weren't quite clear to me. I called out, *"Where am I? Is someone here? Please tell me what's happening? Where is Jenny? Help me please, where am I?"* I could not move a muscle I didn't have any feelings anywhere. Just as I was about to scream once again a woman walked into my room. She was dressed in a white uniform, my imagination was swimming, I could not make sense of what was going on or where I was and why. *"Nice to see you are awake, welcome back to the living, Mr. West. You are in Lenox Hill Hospital where you have been treated for gunshot wounds to your left leg and right side and lower back. You also received a pretty bad bump on your head, but now that you're awake you'll be fine. You have been here for a week but don't worry everything will be fine. The Doctor will be by in a few minutes, so just relax and try not to move too much, we don't want you to pull out the stitches. Glad to have you back with us Mr. West,"* she said as she adjusted the pillow beneath my head.

I can't explain how my mind was working, everything seemed all mixed up. I remember being at the restaurant and then someone started shouting to get on the floor. I saw Jenny looking at me with an expression of *'Help me'* and then blank, nothing left in my memory. I was not in my own body, I seemed to be floating on air and felt nothing. I kept saying, *"Help, help I'm flying away. Where am I?"* over and over again.

I don't know how long I was in this state of mind but I was abruptly prodded by a man wearing a white pair of pants and a shirt to match and a stethoscope hanging from his neck. He kept saying, "Mr. West, wake-up, I'm Doctor Wilson and I'd like to examine you," he said as the nurse was busy cranking the bed. Slowly I was coming back to life as the Doctor began listening to my chest and banging his fingers on my back. Then he took a knife or some other object, I could not see all the way down to my feet and began scratching the bottom of my feet. I could not help it as my toes began to move as he scraped and he said, "*You are going to be fine, everything seems to be working as it should. You may be a little groggy, Mr. West, but that will wear off very soon. We had to keep you sedated because you received a blow to your head and we wanted to make sure that you did not have any internal bleeding. Everything seems to be returning to normal, you'll be out of here in a day or two. Your leg will feel stiff for a while but that will go away In a few weeks, the rest of your wounds are healing very nicely and with time you'll forget them, that's for sure and as long as you exercise as often as you can, all will be well. Please try to relax Mr. West, you are in good hands,*" he said.

"*Thanks Doc, but please tell me what happened to Jenny? Why isn't she here? What day is it? Please bring me up to date Doc, please!*" I said.

"*Mr. West, you have been through a lot and it would be best if you rested, you'll need all your strength to get better. I can't answer your questions because I don't know the answers, but I promise you that today someone will come and see you and tell you everything that happened. I know that you have been here for seven days and today is the first day you have been conscious. We had to keep you sedated because we wanted you to rest easy and heal. Now that you are on the road to recovery, we will have you up and around in a few days and you'll start to feel quite normal again. Now please relax, I'll have the nurse bring you some food, I'm sure you must be* hungry. *You haven't eaten for a week so take it easy and eat lightly until you adjust once again. I wish I could tell you more Mr. West, but I don't know anything other than your condition, please relax and let us make you well,*" he said with a smile and a gentle touch.

"Thanks Doc, when will this someone come see me? Where is Jenny? Is she alright? You must know that information and if not, who does?" I asked as tears began to run down my cheeks. I was upset and all I could think of was Jenny.

They forced me to sit-up by cranking my bed to a new position and brought me a tray of orange juice, water, and a piece of toast. The nurse told me to drink slowly and chew the toast thoroughly and to try and relax. Everything will be okay she had said, but as far as I was concerned nothing was okay and it didn't look like anything would be for a long time. I was very upset over the fact that no one was able to give me any details about Jenny. If she was alright why hasn't she visited me? I realized I was tormenting myself with all these unanswered questions but I could not help myself.

Finally a man arrived and showed me his identification. He was detective, first-class Martin Ball. He was tall and looked as if he had been around the block a few times. His smile was soft and he made me feel more relaxed. "*I'm Detective Martin Ball, I'm so glad to see you sitting up. I have been here almost every day to see how you are doing Mr. West. Do you feel up to answering a few questions?*" he asked

"I won't answer any of your questions until you tell me what happened and where is Jenny?" I said.

"*I'll be happy to bring you up to date Sam, I hope you don't mind if we keep it on a first name basis, I'm Martin,*" he said.

"That's fine Martin, please give me the truth. I didn't mean to infer that you would lie to me, I just meant I want all the facts, good or bad," I said.

"*Last week, if you remember, you went to Luigi's for dinner with your girl Jenny. If you remember there was a terrible scene when* three gunmen entered the restaurant and attempted to hold up the place. They threatened to shoot anyone who did not follow their instructions. Their instructions were directed to all the patrons, waiters, and anyone else who worked there. They were all told to empty their pockets and place the contents into a sack that one of the men was carrying around. They made it clear that this meant all people, the staff as well, no exceptions. What happened next was still unclear but all hell broke out as someone started shooting. It is still not clear if the shooter was one of the robbers or was one of the customers or a staff member. Right now it doesn't make any difference any longer because the damage has been done. The place was a madhouse when the bullets started flying and many people were wounded. While this was happening one of the chefs managed to call 911 and we dispatched our officers. During this wild scene, you were shot in the leg and back and as you tried to reach Jenny someone hit you on the head or you banged your head on the hard floor when you fell. A witness said that one of the thieves hit you on the head with the butt of his gun. In any case you were found unconscious and bleeding pretty badly from your wounds. The paramedics arrived but could not enter the Restaurant because of the gun battle going on. It took us another fifteen minutes to subdue one of the robbers while the other three evaded our officers by going through the ceiling to the roof and then making their escape by jumping to the next building. The buildings had a space of ten feet between them. But these guys were desperate and jumped anyway. One of them didn't make it and was killed when he landed on the concrete below. Now we have one in custody and one in the morgue and we also have three dead people that were killed in the restaurant. I am sad to say Sam, Jenny was one of them. A stray bullet passed right through her heart and she was killed instantly," he stopped talking or I stopped hearing when he said Jenny was killed. I lost it and began sobbing uncontrollably. Jenny killed, I could not believe what I just heard. My girl, my future wife, I loved her with all my heart and now she was dead.

The Detective didn't know what to do with me, a blubbering person I guess, as he called out for the nurse. *"I broke the news to him and he lost control of himself. Give him something to calm him down. I'm afraid he might hurt himself,"* he said as he moved away from my bedside.

When I woke up it was dark outside and the detective was gone. No one was around and I tried to put my thoughts together. I knew I had to be strong for Jenny's sake and her family. I couldn't imagine how they felt, their only Daughter gone forever, it must be devastating for them. I know it was devastating for me, my life seemed worthless. I felt like shit and wanted to disappear and bury my head in sand. Life was so important to me before this happened and now, nothing seems to be right.

I spent another three days in the hospital in a state of deep depression. On the fourth day I finally got out of bed and started walking and still feeling very sorry for myself. I walked the corridors of the hospital even though my leg and back ached. I wanted to inflict pain on myself, I believed that if I suffered it would make things better. I walked and walked until I was exhausted and I finally sat down in the atrium at the end of the long corridor. I sat there staring out the window and seeing nothing at all as I could not focus on anything. I kept staring at the buildings that looked back at me and said nothing at all. Not realizing that anyone else was in the room I began to cry softly as I thought of Jenny and felt sorry for myself once again. All of a sudden I heard a soft voice saying, *"It can't be all that bad, can it?"* A young very attractive girl was sitting on the chair facing me. She was very beautiful with a smile that would melt anyone's heart. Her eyes were blue and very soft as she looked at me and repeated, *"It can't be all that bad. My name is Susan, what's yours?"*

"I'm Sam, Susan, Sam West, it is a pleasure to meet you. I'm very sorry if I have brought your spirits down, I didn't know anyone else was in the room. I'm not very good company right now," I said.

"I'm Susan Weiss and it is a pleasure to meet you Sam. Do you mind talking about it? It's alright if you don't want to, I'll understand. While you are thinking it over Sam, let me tell you a little about me. I'm here Sam because I don't have much time left on this earth. I have a disease called leukemia and they tell me it's not curable. I don't know how long I have left to live as this is the first time I have ever been confronted with anything like this. My biggest concern in life used to be, if my hair looked good or, would that boy next to me in school like me. Now I realize how silly all that was as I'm faced with a much shorter life than I thought I'd have. I decided Sam that I must enjoy every second of this life as it is the only one I'll ever have. I realize that no one has a specific time that their lives will last, no one. Some live for a long, long time and others live a short one. But what I realized Sam, is that whatever time we are allotted we'd best love it and embrace it with all of our hearts. There is no time to cry over things that we don't have especially the ones we have no control over. We should be thankful for every moment of life we are so lucky to have and share with others. Just as I'm enjoying every second I'm sharing with you Sam, because it may be the last second I will ever have. I might not be here tomorrow but I am going to savor every second I have here and these few moments with you. I know not everyone can think this way but not everyone is faced with a decision of whether the sun will rise tomorrow or not. So Sam, what can be so bad that you want to put yourself into a state of depression? Please tell me Sam, I promise to be a good listener," she said with a smile on her face.

"I don't know where to begin Susan. I was a happy guy and worked hard at my job every day. Then one day I met this wonderful and beautiful girl named Jenny. I fell madly in love with her and she felt that same way about me. A few weeks ago I asked her to have dinner with me at a very nice Italian restaurant. I planned to ask her to marry me and this was the night I was going to give her my pledge of love and companionship forever. As planned we went to Luigi's Ristorante and ordered a bottle of wine while we read the menu. We ordered our food and began talking when I asked her to marry me and she said yes. As a matter-of-fact she was so thrilled she jumped up from her seat and came to me and kissed me right there in the restaurant in front of everyone. Many of the other diners clapped their hands and few said congratulations. I was floating on air and so was she and then the World came crashing down on us. Just as the waiter approached our table, some people burst into the Restaurant and declared that it was a hold-up. We were instructed to empty our pockets and place all of our belongings into the bag that was being passed around. I was in a panic because I didn't want to see Jenny get hurt and I also didn't think clearly because I didn't want to empty my pockets for these crooks. Although I didn't buy Jenny a real ring yet, I did pick-up a very inexpensive one at the five & dime. It wasn't worth anything except it was a symbol of our love, especially mine. Jenny made it clear that a ring was not necessary and never would be. I quickly slipped it to Jenny and told her to slip it on her finger hoping they wouldn't notice it and leave her alone. All of a sudden someone in the crowd started firing a gun at these crooks and all hell broke out. I was hit with a bullet in my leg and back, and when I fell to the floor, I either hit my head on the concrete floor or someone hit me over the head, I can't remember. I awoke right here in this hospital to the terrible news, my Jenny was shot dead in that Restaurant. My one true love was taken from me. Why wasn't I the one killed? Why did she have to leave me like this? My heart is broken and life just doesn't seem the same anymore and now I have met you and we are both looking out a frosted window as the future looks bleak for us," I said as I wiped away a tear.

"Let me tell you something Sam, and please listen very carefully. My window is not frosted, no Sam, it is as clear as it possibly can be. My heart is not sad, no Sam, it's jumping for joy because for some unknown reason I have met you and you have made my day complete. Sam, please listen to me, you had no control of the events that took place in that restaurant. The events that took place were pre-ordained by a higher power and no matter what you could have said or done, it was going to happen. Now Sam, Jenny has gone to a better place and she has gone with a happy heart because of the man she loved, the one she was going to share her life with, and loved her just as much. In her heart she knows that she will always be in your heart for as long as you live. Now Jenny would be very sad if you acted as you are doing right now, she would not expect her lover to cry and be depressed when the celebration of life must be carried on by you, her partner. So Sam, take my advice, throw away that heavy heart and from this moment on start seeing life as it should be seen, with love and happiness. Jenny will always be that portrait in your mind's eye and she will be watching over you and she will expect to see you happy and living life to its fullest," she said as she held my hand and squeezed it ever so gently.

"Susan, you are one smart and brave girl and thank you for spending your precious time with me. You are right and I realize what a fool I am. I know I didn't lose Jenny because she will always be here in my heart and mind and she'll guide me to do the right thing always. I guess it was meant to be and I promise to be a better person," I said as I held on to Susan's warm hand.

"I'm tired Sam, would you mind walking me back to my room. I really can't stay erect for too long, I don't know why, but I get so very tired and I'm only twenty-three. I am so happy Sam that you realize how foolish being sad is. Don't waste any energy on negative things as they are only a zap of one's strength. I'm in room 427, it's just around the corner. Sam, can you please hold me, please take my arm, I need someone to lean on right now," she said as I locked my arm with hers. She was warm and soft and it felt really good. Susan made me feel better and now I was helping her. I forgot my own cares as I was wrapped-up with her. Deep inside I hoped she would not leave too soon, she was far too sweet to go at such a young age.

"I'm in room 431 Susan, you can call me anytime. If you feel up to it later, come by and visit me. Here we are at your room, I'll let you rest for a while before I come back to see you again, I hope it's alright with you," I said as I kissed her gently on the cheek and squeezed her hand gently.

The next three days went by so quickly and, although it's hard to believe, they were the most wonderful days of my life. I spent them with Susan holding her hand as she lay in her bed and we had long talks about things that perhaps meant nothing at all but sounded great to us. I could see her getting weaker each day while I was getting stronger. I knew the day would come when I would be released from the hospital and finally it did and, believe-it-or-not, I was sad to leave Susan behind. I went over to see Susan and tell her that I will be back each day to visit. I found her lying in her bed as she was getting another blood transfusion and kissed her gently on the lips and told her I'll be back tomorrow.

The next day, as promised, I went to visit Susan. I could hardly wait to see her again and couldn't believe I was falling in love with her even though there wasn't any future in it. I realized that no one has any control over their feelings and love has no barriers, it will find you and take hold of your heart and mind faster than anything you can imagine. I spent the day with Susan and although we didn't do anything because she was now too weak to take a short walk we still had a great time. I kissed her good-bye and told her I would be here again tomorrow just after lunch.

I went into the store to see my Boss and tell him that I will start working next Tuesday. It was Thursday so I still had a few days to visit with Susan before resuming my duties at the store. I will make sure I visit with her every day after work and all day on my days off. My Boss was excited to see me and avoided asking me any questions about the robbery and Jenny's death. I could see the pain in his face as he tried to keep the conversation light. I finally said, *"Ralph, please don't worry about saying anything wrong. There is nothing you can say that is wrong, so please relax. What happened, happened and can't be changed and we all must move on. I am sorry I had to miss so much work but am grateful that you took such good care of my customers and made sure my pay went into my bank account. I was madly in love with Jenny but I can't change what happened and must start once again. I love you guys and will do my best to be the best salesperson here, now let's get the show on the road,"* I said with a big smile on my face and went to my desk to see if there was any messages that need my immediate attention and then left to go to the hospital to visit Susan.

I arrived a little after lunch and proceeded directly to Susan's room. When I opened her door I had a feeling that something was wrong. Her bed was made up and waiting for a new patient. There was nothing in the room that reminded me of Susan, nothing at all. My heart began racing, I was ready to burst out crying when in the back of my head I heard Susan's voice saying, *'Don't cry for me Sam, please be happy, I'm free at last.'* My mood changed at once and a smile came into my head as I walked over to the nursing station to inquire about Susan. *"Hello there Sam, I hope you are feeling better?"* Nurse Maggie said to me.

"Yes I feel a lot better Maggie. Where is Susan, Maggie? Her room seems to be all made-up and ready for a new tenant," I said.

"I'm sad to say Sam, Susan passed last night. She left this note for you and asked the night nurse to make sure you get it. She must have had a feeling that she wasn't going to last much longer. She was a brave girl and had a great outlook on life. We'll miss her a lot around here Sam, she was an inspiration to us all," Nurse Maggie said as I walked away with Susan's note in my hand.

I didn't want to read the note in the hospital, I decided it could wait until I get home. I took the train home and don't remember the trip at all as I was so engrossed in thought about the few days I spent with Susan and how inspiring she was to me. I wondered if it was possible to love two women at once. I guess it is possible and can only stand as a testament to one's ability to be kind and love deeply, and Susan showed me how true that was. My life was enriched by knowing her even if it was only for a very short period. I arrived home and sat down on my sofa and opened Susan's note:

Dear Sam,

My time has come for me to leave here and find greener pastures. I just wanted to thank you, for being so wonderful to a dying girl. In the short time I got to know you I fell in love with you Sam. Not because you took a dying young girl into your heart but because you are a good person and I, in my last days, was able to help you see the light. Thank you again Sam, and please remember me and try to live up to the ideals we talked about. And Sam, thanks for loving me even if it wasn't for real, even though I think it was genuine. Thanks Sam, I'll be watching over you and you have my heart forever,

Love forever,

Susan

I folded the letter carefully and put it back in the envelope. A tear ran down my cheek and I said out loud to Susan, *"I'm sorry I cried a little but the tears are warm as is my heart and these feelings I have for you are very true, I do love you Susan. Rest easy, I'm here for you, always."* I sat there on my sofa for a long time just thinking of the great few days I spent with a wonderful person. I didn't have a photograph of Susan because she didn't want me to have one as she now looked. I really didn't need one, she'll never be out of my mind and shall stand tall with Jenny to help guide me through the rest of my life.

A New Beginning:

IT HAD BEEN SIX MONTHS SINCE JENNY AND SUSAN HAVE come into and left my life. I have worked very hard in the store and was voted the top salesperson in the store for the month of December. Benny has been in a few times and has told me very little about the progress being made on the Bank robbery investigation. As far as I was concerned it was a thing of the past as a year and a half has passed. I read in the papers where Tyrone was sentenced to two years in prison for his part in the robbery. He also returned about half of what he stole to the cops. I wondered who gets that money. It's not as if they really know whose cash it really is as most people would not declare this much cash. Naturally I could not make an inquiry and knew for sure that the Mob would not dare declare their losses. I'll bet the Mob was really pissed-off when the papers said that Reggie gave back the funds. Oh well, that is the way the cookie crumbles.

I hadn't touched the hiding place in all this time and didn't even try to move the stash. All I did was check that the area was undisturbed and that was good enough for me. It was a pleasure to have electricity in the cabin. The funny thing about that was all I needed was one light bulb and one outlet and for all that they had to run an electric wire from the pole which was about seventy-five feet away from the house. They charged me five hundred dollars for the wire and gave me twenty-four months to pay for it. Each month a charge of twenty dollars appeared on my bill, under the heading *Connection Charge*. It was my pleasure to pay this charge and have the one light whenever I was there. My next project was to build an extension to the cabin so I could have a bathroom, a bedroom, and a kitchen too. Soon it will happen and I'll have a real place I can call home. In the meantime I'll come up here and breathe the fresh air and think of Jenny and Susan and be at peace.

The time was fast approaching the two year mark since the big project. Who would believe that it has been so long since I put that project together and pulled it off. I felt the coast was finally clear and it was time for me to make decisions about my future. What shall I do with my life? If I stay with this job I will eventually become the boss of a few of the salespeople, but ultimately I will be nothing more than a glorified men's suit salesperson. I wanted better things for myself and seeing that so many people I knew left New York for California, I started to read all about life in the land of sunshine and Hollywood personalities. The stories and adventures of show people intrigued me as they sounded so exciting. Watching the Rose Bowl on New Year's Day was one of my biggest inspirations to get up and leave New York for the warmth and excitement of Los Angeles.

I had a few problems associated with my intended move. One of the most difficult problems was how to transport my stash from here to there. I also had to sell my piece of heaven in the mountains. The most uncomfortable part was to tell my Boss that I am leaving the company. Should I tell them I am relocating to California or should I give them another destination? My thoughts were very mixed about the whole thing because I allowed my imagination to carry into directions that do not exist. For example, I thought about the cops, what if they started to suspect me for the robbery that was now almost two years old. When I returned to earth, I was able to think logically and asked myself why I even entertained that kind of thought. If they haven't talked to me yet, why should they start now? After taking every precaution possible I felt my tracks were well hidden and no one could possibly connect me with the robbery. Now that I was thinking straight again, I could continue planning my new life in a far off place that is always warm. I can even spend some of my hidden treasure and enjoy the benefits of my hard work. I could easily go into some small business or just take it easy for a while. No one was bothering with a guy like me and if for some reason they wanted to look into my life, they would find a guy who lost his future wife and who almost died in a robbery, all very logical reasons why he would want to start all over again elsewhere. *'No Sam, there was nothing to worry about except what day you will leave for that new life, that new beginning.'*

The year was coming to an end and I spoke with a real estate agent in Lake George and she felt it would be best to offer my piece of land for sale in the late spring. We both agreed that it has a lot more appeal when the snow is gone and the ground is dry so we set a date for May to start actively showing the place. That would give me a little window to dig up my treasure and move it all to Manhattan. I decided that I would drive to Los Angeles and take only a few possessions. There was no need to fill the car with unnecessary clutter and I could buy new stuff once I was settled in L.A. The other project was to get rid of my apartment. I didn't own the place but I was under *rent control* and could continue to renew my lease year after year with modest rent increases as governed by law. The beauty of my place was that because of the rent control the cost of living there would remain low for all time. Once I move out the landlord can raise the rent significantly and the new tenant will come under rent control from that time on. If I subleased the place I could make sure the new person avoided that increase. I had no intention of ever returning to New York so why I worried about this was beyond me. Every day I thought about it and every day I realized that I was only creating a problem for no good reason and finally decided to advise the landlord that I will be moving out by June 1 and would like to have my security deposit mailed to my Mom's address in N.Y.

My Mom, well, that was another drama as my Mother was very upset with me because she was from the old school. When I stopped in to see her and told her about my plan to live L.A., she went ballistic. *"Sam, you have a wonderful job. You have been there for years and soon you will get a promotion. Why throw all that away? Sam, I know how you feel after losing Jenny but this is your home. New York is where you grew up and this is where your Mother lives. Please Sam, please think about it, I need you here,"* she said.

"Mom, please understand I need a new start. I'm not getting anywhere in my job. I know it looks good from the outside but believe me Mom, it's a going nowhere job, and I just don't feel it's my future. I'm not getting younger and it's time I made new roots, and in California I know I can start fresh. Maybe I'll meet a nice girl and get married! I have to get the past out of my mind if I'm to move forward. There are too many bad memories here in New York and the only way I can start over is to find a new place far away. Look at the bright side Mom, once I'm settled I'll send you a ticket and you can fly to L.A. and spend as much time as you like with me. Maybe you'll like it there and want to move there as well. Who knows Mom, what terrific things we'll find on the other side of the earth? I love you Mom and want to see the best for you and all I want is for you to see the best for me. Los Angeles is a new place for a new beginning and maybe my life will become more enjoyable, maybe I'll be happy once again," I said to her as I hugged her.

"You are right Sam, I'm sorry I was just being a selfish Mother who wants her Son close by. Deep in my heart I know this could be a very good move for you Sam, so do it and I am with you. I love you Sam, you are the only one left in our Family so naturally I want to hold on, but I want you to go and be happy this is the truth, go in good health Sam and remember you can't stop writing and calling me at least once a week. I'm sorry for crying Sam, but a Mother never stops worrying about her child, never." She said as she hugged me and kissed me on the cheeks.

Ever since I have moved on my own I visited my Mother every two weeks just to say hello and give her a hug. She has lived alone for over ten years since my Dad died and she has never complained once. She worked for a manufacturing company for over twenty years as their chief bookkeeper and is now a mainstay in the company. She has never complained and paid my college tuition without complaint and has never denied me anything. She paid the taxes, even though they were small, on the piece of land in Lake George and never once went there since my Dad died. She was a great woman and she deserved my loyalty and love always.

I decided not to tell my Boss until May that I was leaving and was going to live in California, or should I tell him somewhere else just in case someone like Benny might ask. I decided it would be best if my start would be brand new and to do that I have to break all ties. I will tell my Boss I'm moving to Florida because of the warm climate. I can use the excuse that my back hurts during the cold season and I want to forget the terrible ordeal I went through last Christmas.

I felt a one month notice was fair and would allow him time to find a replacement. I would tell him that I would gladly help train my replacement and shall make sure that all my clients are well taken care of at all times.

The Trip:

THE TIME WAS NEAR AS WE WERE IN APRIL AND I HAD decided to give my notice on May 1st. I was at my desk experiencing a slow period and decided to pick-up the Daily News that was sitting on my desk. I don't usually read the paper while at work as it sends the wrong message. What if a client walked in and at first glance would see me reading the paper. Their first impression is that this is not a very busy place and then, perhaps they might think we are neglectful at our jobs. But for some reason I thought it wouldn't hurt so I picked it up and started turning the pages when I noticed on page five an article about Tyrone. Of course, it took my full attention as I read that he was being released on parole after serving nine months of his sentence. He would be a free man in a week and I began to think why he was being given such a break. My first thought was that the cops wanted to keep him under surveillance to see if he contacts anyone else. Then I guessed they wanted to be sure he didn't have any more loot. Naturally I really didn't know the reasons but I couldn't help myself from guessing what they might be. I was not concerned at all because there was no way he knew who I was and no way in hell he could ever find out. As I sat there wondering what their reasons were and with coincidence at one hundred percent, who walks into the store? You guessed right, Benny Guarino, my Mob connection, so to speak! I looked up and my heart skipped a beat as the entire scenario came into my mind. *"Hi Ben, how are you?"* I said in my usual cordial manner.

"I'm great Sam, thanks for asking and how are you doing? You look pretty good my friend, he said.

"You are aren't due for a new suit for another month at least, so what brings you by to see us? It's a pleasant surprise Benny, I'm always happy to see you," I said with a big smile.

"I was just in the neighborhood and decided to stop by and say hello. By the way Sam, did you read in the paper today that one of the guys who robbed the Bank is getting out on parole?" he said.

"I sure did Benny. Do you think it is right that a guy gets out so early for such a big crime? I think the cops have another plan for him, what do you think?" I said.

"I think you are right Sam. It's a little funny that he only serves a few months and then gets out. I'll bet he is going to take them to the money! I did read that he turned over a few bucks to the cops and add that to the money he turned over to us that should amount to a lot of bread. Of course Sam, no one knows exactly how much money was actually taken because it was never published in the papers. I'll bet the cops and the Bank know how much but aren't going to let the public know. I also think there was a few more guys in on the robbery, there is no way that two guys alone can pull off a deal like that. Oh well, we'll never really know and between you and me I don't really care. We got most of our money back and that is all I care about. How about you Sam, did you recover your bread?' Benny said.

"I got back all my money. It wasn't a lot but the Bank stood good for it and a few weeks after I filled in the claim form I received a check for five hundred bucks. That was all I had in there, I was saving for my vacation and thought if I put a few bucks in my safety deposit box I won't see it and I'll save. Thanks to the Bank I lost nothing," I said with a smile.

'Well Sam, enough of this crap. We aren't detectives and who really cares. It just makes interesting conversation between friends and especially us because we both used the same Bank. I don't need *a suit yet but will be back next month to pick-up a new wardrobe. I hope the new styles will be in by then?'* he said as he turned around and started walking towards the exit. Just as he turned to wave good-bye I saw the front door open and someone entered carrying something and in a flash started firing a machine gun at Benny. Bullets struck him everywhere as his body seemed to fly in every direction as the bullets tore him apart. He was dead in seconds and blood was everywhere. People were screaming outside the store on Fifth Avenue and everyone in the store seemed frozen in time. The shooter turned around and calmly walked out blending right into the pedestrian traffic and disappeared. I was shocked and could not move, I've never seen anyone get killed except in the movies and it didn't seem as violent as this. Certainly I was in a gunfight when I lost Jenny but I got wounded and hit my head when I fell on the floor so I missed all the action. My friend Benny was no more, pieces of him were strewn all over the floor and no one, yes no one would go over to where he was lying. I was one of those who didn't move, who didn't run to help Benny and now I felt guilty and started to shake. I fell to the floor as my legs gave away and I was sobbing openly and loudly for my friend Benny. I didn't think I was a coward but I didn't lift a finger to help him at all. It all happened in less than thirty seconds but I couldn't fathom the time. To me it felt like it was a long, long time. My head was spinning and my heart was racing so fast I could hardly catch my breath. All of a sudden the World came alive again with screams and shouts, "Call *the police, get help. Is everyone alright?"* I now heard everything and saw that there was complete chaos in our store. Someone had to take charge or this situation was going to get out of hand. I began shouting, not in a belligerent way but loud enough to get everyone's attention. *"Listen to me, I know this is a very sad time in our lives, but we must remain calm and remember what happened. The police will be here any second now and they do not want us to screw-up the crime scene so don't look at the dead person and try to get hold of yourselves. Stay where you are and try to be a proper witness, the police will need your help to catch the people who did this. I know it's hard to do but we must be strong at a time like this. It all depends on us so take a deep breath and stay calm, please!"* I tried to keep talking as long as I could without sounding stupid. I was never a good public speaker and I wasn't much of an improvement this time. I kept on speaking simply because someone had to keep everyone calm. I felt if I could keep their minds off the situation that just took place, they will, at least, be quiet. It seemed like it was taking the cops forever to get here. When they finally arrived I looked at my watch and couldn't believe that it was only six minutes since the first phone call went out to them. This was a scene that we only happened see in movies, as a matter-of-fact it was so surreal that I was actually waiting for someone to yell, 'CUT' and the body would be put back together for the next scene. Once the cops arrived the noise returned and freaked me out as people cried and others fainted while the cops were yelling out orders that no one really heard. Once the paramedics arrived things seemed to calm down a bit. I think when they covered the body parts it helped many of those in the store, which numbered about thirty, to calm down even more. The next wave of humanity to arrive were the detectives who didn't help the chaotic situation much more. It was a mass of humanity trying to put together something that can never be brought back to life. The shock effect of this event was far beyond anyone's imagination, especially the noise of the guns being fired and the body parts of the victim flying into the air. I'm sure that most of the people in the store had seen some sort of gangster movie in the past, especially one of the Mob wars in Chicago during prohibition, but reality was far different than the sound and visual effects of a movie. To add to all this the detectives that arrived on the scene were not very nice people and didn't take into account that the potential witnesses were in a state of shock. Their patience and understanding went out the window when it came to the questioning of the people. Of course, no matter how bad one felt or how badly one displayed their shock no one was permitted to leave the store before giving their statements to one of the policemen. This didn't help anyone's disposition including mine.

Four hours later I was told I could go home. As I left the store I saw a clean-up crew arrive to try and get the store back to normal for tomorrow's day of business. As far as I was concerned this place will never be the same again. I don't know how I will be able to finish out the last four weeks before I leave for California. I decided to eliminate those thoughts from my mind and see how tomorrow plays out.

The Big Move:

NEEDLESS TO SAY THE EVENTS THAT TOOK PLACE A FEW days ago didn't help anyone's mood at the store. The result of the events that took place was that when the store opened the next morning there were about one hundred people lined-up to get in and gawk at the area where Benny's body was. Some Mob guy got killed and the public wanted to see the blood and anything else that would satisfy their curiosity. Some brought flowers and others just stood there and stared at the spot on the floor. The area where the body, or shall I say pieces of the body was the day before, were roped off with little signs saying, Police line. *Do Not Cross*. None bought suits, but many wanted a shirt, or a tie as a memento of Benny Guarino's death. It was eerie to watch all this at least that was how I felt. My Boss was thrilled with the free advertising the store was getting and the possibilities of local radio and television stations calling to arrange interviews. He expected the store to set all kinds of new sales records because of this. All he wanted was to figure out a way he can capitalize on this even more than just the free advertising. He came over to me and said, *"Sam, what do you think we can do to drum up more business while this is hot in the news column? What do you think of a special, like a suit with two pair of pants for seventy-nine bucks and a free necktie thrown-in? I think we can come up with something really special that will put Bond's sales on the run. What do you think?"*

   "I think it's really a good idea even though I don't think its right to take advantage of one's death. I realize that anything that has to do

with the Mob is news that everyone wants to hear about it. I heard that when there was a public killing in Chicago during Capone's days the public visited the place for weeks after it happened so I guess New York is not any different. I think you should take advantage of it and offer some kind of very special sale. Do it while this is hot news, remember Boss, it will be old news in a few days," I said.

"You're right Sam. I got an interview tomorrow on CBS and, NBC wants to come here and take pictures and interview some of the staff. You knew Benny better than anyone Sam, would you mind being in on the interview?" he said as the look on his face showed his excitement.

"I really don't want to be exposed to the public, but if it helps you promote the store, I'll be happy to say a few words. The one thing I do owe Benny is to say something nice about him. After all he was my best client and would continue to be if this didn't happen. Besides all that Boss, he was a very nice man and always treated me with great respect," I said.

"Thanks Sam, I'll let you know when the interview is scheduled and, Sam, there will be a travelling bonus for you as well," he said.

"Boss, I'm not giving the interview because I want a bonus. I'm doing this because I feel I owe Benny a lot, because he was a very nice and kind man regardless of his affiliation with the Mob. He was loyal and always paid his bill on time and never made me feel threatened or concerned because of his reputation. No Boss, I cared for him as a nice man and that is what I want to convey to anyone who wants to listen. Of course, I realize that the public would love to hear stories about him and his exploits as a member of Mafia but I don't have any. I will not be selling suits for your company much longer but I'll always remember Benny as a super customer and a very good man," I said.

"Sam, that is fine. Say whatever you want to say but let me tell one thing about this. The public doesn't give a shit about how nice

Benny was, believe me Sam, they won't remember Mr. Nice Guy. But if you embellish his life a little, they'll never forget you and him, that's for sure Sam. It doesn't have to be anything too elaborate but it would be nice to make him into a hero and a crook all at the same time. I'm sure you know what I mean Sam, after-all no one is going to check out what this guy actually did, he's not applying for credit. He was gunned down in the typical Mob fashion. The public would be very disappointed if he was whacked as they call it, if it was a mistake. I'm sure you get my drift Sam, so try to get yourself together and your story straight, after all, we have the chance to go down in history," he said.*

"I understand Boss, I'll do my best. Let me know when the interview is scheduled so I'll be ready," I said.

I was shocked with the direction my Boss wanted the interview to take, but I understood that he wanted to make as much money as he could out of this event. He didn't ask the Mob to whack Benny in his store. But once the venue was chosen and it was his store why shouldn't he make as much as he can? I guess if I was the big boss I would also look for ways to capitalize on this. He was very good to me all the years I worked here and stood with me when I was shot and hospitalized and out of work for at least a month. I was paid every week and he never said a word to me about it. He was a good Boss and I owed him some loyalty and actually owed Benny very little, especially now that he was dead. Even if I owed Benny something he would never be able to appreciate my kindness or my words so all I can say to Benny is that he rest in peace. All I can say about Benny was that he was a good man and he always treated me with respect and always wore very nice suits. I can't imagine why anyone would want to kill Benny. I was very nervous about this interview because it would be the first time I was ever interviewed on television and the whole World will be watching. My Boss was excited and spent the day prepping me for our meeting with one of the representatives from the television station. He told me, probably ten or more times, not to be nervous and just be natural. I think I would have been more natural if he hadn't reminded me over and over that I shouldn't be. He meant well and I didn't have the heart to tell him to stop making me nervous.

The Interview:

WELL THE DAY FINALLY ARRIVED AND I WAS AS READY AS I could be. I didn't want to say too much. The less said the better it is because I wanted to keep a low profile. I didn't need any special publicity especially in view of the fact that I wanted to move on and leave New York. I was not really nervous about the interview but was a little confused how my speech should actually read, finally I realized that I don't need a speech because this is an interview and the moderator will be asking questions, all that is required from me is to answer them and not to elaborate. It isn't easy to face cameras and know that many thousands of people are watching you all over the country. I was a wreck by the time the television crew arrived and when Walter Williams, the very famous news broadcaster, arrived my heart was racing a million miles an hour.

"It is a pleasure to meet you Sam. Let's take a moment to get things organized and the interview will be as smooth as silk," he said in a very soft and soothing voice. *"I'll bet you have prepared a full script for this interview. Well, Sam, throw it away, you won't really need it at all. I will make this interview as easy as eating apple pie for you. Just let me ask the questions and you answer them in an easy way and don't concern yourself with anything else. Just imagine I came into the store to buy a new suit and, as human nature would have it, I would allow my curiosity to take over and would ask you what happened on that fateful day. Well that is what is going to happen and before you know it the interview will be over, so relax and let the show begin."*

"Thanks Mr. Williams, I really appreciate your making me feel at ease. I have never been on the radio or television and am a little nervous. I'll do my best and hope it comes out as you would like it. Thanks!" I said.

I was instructed how and where to sit and how to look at the camera. I was told to act natural and above all imagine that I am in my living room and we are just talking. Try to shut out the fact that there are people out there watching. Above all relax and be yourself, *"I guess that is about it Sam, now let's get started,"* Walter Williams said.

The cameras were now in place and there were wires running all over the place. The floor was cluttered with equipment and wires. We sat in director's chairs as the cameras were being tested and the angles being set-up, especially the angle that they would use to show Walter Williams at his best.

The announcer began the program with an introduction that explained the circumstances and pointing out that this interview was exclusive to the network.

Williams: *"Good evening, welcome to the Walters New Hour. I am Walter Williams and am very pleased to have with me one of the key witnesses to the slaying of reputed Mob Boss, Benny Guarino. Mr. Sam West, welcome to the Walters News Hour."*

West: *"It is a pleasure to be here Mr. Walters."*

Williams: *"Could you please give us a rundown of what happened last Tuesday at the Sy Johnson Clothing Store on Fifth Avenue in New York City?"*

West: *"My day had begun as it usually does as the store opened around 9.30 in the morning. Around noon a very good friend and customer Benny Guarino came in as he usually does every few weeks to say hello and to inquire if the season's new styles have arrived. We chatted for a little while and Benny said he would be in next week to choose the new material and order a few suits. He told me that he was very pleased because he was promoted and* now had quite a few people working under him. I never knew exactly what Benny did for a living but I also didn't think it was my business to ask. It never occurred to me that Benny was a part of the Mafia. He never mentioned anything about criminals or crime to me."

William: "We can understand that Sam, but you must have had a suspicion that he was connected as they say?"

West: "Not really. He did say he was in finance but that was as far as it went. When he came in that day he was all smiles and was telling me about his new position. He actually wanted to thank me for helping him move up the ladder in his company. You see Mr. Williams, a few weeks earlier, his Boss's daughter got married and Benny wanted to make sure he looked his very best at the wedding. Together we picked out a beautiful tuxedo and after making sure the fit was perfect we put together a complete wardrobe including a real nice pair of patent leather shoes. Well when he came to visit he told me how great he looked and that his Boss was very impressed with him and a couple of days later he was promoted. Well, Benny wanted to thank me even though all I did was to recommend some nice pieces of clothing. We talked for a little while and then he said he would be back next week. He walked towards the front door and all of sudden this crazed man came through the entrance door holding a gun of some sort. Before anyone could say or do anything he started firing directly at Benny. It looked like the gun was on fire as the shots continued for what seemed like a long time. Benny didn't have chance as the bullets just cut him in half. Pieces of his body were torn apart and went flying all over the place. It was a horrible sight to see, blood flying everywhere and what was left of Benny seemed to be scattered all over the floor. It seemed like this took forever but when it was all over it took no more than a half a minute. Can you believe that it all happened in thirty seconds and the gunman rushed out the door on to Fifth Avenue and just walked away? Inside the store everyone was frozen for what seemed like a long time, but, as I said, it was only thirty seconds. Then all hell broke out as people began screaming and fainting and I started yelling at the top of my voice for everyone to remain calm. Don't ask me why I did that because I really don't know. I'm usually very quiet Mr. Williams, but here I was trying to get everyone to think about something else just until the police arrived. Looking back on all this I still can't believe that I did that. It was a very difficult experience for everyone and a little more difficult for me because I knew the victim for so long. All I can say about Benny was that he was a great guy and seemed like a very kind and respectful man to me at all times. I'm very saddened by his passing, he will be missed."

Williams: "I'm sure our listeners could imagine how horrible something like this must be. By the way did you know any of his family?"

West: "In all the time that I knew Benny he never mentioned his family or where he lived. The address he gave the store was here in Manhattan and that was all we ever knew."

Williams: "Thank you Mr. West, I am sorry for your loss and hope that this experience is never repeated. By the way aren't you the same Sam West that was seriously wounded in the Luigi Restaurant hold-up a few months ago?"

West: "Yes, I was in the restaurant at the time of the hold-up. I was there with my fiancé, this was the night I asked her to marry me and she had accepted. One minute later she was dead, shot through the heart by one of the crooks and I was shot as well. I am sorry Mr. Williams, the memory of that time is too upsetting, I'm sorry."

Williams: "Thank you Mr. West. I am sorry for your loss and am sure that our listeners feel as I do. Thank you for your time and good-luck."

The interview ended and Williams looked at me and said, "I'm sorry Sam I didn't mean to bring up old wounds. I'm really sorry."

I could not answer because I was too upset. The entire nightmare of that night came rushing back and made me sick. I just couldn't carry on and needed to leave the store and take a walk by myself.

Will I ever forget that night? I asked myself that question often and couldn't find an answer. Perhaps I'm not supposed to ever forget and, as Susan said to me in the hospital I'm lucky to have those memories. All I have to do is to separate the good from the bad and I'll see Jenny, and that alone should fill my heart with joy. I felt a lot better and perhaps this little walk opened my mind to realize how lucky I was to have Jenny even for a short time, after all I could have not had her at all.

The following day my Boss called me over and thanked me for a wonderful interview. He asked me to make myself available to sign autographs. He told me that after the show was aired the phone rang off the hook with callers asking about our hours of operations but most of all they wanted to know when I would be at the store. *"Sorry Sam, you have become a celebrity and we've got to satisfy the folks who want to see you and get your autograph,"* he said. I was not too happy with this turn of events but I had to act as if it was a pleasure to accommodate him. The truth of the whole deal was that I could hardly wait to get the hell out of the store and out of town.

I decided that I was leaving New York at the end of June no matter what. I'll sit my Boss down and explain that this is not the place for me any longer and I must move on. I was still extremely nervous about moving the cash from the very secure hiding place on my land, but I was putting the place up for sale and could not leave it there any longer. I decided that I was going to hide the cash in my car and had a compartment built in the bottom of the trunk. I went to a welding shop in New Jersey and explained that I needed an extra space to hide my valuable stamp collection and some other stuff when I move to Florida. I asked him to construct a metal box that would be attached to the bottom of the trunk and would not be noticed when someone opens the trunk or looks at the car from the rear. After a little discussion he agreed to make me a perfect addition to the trunk floor that will be under the spare tire.

If anyone would look into the trunk they would not see this addition and it was secure because he was welding under the car and it will be as solid as the frame itself. I left the car with him and a week later he called to let me know that it was all ready. When I arrived at this shop late Thursday afternoon he was the proudest craftsman I have ever seen. He couldn't stop telling me how wonderful this job was and how he was thinking of going into business making these for people who need additional cargo space. I was pleased with the job and drove home satisfied that I will be able to put my stash in the new cargo holder and no one will be the wiser. I could hardly wait to dig up my pot-of-gold.

The Revelation:

I LEFT THE STORE ON SATURDAY AT ABOUT FIVE AND DROVE directly to my little cabin. I arrived there at about eight-thirty and was pleased that I could get a good night's sleep. My plan was to get up bright and early and remove my stash and spend the day and making sure the area where I kept the stash was made as nice as possible. I was very excited about finally seeing my rewards after two years of serious discipline. After two years of patience, not succumbing to temptation, being a disciplined guy, now was the time to finally start enjoying it.

I was up at the crack of dawn and began the task of removing my containers. I removed the first one and couldn't wait to open it up. Everything looked like it had the day I'd put it all away. I removed each packet from the container box and placed the unopened package neatly into my trunk's special compartment. It took me a little over an hour to remove all the containers and empty them. I carefully closed my special compartment in the trunk of my car and covered it over with the mat on the trunk floor and placed my usual stuff back on the trunk bed. I was excited that I was able to do all this quickly and efficiently and now all I had to do was to get rid of the used containers and the ground cover sheets. I stood over the area where the stash was buried and tried to decide what to do with the containers. I could put them back into the ground and in years they will fall apart and become part of the soil or I can load them in the car and dump them off at the local garbage dump. I decided that laziness was not the answer so I took the containers and the ground sheets and placed in the car and went over to the local dump and threw them out. I didn't care if anyone found them as they would not yield any clues why they were dumped or who owned them. I also felt, being so early in morning, no one would be around to see me so I was safe all around. I rushed over to the dump and got rid of the containers and other stuff and then went over to the Howard Johnson and had breakfast.

I went back to the cabin and spent the next two hours filling in the earth and making it all look as good as possible. The place was now ready to be sold and I figured I wouldn't ever come back here. I stopped in to see my real estate agent and asked her how she was doing in her efforts to sell my property. She said she was confident it would be sold in a few weeks from now. I reminded her that the price I was asking was more than reasonable and should help the property move quickly, she agreed and I felt better and left for the last time. I felt a little sad that I wouldn't see this little cabin any longer but I was intent on starting a new life and in order to do so I have to give up the old one.

I was back at work as usual on Tuesday and asked the Boss if I could have a word with him. He invited me into his little cubicle that he called an office and cleaned off the only chair in the room placing the papers on the floor. Neatness was not one of his traits, but he was a good boss and treated me very well. *"I'm sorry to say but I am giving you my notice. I hate to leave this job because I really do love it here and have built a solid customer base over the few years I have been at it. Because of what has happened to me over the past little while I can no longer live here in New York. There are too many bad memories and the only way I will be able to become a whole person once again is to get out here and start a new life elsewhere. I have decided to move to Florida and hopefully the past will fade away and I will be able to face life head-on once again. I'm leaving and won't be coming back and want to thank you for your kindness when I was wounded and the support you have* shown me over the years. This incident with Benny was the straw that broke the camel's back. I have had enough and must admit I'm sad to leave New York and this place as this has been my only job since graduating university, but as I said, there is too much baggage here. I'll be leaving at the end of June which should be enough time for you to replace me. I'll introduce my replacement to all my clients and explain that I'm leaving because of very personal reasons and nothing to do with the shop. I just want to thank you for being so kind to me in my hours of need and hope that we will remain friends for all time," I said with a tear in my eye.

"Thanks for giving me plenty of notice Sam, I really do appreciate it. I cannot blame you in the least for this decision Sam, I just didn't know what took you so long to make it. Anyone who has experienced the terrible times that you have would have run away a long while ago. Of course, you have my blessings and yes I also hope we will be friends for years to come. Thanks for giving me notice, filling your shoes will not be easy Sam, you have been a great asset to the company. All can say is good-luck and if you ever need anything please don't hesitate, I'll be here to provide it if I can. Sam, you are a mensch, thanks again!" My Boss said.

The Trip:

FINALLY THE MONTH ENDED AND I WAS READY TO HIT THE road. I had my entire trip mapped out and figured I'd take as much time as I liked getting to California. After all I wasn't in any rush and didn't have anything waiting for me at the other end. I had plenty of money so that wasn't an issue and I have never seen the country past New Jersey. I was going to take my time and savor each and every mile and see sights I only dreamed of. My plan was to take Route 66 most of the way. Perhaps I will meet some nice people along the way and will learn all about America, first hand.

Driving from New York to Los Angeles with over a couple of million dollars in the trunk of one's car is not as relaxing as one would think. I had no idea how long it would take me to get to L.A. perhaps a couple of months. I had decided to play it by ear and what will happen will happen, there was no rush. I was thankful that I had built the metal box into the bottom of the trunk to keep the money safe. I didn't unwrap the money when I removed it from my underground hiding place in Lake George. I figured that I would be going through heat and rain and who knows what other weather changes would take place. I felt it was best that it remained covered and protected until I reach California. I placed a blanket over the bottom of the trunk floor and then put my suitcases in the trunk and threw a bunch of other items over that. I had a few thousand dollars in my pocket and I figured that would be more than enough for the trip to the West coast. I arrived in Las Vegas and was overwhelmed by the Vegas Strip. I have never seen any place like this and for a moment wanted to stay there forever. I spent the next week at the Sands hotel and had a great time.

Just as I was ready to leave, I met Amber, she was the most beautiful woman I have ever met and I just couldn't leave her behind. I asked her if she was willing to leave Vegas and come start a new life with me in Los Angeles. She looked at me as if I was nuts but after an extra day or two she agreed on the condition we get married.

Amber and I settled down in Long Beach and bought a small house and unfortunately did not have any children. We did see a few doctors but finally gave up and accepted the fact that it would be us. We talked about adopting a child but gave up on that idea because we felt that Amber's background would not stand up to scrutiny. She was a dance hall girl that performed at one of burlesque house before joining the staff at the Sand's hotel. She luckily met someone who knew someone and that was how she got the job being a hostess at the Sands. I explained to Amber, way back then that a very dear uncle died and left me a few million dollars. She never questioned me any further and convinced me that keeping the money in our house was not practical nor safe and insisted she make some investments with it. She bought a few rental properties in Long Beach and slowly moved most of the cash into wise investments. She was a lot smarter than I and invested one million of our money and we never had a financial problem ever again.

Oh by the way, the case of the safe box was closed by the NYPD and the FBI as case solved. I guess they got their men when they prosecuted Reggie and Tyrone. Due to the fact that only a few thousand dollars was ever claimed, the authorities felt they had recovered all the money stolen. The one sad part was that the money recovered was returned to the bank, but never distributed to the Safe Box holders. Oh, yes, that's right I got my $500.00 back because I made a claim. What a fitting end!

Printed in the United States
By Bookmasters